THE JADE ARROWHEAD

JESSICA McCLELLAND

RED SKY inc.

Red Sky Inc.
Grand Junction, Colorado.

First printing: 2013
Second printing: 2018

PRAISE FOR THE KILLDEER SERIES

You'll be compelled to race through North of the Crazies by Jessica McClelland's easy and addictive prose, but that means you'll lose the detail and the accuracy that make her a truly fine writer. Her knowledge of the contemporary West and her abilities as a storyteller makes her a welcomed addition to the new class of crime fiction authors.

-Craig Johnson, author of the Walt Longmire Mysteries, the basis of A&E's hit series Longmire

Jessica McClelland's Snow at Midnight bursts out of the chute with a fresh new voice an authentic Montana sense of place, and a flawed but endearing protagonist readers will cheer for. Welcome aboard, Marley Dearcorn.

-C.J. Box, New York Times bestselling author of Force of Nature.

Ms. McClelland's gritty and endearing heroine takes you for a wild ride through the Montana countryside filled with murder and intrigue.

—Sam Morton, Winner of the Wyoming State Historical Society Award for Historical Fiction.

BOOKS BY
JESSICA McCLELLAND

SNOW AT MIDNIGHT
DRAWN TO THE MEAN
THE JADE ARROWHEAD
THE BUFFALO FENCE
NORTH OF THE CRAZIES
JIM CREEK HILL
WATER RIGHTS

THE JADE ARROWHEAD

CHAPTER 1

"Guess how many times I've been struck by lightning?"

"Loy, you've never been struck by lightning," I said.

"Not me," Sheriff Shucraft said, suppressing a laugh. "That's what Willy said to me the day I went to arrest him."

"Willy, the ranch hand from the Lazy Ox-Yoke? When did you arrest him?" I asked.

"Day before yesterday. I got a tip. Marley, can I tell this or what?" he asked.

I felt a small surge of guilty pleasure from news that the ranch hand who had given me so much trouble over the winter months was behind bars. Willy and his gang of followers, who occasionally crossed the line between legal and illegal when they felt like it, had confronted me on a lonely mountain trail and I considered myself lucky to have gotten away with only a few scratches. It could have been a lot worse.

I was more than ready to hear about a little bad luck that the belligerent ranch hand was enduring. "Okay, I'll quit interrupting. Tell it."

Loy stood over my desk at the Fable branch library. It was slow for a Tuesday, and since no one else was in the tiny library at the moment he felt safe confiding in me. I pulled my loose strawberry blonde hair into a snug ponytail, sat back in my chair, and folded my hands in my lap to give him every impression I was a captive audience. I'd known Loy since high school. The fact that he was sheriff of our small county had never really changed that Loy was my oldest friend, who just happened to carry a gun for a living. Although Loy had shamelessly pursued me off and on for years, I had decided after we graduated high school that a relationship between us would never happen. He was far too valuable to me as a friend to risk losing him due to a failed romance.

"So the day before yesterday I needed some fresh air," Loy said cryptically. "You know, up in the woods. I'm taking in the sights, and here's Willy, and he's mucking around in the trees off that trail that goes up above your dad's little caretaker's house. Not too far from the end of that trail that's right above the silent spring? Anyway, he's in a clearing in the trees, and next to him is a fifty-five-gallon drum and sticking out of the top of it is this moose head."

"A moose head?" I asked.

"And it's a bull. Willy is trying to stuff the thing inside the drum when I come across him. This moose head is huge, right? And the antlers are all in velvet, but they are too big to fit in the drum. So, Boy Genius is standing there holding the lid of the drum and he's trying to shove the thing inside . . ."

The sheriff had to stop and take a breath. He was laughing so hard it was taxing his ability to tell a good story.

"What did you say to him?" I had to press my lips together to keep from laughing.

"I says to him, 'Willy, that yours?'"

"And what did Boy Genius say?" I asked.

"He looks me straight in the eye and says, 'Sheriff, I've never seen that moose before in my life.'"

"To which you replied."

"I says, 'Willy, I can see from his expression that he recognizes you.'"

I finally laughed. "Did you really say that?"

"I did. And Willy? He looks down at the moose like he's trying to figure out if I'm kidding."

"Did the moose have any comment at this point?" I asked.

"I think he invoked his right to counsel," Loy said. "But then Willy starts telling me about the times he's been struck by lightning."

"What has that got to do with the severed moose head he's trying to shove into a fifty-five-gallon- drum?" I asked.

"A great deal, I guess," said Loy. "Willy tells me, 'Sheriff? I've had nothing but bad luck my whole life. Your worst day on earth ain't half as bad as my best day.'"

"How many times has he been struck by lightning?" I asked.

"Twice. But that's beside the point," Loy said. "He starts telling me he is innocent, that all he did was go up to check on his bait barrel. He and his buddies want to go bear hunting in the fall and they have a bait barrel on that section of land above your dad's property. When he gets there he finds this head sticking out of the barrel."

I was mentally adding up the number of years that Willy would be spending in jail. "It's illegal to bait bears in Montana," I said.

"I pointed that out to him," Loy told me. "He must have accidentally been looking at the hunting regulations for Wyoming."

"And how did the moose get in the barrel?" I asked. "Maybe it was a suicide?"

"He says he doesn't know how it got there, and it must have fallen in." The sheriff was doing his best to hold it together.

"Why were you going to arrest him, again?" I asked.

"He's a convicted felon," Loy said. "He spent a year in state prison for illegally guiding four out-of-state hunters down on the outskirts of Yellowstone Park to shoot trophy bull elk that wandered outside the boundaries. A little birdie told me that Willy was pretending that the conviction didn't really apply to him and had taken to carrying a gun with him again. Which just happens to be a violation of his parole."

"That little birdie didn't happen to be my father?" I asked.

Loy ignored the question. "Willy had a rifle slung over his shoulder."

"Did he say the rifle wasn't his?" I asked.

Loy pulled a chair over to the desk and sat down. "Nope. Even better. He said that it was his old rifle, one he'd gotten for Christmas when he was a kid. He said he had gotten it before his conviction, so it didn't count. When I told him that since he was a convicted felon he couldn't be carrying a rifle at all, he said that he thought it just meant he couldn't buy any more new ones."

"Well, it makes perfect sense to me," I said.

Loy chuckled. "I think he was truly surprised when I arrested him."

"Admit it," I said, leaning back in my chair. "You love your job."

He laced his big hands behind his head with a cocky grin pasted on his wide face. "Today I love my job."

"Oh, really?" I asked. "Why is today special?"

Loy grinned like a rodeo clown. "Because Wendy said she would go out with me tonight."

"See? I told you if you were persistent she would be interested."

"But there is a catch," he said.

I felt my pleased smile shift into a suspicious smirk. "Does this catch have something to do with me?"

"It might," he said. "Can you babysit Wendy's nephew this evening?"

I suppressed a deep groan. "Hugo? He's ten years old."

"And? He's a great kid," Loy said.

I fiddled with some papers on my desk. "I don't know."

"Come on, Aunt Marley. It's just for a couple of hours. Wendy and I are driving into Parkman to try out that new restaurant. You know, the bistro?"

I felt my shoulders slump. "It's not that I hate kids, Loy. I just don't know what to say to them."

"Talk about boogers and how gross girls are and you two will be fine," Loy told me.

He got to his feet and started to slink towards the door.

"Hey, I didn't say I would do it," I said.

"You didn't say you wouldn't," he replied.

"What if I have plans?"

"You don't. And I already sort of told Hugo that you would be coming by to pick him up."

I felt my spine crumble when he shot me his best pretty-please look. For a burly sheriff, Loy could spin the resolve right out of a girl when he put on his puppy-dog eyes.

"Alright, I'll do it. What time?" I said.

"Why don't you swing by Wendy's around five thirty?"

"I guess I can do that." There went my quiet evening with Leif. We had a bag of microwave popcorn and a movie that would have to be put on hold. But Leif wouldn't mind. He was the most understanding, easygoing man I had ever met.

Loy pulled his baseball cap down tight. "Thanks, Hun. If we will be any later than ten, I'll call."

"Ten? What am I supposed to do with Hugo for four and a half hours?"

The sheriff shrugged. "I don't know. Why don't you go up on the ridge above your dad's place and check out the guy digging the hole?"

"What guy?" I asked.

I stood up and smoothed a wrinkle in my navy blazer. Since I was a part-time librarian now, I'd been able to bring my office clothes out of retirement and dress like a grown-up once again. No more mud-encrusted boots and torn blue jeans for me. The time I'd spent working as a landscaper was over, and from now on I planned to stick to working jobs where the biggest hazard to my health was eye fatigue from staring at a computer screen. No more boulder hopping or sunburns for me.

The sheriff sighed. "There's some guy from the University of Wyoming up on the ridge behind your dad's place searching for fossils. Marley, don't you ever stick your head out from that rock you're living under?"

"You mean an archaeological dig?" That seemed odd to me. My father had never given anyone permission to dig on our property. Not since Grandpa had died.

"Well, sort of," Loy said. "Your dad told me this guy from the University is a graduate student. But he's not an archaeologist. He's some kind of a dinosaur hunter."

"We don't have any dinosaurs on our property. That I know of." This didn't sound at all like my father.

"I'm just repeating what I heard. Wendy said your dad mentioned it to her, and Hugo hasn't been able to let it go since. The kid is into that sort of stuff."

"Dad has collected a bunch of arrowheads over the years," I said, frowning. "Maybe that's what this grad student is looking for?"

"Nathan said the guy is looking for fossils," Loy told me. He tipped his hat brim and pushed the door open. "I'll let Wendy know you will take Hugo up to see the great discovery. Don't forget, five thirty."

I sat at my desk pondering the situation, trying to reconcile what I knew about my father with what Loy had said. It wasn't like my father to allow diggers on our property. For as long as I could remember, the Dearcorn ranch had been off-limits to what my father called "pot hunters," and I didn't understand why he would suddenly change his mind about it now. But time was slipping away, and I had work to finish up before the library closed for the day. And I had a kid to entertain.

After scanning a pile of returned books back into the computer, I tidied up the small log-cabin library and started shutting down the lights. It was almost five and we closed at that time on Tuesdays. Our one public access Internet computer had not been turned on once. It was a gorgeous summer day and nobody was interested in being inside when the mountain beckoned with its wildflowers and whispering aspen trees. At precisely the top of the hour I locked the front door and flipped the open sign around to say closed. Then I called Leif to give him the news of my change of plans.

He answered on the third ring. That was good. It meant that he wasn't in the middle of an important phone call.

Leif was an international businessman, and even though I didn't know precisely what he did for a living, I knew that it wasn't unusual for him to be chatting with someone on the other side of the world at odd hours.

"Leif Gable," he said with his typical greeting. He hardly ever answered a phone with the word hello.

"I'm on babysitting duty tonight," I said by way of a greeting.

"Oh?" he said. "For who?"

"Wendy Martinez. Her nephew is staying with her for a few weeks here in Killdeer. I guess Hugo's mother thought it would be good for the kid to spend some time out in the country with his aunt over the summer, and you can't get much more country than Killdeer. So, sorry but we have to change our movie plans for tonight."

"That's fine, Marley."

I could hear in his voice he was a bit disappointed, but I had some good news that I knew would cheer him up.

"Why don't I make it up to you and buy you dinner tomorrow night in Parkman? There is a new bistro in town," I said.

"I think that sounds perfect," Leif said. "If you make the reservation, I will drive."

"That's a deal," I said. "I'll be home in a bit to change."

I hung up the phone and locked the door behind me as I left for the afternoon. The library I worked for wasn't down in the valley in my small hometown of Killdeer. Instead, it sat on the mountainside, in a tiny town called Fable. Fable was such a small town I wondered how the county could justify maintaining a branch library in a place so remote, but it supplied me a job so I didn't wonder about it too hard.

I climbed into the black SUV that Leif was graciously loaning me. It was ridiculous, to my way of thinking. The black vehicle was a shiny, brand-new BMW sport-utility, and it made me nervous just driving it to the grocery store. It was worth more than I had paid for my first house. But until I could afford to have my battered old Honda repaired I was stuck with it. I pressed the ignition button, it occurred to me that it had been nearly six months since the Honda had been towed away to be fixed, and I hadn't seen it since. Leif had mentioned to me that a repair bill would be forthcoming for the Honda, but I hadn't seen one in all this time and I was starting to think that I never would.

One more thing I would eventually need to discuss with him.

I had fallen into the situation with Leif Gable by chance. I'd given up living at my father's little caretaker's house on the ranch as a favor to my friend, Wendy. She had needed a place to stay, and I'd offered my little house to her as a favor. My spontaneous gesture had left me homeless, or worse, staying full-time with my father like a wayward teenager. Leif had a beautiful home at the end of the valley just down the road from my father's ranch. We were neighbors, in a manner of speaking, and he had surprised me by asking me to housesit. I'd agreed to do it for him as a favor. At least that was how it had been six months ago.

As I drove down the twisting tree-lined road out of Fable I realized I had to accept the fact that my relationship with Leif wasn't as simple as I had fooled myself into believing. He'd been so patient and casual I hadn't even noticed that I was falling into a relationship.

I had started out as his tenant while he finished his messy divorce back in Washington, D.C., and I had graduated to roommate when he had come back to Montana in December. It was now early June and Leif and I had settled into a quiet and comfortable routine. I worked a couple of days a week in the library, and he did . . . whatever it was he did for a living.

I knew Leif was a businessman, and I also knew he worked for the government from time to time. He was usually managing the daily operations of two companies that were headquartered somewhere in Massachusetts, but sometimes he disappeared for several days and it was during those times he was doing his freelance contract work. Leif was something called a forensic accountant. Since balancing my checkbook was often a challenge, I knew instinctively that doing investigative accounting for the government wasn't something I was qualified to make small talk about, and I never brought it up.

When he returned from his unexpected trips I never asked him about them. He never volunteered any stories, and we left the topic alone. It was my way of maintaining the illusion that I wasn't a part of his life, that I was simply a girl he was spending time with until someone classier came along to fill the relationship void in his world.

At least, that was what I had been telling myself. I knew I wouldn't be able to make it through the summer without sitting down with him to have an open discussion. But for now I was content to pretend it didn't mean that much to him. That way I could pretend it didn't mean that much to me.

At the bottom of the steep hill I turned left and I drove by the pasture that marked the farthest edge of my father's ranch. Our little thousand-acre spread was situated a ten-minute drive outside of Killdeer, population 901 when everybody was home. It was in a prime spot. My family had owned the land for four generations. Dearcorn Ranch, as it had been called since 1911, flanked a long stretch of U.S. Forest Service land that marked the western boundary of the property. To the north of the property a stand of aspen trees crowded together, sheltering us with privacy, and across the road from our place to the east sprawled a vast stretch of state land. We had the good fortune to be surrounded by neighbors who couldn't ever build.

My father had retired a few summers ago from cattle ranching, and now he amused himself with planting alfalfa in the spring on the prime pastureland that lay between the mountain and the county road, and in the winter he went half-mad with boredom. Some days I missed the cattle, even though they had been a source of unremitting hard work and heartache.

When I drove past the dirt road that led to my father's ranch house, I wondered if my best friend, Irene Baker, was there this afternoon. She and my father had finally ended their footloose days and were now in a relationship that could only be described as torrid. I knew to call my father before spontaneously popping by for a visit these days.

When I parked in the wide gravel driveway at Leif's house I could see him sitting on the porch wearing his telephone headset and talking. His expression was impatient, and it was plain to see he was embroiled in a business phone call that was rubbing him the wrong way.

He gave me a wink and a smile as I went inside to change out of my office clothes. I slipped into a pair of jeans and bright yellow T-shirt and pulled on a pair of hikers. I gathered my strawberry blonde hair in a wad, crammed it underneath a baseball cap and went back downstairs through the huge living room to the kitchen. It had taken me weeks to get used to living in such a mansion. Leif's house was a two-story log masterpiece he had built as his ultimate retreat, and even though the countertops were polished granite and the walls were covered with original oil paintings, the place still managed to look as if it belonged in the deep woods. It was nestled in the trees at the base of the jagged limestone cliff that encircled it like a giant horseshoe. Pine trees surrounded the house on three sides, hiding the home from the world. Leif preferred it that way.

I fixed him a tall lemonade and crammed the glass with ice. It was a beautiful summer day, and though there was a pleasant breeze it was still warm on the porch.

He glanced up as I put the lemonade next to him on the glass tabletop. He gave me a grateful smile and mouthed the words "See you later" before turning his attention back to the phone conversation. Leif spent so much time on the telephone that he wore a headset constantly during working hours. He mentioned to me once that it wasn't uncommon for him to talk on the phone for seven hours at a stretch.

It made me grateful I was a librarian and not the head of an international company.

I drove to Wendy's house with the windows rolled down and the radio turned up. The only clear signal on the dial was a country station out of Parkman that played an awful lot of Taylor Swift. Today, I didn't mind. It was summer. The sky was clear and even the chirpy voice of a teen pop idol sounded believable.

Wendy Martinez lived in the small caretaker's house that was a part of my father's ranch. I had invited her to move in after she and her husband, Joe, had split up. She owned a yarn store in Killdeer, Wee Wooly's Yarn Shop. I marveled that she had managed to keep the business going without her husband's secure income backing her. She had previously lived a glitzy lifestyle as the wife of a bank president. Though she was poor as a college student these days, she seemed happier.

I parked and saw someone who I assumed was Wendy's nephew standing on the deck. He was skinny and, like most ten-year-old boys, constructed mostly of knees and elbows. But his smile was big, and looked more game than mischievous.

"Are you Marley?" he asked.

I stopped at the bottom of the stairs. "I'm Marley. You must be Hugo."

"What kind of a name is Marley for a girl, anyway?" he asked.

"What kind of a name is Hugo?" I asked without a moment's hesitation.

He grinned. I wasn't going to talk to him like most adults and answer his questions with a patronizing tone. He seemed to brighten.

"Mom named me after the writer," he said.

I frowned. "Which one?"

"Victor Hugo," he said. "Mom said she loved his books so much, but that the name Victor sounded too Russian, or something. So she named me Hugo instead."

"Marley was my grandfather's name," I told him. "My father really respected my grandfather and so he named me after him."

Hugo thought about that for a moment. "Okay."

I seemed to have passed some sort of test, and Hugo bounded down the stairs.

"Don't you have to tell your Aunt Wendy you are leaving?" I asked.

"She knows." He shouldered a camouflage, boy-sized backpack and climbed inside the SUV without a second glance back at the house.

I saw Wendy appear in the big picture window and give me a wave. She was trying frantically to cram in an earring, and she clumsily bumped the front door open with her hip.

"Thanks, Marley. I really appreciate this. Do I look okay?"

Hugo leaned out of the car window. "You know we only have two hours of viable sunlight left to go see the dinosaurs."

I gave Wendy a questioning look. "Viable sunlight?"

She smoothed the fabric of her cheerful baby-blue sundress. "My sister talks like that all the time. She's a curator at the Pennsylvania Museum."

"It's called The Penn, Aunt Wendy," Hugo said from the car window. He deliberately made a show of buckling his seat belt.

Wendy gave a small laugh. "He's . . . ah, really bright." She said it like an apology.

I glanced over my shoulder at the young Indiana Jones sitting gamely in my front seat. He pulled out a pair of binoculars and started scanning the trees. Since the caretaker's house was surrounded on three sides by forest, I didn't think the binoculars would do him a lot of good. He didn't seem to mind.

I couldn't help but smile. "You know, Wendy, I think we will get along just fine. You and Loy have a good time tonight on your date."

She flashed relief with a smile and gave Hugo a quick wave before heading back inside.

I climbed in the SUV and started the engine.

Hugo laced the binoculars around his neck by the strap and watched the trees whip past as we drove down the road. One knee was plastered with three smudged Band-Aids. He swung his legs as he talked.

"Did your family come here a long time ago?" he asked.

"Yes," I said. "My great-grandmother was a homesteader here in the early nineteen hundreds."

"Did she ever kill any Indians?" he asked.

"Hugo," I said. "That's not very nice."

He didn't miss a beat when he answered, and turned his head to look me straight in the eye.

"I didn't mean it like it was a good thing."

I relaxed a little. "No. She didn't ever fight any Indians."

"That's good," he said. "'Cause the indigenous peoples of this area have a rich history."

I swiveled my head around to stare back at him. "Do you even know what the word indigenous means?" I asked.

"Yes. It means belonging to a certain place," he told me.

"Did your mother teach you that?" I asked.

He lifted his binoculars to stare at a sparrow hawk grooming on a fence post. "She studies primitive cultures in Mesoamerica."

"So how come it is you know so much about the native people of Montana?" I asked.

He lowered the binoculars as the sparrow hawk took flight.

"Mom says that our history is important because we need to know where we came from," Hugo said, quite seriously.

"I guess I'd agree with that," I said, thinking about how important it was to me that I had my connection with Killdeer. The entire population of the town was less than a thousand people, but somehow it always seemed bigger to me.

"And 'cause I sort of wish that things had been different during the Indian Wars," he said, almost as an afterthought.

"Oh?" I asked. "I do too. But how do you wish they had been different?"

He adjusted the binoculars and scanned the peak of the mountain, searching for something that only an open imagination could see. Then his mouth curled down in a troubled, thoughtful frown. "I wish the Indians would have won."

CHAPTER 2

Hugo and I parked with the nose of my SUV practically touching the back bumper of the brown University of Wyoming geology van. The rough-looking van blocked the gate access, but apparently the graduate student had decided he didn't feel comfortable driving up. We squeezed through the narrow gap between strands of barbed wire and started walking up the dusty track that led to the top of the ridge.

"Will we find any arrowheads?" Hugo asked, looking around with obvious excitement. "This is a perfect spot for that."

"I don't know," I said. "Maybe. I think my father has an old box of arrowheads someplace that my grandfather picked up over the years."

The sun was a bit too bright and cheerful, and before we were halfway up the ridge I was sweating and wishing I had brought a bottle of water.

We walked up the rutted track side by side, and Hugo kept up a running commentary on the types of bugs he spotted, the likelihood of finding a rattlesnake, and the sad fact that ancient Native Americans didn't have things like ice cream and Neosporin.

"I see some dust," Hugo said.

Plumes of cast-off dirt floated in the air. It wasn't difficult to see the dig site. I walked past a healthy clump of milk thistle and over the spine of the ridge, my boots leaving perfect tracks in the soft dirt.

We stopped when we crested the ridge, but before I could announce us to the graduate student, Hugo was already scampering down the other side madly.

"Hey! What kind of dinosaurs are you digging up?" he called.

A slender young man, maybe thirty, spun around with a yelp and nearly fell backwards. He held a small shovel in one hand and was coated with a thick layer of the gray dust.

"Sorry." I gave a friendly wave and followed Hugo down the hill. "I'm Marley Dearcorn. Nathan's daughter."

The grad student pushed his floppy hat back from his forehead and laughed. "You startled me," he said. "I haven't seen another person up here for two days."

"Are you digging up a T-rex?" Hugo asked. He was so anxious to climb down in the hole he was dancing along the edge.

The young man pushed the tip of his shovel deep in the ground and left it standing at attention while he bent down for an old army canteen. He took a long drink and shook his head. "No T-rex here. This is a Jurassic formation. I'm looking for something very rare, called a Megalosaurus."

Hugo was scanning the hole, both arms flapping with excitement. "Megalosaur? I've never heard of that. What is it?"

"It's sort of like an ancient cousin to the T-rex," the grad student said, taking a handful of water from his canteen and splashing it on the back of his neck.

The young man gave me a smile—he was actually enjoying the questions—and after he tightened the screw top of his canteen he dropped it to the ground and held out his hand.

I watched where I put my feet, being careful not to step on anything that looked important, and I leaned forward to shake his offered hand. My hand came back covered in dirt.

"I'm Jimmy Burke. I'm with the University of Wyoming's paleontology department."

"A paleontologist?" I said, trying to remember the brief conversations I'd had with the Forest Service diggers back at my old job with the Fish and Wildlife office. "So, you're not an archaeologist?"

Jimmy gave a half smile. "Nope. I don't dig up people."

"My mom digs up people," Hugo said, a wide grin on his face.

Jimmy blinked once and stared at the boy. "She does?"

"My mom's work is in Mesoamerica, mostly. She says that it's the white man's burden to preserve ancient cultures. I'm Hugo," he said, his sharp eyes appraising Jimmy.

"Hello, Hugo," Jimmy said, his own expression shifting from amusement to thoughtful consideration. "Who does your mother work for?"

Hugo was practically bouncing with excitement.

"She works for The Penn," he said, happy to be having a deep discussion with a fellow scientist.

Jimmy's face registered confusion, so I volunteered a little backstory. "The Pennsylvania Museum," I said.

Jimmy shrugged. "I'm not familiar with it, but if they are an anthropology museum I wouldn't be."

"What have you found?" Hugo asked, ignoring us both completely and concentrating on the hole.

I could see from a quick glance that the topsoil was peeled back about a foot, exposing a darker layer of the grayish mudstone that made walking along this ridgeline in a rainstorm practically impossible. Once this soil got wet, there was no dealing with it. The dirt stuck to everything when the rains came. But when it was dry it crumbled away with the proper application of a pick and shovel. More than once I'd had to come up on this ridge to help my father repair our ancient barbed-wire fence, and in late August after the ground had baked for a couple of months, the soil was more like concrete than dirt. June was a good time to be digging up here.

"I haven't found much," Jimmy said. "Just a few bone fragments. But it's a good sign that I found them. It means there is something down there."

I knelt down and filtered a handful of soil through my fingers. It was warm to the touch, and powder-dry. "So, Jimmy. How did you know to even look here for dinosaurs?"

Jimmy took two steps towards the edge of the hole and eased himself down onto the grass lip surrounding the dig site. He was coated with dirt, and even though it was a sunny day he was covered head to toe with clothing. He wore an old white dress shirt that had obviously been recycled from a Goodwill store. The cuffs were buttoned down to his wrists and the collar was pulled up as high as it would go. I recalled from my days working as a landscaper that unless you wore clothing over every square inch of skin, the Montana sun would gladly blister you raw.

Jimmy pulled a half-melted Snickers bar from his shirt pocket, took a bite of the gooey chocolate and talked while he chewed. "I wasn't sure I would find anything at all. This site hasn't been dug for a long time. The documentation for it was lost in a fire at the University back in 1981, and I was going more from rumors than from actual quarry maps."

"This was a quarry?" That was news to me.

He wiped a smear of chocolate off his lip. "More than thirty years ago, at least."

"But if the maps were lost, how did you find it?" I asked.

"Haven't you ever heard of Dr. Clifton Myers?" he asked.

I shook my head. "I don't know much about the academic field."

Jimmy swallowed the remains of his Snickers bar and carefully folded the wrapper inside his shirt pocket. "Clifton Myers is the curator for the Colorado Museum of Natural History at Boulder. He's the big tuna who found this place back in the 70's when he was a student at the University of Wyoming."

Hugo eased his way into the hole and dropped on all fours. He began sifting through the dirt with eager hands. I started to say something to the boy, but Jimmy shook his head at me. "He's fine. There's nothing in there he can hurt. I don't think I'm to the bone layer yet."

"If you find anything," I said to Hugo, "let Mr. Burke here know about it right away."

Jimmy leaned back and laced his fingers behind his head. His hat tipped up and I could see a ratted mess of blond hair, bleached from too much sun, poking out from under the dusty brim. He didn't look very much like a Mr. Burke to me.

"Back when this was a quarry, Clifton Myers found two megalosaur teeth," Jimmy said. "They are very, very rare and there isn't that much known about them. I'm doing my graduate work on megalosaurids and since this was the last place anyone found teeth from that particular family, this is where I came to look."

"Aren't you a little old for a grad student?" I gave Jimmy a lopsided smile so he would know I was teasing him.

He pushed his smudged glasses back up on the brim of his nose. "I started college late, and then I had this crazy idea that I wanted to be a political science major for three years, but luckily I came to my senses. What's your field of study?"

"I used to work for the Montana Fish and Wildlife office, over at the little branch office up in Helena. But now I'm a librarian, not a student."

"Hey you guys?" Hugo said. He was bent over a spot in the hole, scrutinizing it.

"A librarian?" Jimmy said. "What kind of retirement package do you get?"

"Hey, Mr. Jimmy?" Hugo said, more insistent.

"Looking to change your major again?" I asked.

"I found something!" Hugo bellowed.

Jimmy shot me a wink. "I'll bet it's an old pop bottle top."

"What did you find, Hugo?" I was happy the boy seemed to be genuinely enjoying himself.

"Something that I don't think should be here," Hugo said.

"Is it a horned lizard?" I asked. "There are lizards all over the rocks up here."

"I think it's a tooth," Hugo said.

Jimmy was on his feet and in the hole faster than I could blink. He pulled a worn paintbrush from his back pocket and dropped to his knees beside Hugo. "Show me," he said, all trace of humor gone from his tone.

"It's right here." Hugo pointed carefully.

Jimmy teased the dirt aside with the paintbrush like he was performing surgery. I couldn't resist and I joined the two of them in the hole, being very careful not to step anyplace that Jimmy hadn't already walked. I dropped to my knees beside them.

"That would be lucky," I said.

Jimmy seemed to have lost the ability to talk. He was staring at the ground, his eyes shining with glee. Another stroke of the brush revealed a black shape poking through the dirt. It was the size of a broken butter knife handle, but more rounded. The bone had a slight curve as it tapered to a jagged point. It was black, unlike the gray soil surrounding it, and the surface looked slightly shiny.

"Great job," Jimmy said. "That is a very nice rib-bone fragment. You may have just found me my master's thesis."

Hugo knelt back, pride and satisfaction filling his face. "Cool! I can't wait to tell Mom."

I felt something dig into my knee and I shifted to the side. "Ow. I hope I didn't just crush another one of your dinosaur bones."

I leaned back, my knees resting only a couple of feet from where the bone fragment lay in the loose soil. Jimmy extended his brush and began cleaning the spot.

"Maybe it's a claw," Hugo said. He watched, wide-eyed, as Jimmy brushed away the dirt.

I had to laugh to myself. The two of them were like prospectors who had just found a gold nugget. But I had to admit their enthusiasm was infectious.

Jimmy blew on the loose dirt and frowned when something appeared. He paused for a moment and glanced back at the rib-bone fragment he'd just uncovered, and then looked back to the spot where I'd just been kneeling. His frown deepened.

"What's wrong?" I asked. "Did you find a pop bottle top?"

I stopped teasing him when Jimmy looked up, his face perplexed. "This," he said, pointing to the ground, "should not be here."

He leaned back far enough that I could get a good look at the object he had uncovered. I could see the rough outline of a smooth edge, similar to the rib bone in many ways. But when I leaned down and really examined it, I sat up and shared Jimmy's shocked expression.

"What is it? What is it?" The boy wiggled between us and stared at the ground. He gulped air. "That's an arrowhead."

"I'm no expert." I met Jimmy's eyes. "But what is an arrowhead doing in a layer of rock that has dinosaur bones in it?"

Jimmy's face shifted from shock to confusion, and finally settled on despair. "There goes my thesis."

Hugo was still sandwiched between us. "Oh, it's re-, re-something."

"Re-working," Jimmy said. He sat back on his haunches and rubbed his forehead. His face was set with disappointment. "It's classic re-working. I really needed this site to be pristine. Obviously it's contaminated with younger strata. This arrowhead is totally out of context. I can't believe this!"

I must have looked confused. Jimmy held out his hands, gesturing as he explained.

"Sometimes an object from one stratum becomes embedded in a layer of sediment that is far, far younger than its own. But I've never seen re-working like this before. I think my master's program just got a major setback."

Jimmy dropped his paintbrush and rested his forehead in his palms. Hugo edged around him and scooped up the brush. With fast, clumsy strokes, he uncovered the arrowhead so that I could really see it for the first time.

It was in perfect condition. The arrowhead was larger than the rib fragment, but not by much.

"I've got an identification book in my pack," Hugo said with excitement. He dashed towards the top of the ridge and over the crest of the hill in a mad sprint. I could hear him running down the other side towards the SUV.

Jimmy seemed to be recovering his good humor, and laughed. "Only I would find an arrowhead in a Jurassic quarry."

"Will you be able to use this place now for your thesis?" I asked.

Jimmy halfheartedly picked up his paintbrush and cleaned around the arrowhead. "I don't know. Maybe."

As he brushed away the soil from around the arrowhead, Jimmy's face froze with surprise. "What the . . . ?"

I watched as he began to brush faster, pushing the soil aside with frantic strokes.

Jimmy knelt down so far his knees were tucked to his chest. He kept brushing away the soil with methodical motions. It crumbled and scattered as he worked, and when the dirt was too compact he used his hands to loosen it before taking up the brush again. He pulled a worn dentist's cleaning tool from his pants pocket and carefully pried the dense soil aside.

I couldn't resist the urge to help, and soon I was on all fours beside him, carefully moving the dry soil away and watching Jimmy so I could copy his moves.

He leaned back after we had removed another layer, and took in a huge breath of air. Like he was blowing out candles on the world's largest birthday cake, Jimmy blew away the powdered dirt to expose the ground.

"I think you need to change your major again," I said.

Jimmy looked back at me with an expression of utter disbelief. "I'm not qualified to do this. This," he said, waving his arms at the ground. "This is way out of my league."

"Four, five, six . . ." I counted the objects lying in the freshly exposed soil. "There are at least a dozen arrowheads here."

Jimmy snatched the brush again and moved closer to the place Hugo had discovered the rib fragment. He removed the muck and kept blowing away the dust until I was sure he had to be seeing stars. I was afraid he would pass out at the rate he was huffing and puffing.

Jimmy paused long enough to catch his breath. "I think this is an artifact site. My dinosaur bone may be the anomaly here."

Hugo came sprinting back with his backpack slung over one shoulder.

"Wow!" Hugo said when he saw the cache of arrowheads. "Look at them all."

The boy dropped to the ground and practically stripped the zipper on his backpack getting it open. He dug around inside until he found a tattered book squirreled away at the bottom, and pulled it out with a triumphant grin. Hugo started flipping through the book, searching for a match to the arrowheads we had uncovered.

I didn't want to feel totally useless so I gingerly took the paintbrush and started to carefully clean away the loose soil, hoping to find the last of the arrowheads.

"If you find anything," Jimmy said, "don't pick it up. I want to photograph everything the way it is before I start to sketch a quarry map."

"Ah, Jimmy?" I asked. "How big did they make arrowheads?"

"Why?" he asked, abandoning his spot and crouching beside me.

"This seems a little bigger than that." I had fumbled across something solid that seemed like it was buried deep in the ground. Whatever it was, it was definitely bigger than the arrowheads we had uncovered.

Jimmy pulled the brush out of my hand and went to work. Something round, blunt and black emerged from the soil.

"That is not an arrowhead," I said. The hard surface was rounded and smooth, curving back and vanishing into the ground.

It looked more like a snout sticking out of the dirt than a rock.

Jimmy looked pale even under the blazing late afternoon sun. He stared at the thing, his jaw slack.

"Is it important?" I asked, a little concerned about his sudden silence.

"Ah, yeah. It's important."

The young paleontologist almost fell backwards as he tried to sit down. He looked light-headed.

"Jimmy, are you alright?" I asked.

"I will be," he said.

"You want some water?" I asked, searching the ground for his canteen.

"No," he said, letting his eyes fall on the black object poking from the ground. "I want a National Geographic film crew. They are going to want to see this."

CHAPTER 3

"That's impossible," Jimmy said, for the fifth time in as many minutes. He had worked for nearly half an hour to uncover as much of the site as he could.

"So this isn't, what, reworking?" I asked.

I watched him as he frantically but cautiously cleared away the soil from the bone I'd uncovered. He muttered the words "it goes" again and again as he scooped the dirt aside. Apparently, it goes was paleontologist talk for a bone that was complete and not just a fragment. After staring at the ground speechlessly for a moment, Jimmy stood up like he was addressing Congress.

"Everybody off the site," he said.

"You mean, me and Hugo?" I asked, looking around.

"I mean nobody comes up here. Please, both of you don't say anything to anyone. I've got to take some pictures and make some phone calls. I need to call the University. There is no way that they are going to believe this!"

"Believe what?" I asked.

Jimmy was practically bouncing with excitement.

"This," he said, pointing at the bone, "is a premaxilla."

"Is that some species of dinosaur the Discovery channel forgot to tell me about?" I asked.

The grad student rolled his eyes. "It's the nose. It's a dinosaur's nose. And you know what that means."

"He means there is a skull underneath it," Hugo explained to me helpfully.

Jimmy kicked up a cloud of dirt as he rushed to his field pack.

"A skull is important, right?" I asked.

Hugo wiped away a film of dust that had collected on his face. "It's the most important part you can find."

The kid looked like he was accustomed to being coated in dirt and I imagined that he'd spent more than one summer tagging along with his mother on digs similar to this one.

Jimmy pulled a digital camera from his field pack and fiddled with the settings, mumbling. "How am I going to secure this place tonight? There will be people crawling all over it if we don't do something."

Hugo scratched his nose. "Hey, I've got an idea. Why don't I go get some sleeping bags and we can spend the night up here guarding the site?"

"What?" I asked.

Jimmy's face lit up with hope at the suggestion. "Could you?"

"No way," I said. "Listen, nobody ever comes up here. Just throw some dirt over the arrowheads or something."

"You don't get it, do you?" Jimmy told me.

His face was red and one pulsing vein stuck out on his neck.

"I get that this is important," I said. "But unless you make a big production out of it nobody will even know you are up here. This is Killdeer, Montana. We have more gophers than people."

Jimmy paced the hole as he tried to maneuver into position for a shot with his camera. "I don't think you grasp the gravity of the situation here," he said as he started snapping photos.

"He means that it's valuable," Hugo said.

"You mean, valuable as in worth a lot of money?" I asked.

"No, no," Hugo told me as he stepped out of the hole and plopped onto the grass. "Like, historical."

Jimmy's face pinched into an expression of complete exasperation. "Okay, let me explain this in a way you can understand."

I backed off of the site and sat down beside Hugo. I gave Jimmy a patient smile, with difficulty. "Alright. Explain."

Jimmy lowered the camera and leaned towards me. "In 2009 a triceratops skull sold at Bonhams auction house in New York for $242,000. That was just a triceratops. This is possibly a Megalosaurus. An ancient cousin to the T-rex, and very, very rare. Even if it's just an Allosaurus skull, it could still be worth about a million bucks."

"A million bucks?" I was glad I was sitting down.

Jimmy resumed snapping pictures. "Couple that with the anomaly of the arrowhead cache, and this site is impossible to value monetarily."

Hugo gaped at Jimmy. "A million dollars?"

"So you still just want to throw some dirt on it and walk away?" Jimmy asked.

I felt my mouth hanging open and managed to close it before any flies could become a late lunch. "Maybe we should go talk to my father about this."

"I need him to sign some papers," Jimmy said. He took several more pictures before replacing the lens cap on the camera.

"What sort of papers?" I was still thinking about the possibility that my father would be able to take that dream vacation to Belize that he'd always talked about.

"I understand if Nathan wants to sell the fossil. If it's valuable, I'd want to sell it too. But I want some time to study it first. Do you think he could grant me that?" Jimmy asked.

"I can't say what he will do," I told him.

"Hey, won't the museum in Wyoming get the dinosaur?" Hugo asked.

Jimmy shook his head as he shoved his camera back inside his pack. "Not unless Marley's father will donate it. This is private land. Anything that is found here belongs to Nathan Dearcorn. I'm not really sure about the arrowheads. I think they belong to Nathan, too. Honestly, I don't know that much about artifacts."

"You could have kept this to yourself and we never would have known there was anything of value here," I said, looking at Jimmy with scrutiny. I was deliberately baiting him to see what he would say. Having a possible fortune buried in my father's backyard, so to speak, made me think that it might be a good idea to determine what team Jimmy was batting for. His, or ours.

"I wouldn't ever do that," he said. "This is too important. Besides, you can't just take a fossil out of the ground and haul it to some auction house these days. Everything has to be documented and released legally before it can be sold."

Jimmy was telling me the truth, as far as I was able to judge. He didn't seem to have any agenda other than getting time to study the fossil.

But I thought I would tag along when he went to talk to my father, just in case.

"They are Clovis points. At least, I think they are," Hugo looked up from his arrowhead book, his face beaming.

Jimmy dropped his field pack and eagerly knelt down. "Let me see that."

The two of them crouched over a tiny pocket guide to arrowheads and bumped foreheads as they studied the text.

"Are they old?" I asked.

"They have to be," Jimmy said. "But I'm not sure of the actual age."

"It doesn't say in the book," Hugo said. "My mom's got a better book than this one at home, but it's really big and heavy and she said I could only bring seven books with me on this trip 'cause my suitcase was already too heavy, and so I couldn't bring it."

"Maybe you could call your mom and ask her about them," I suggested.

Jimmy jumped up. "We can't tell anyone about this until after I've had a chance to call the University. I have to map this site and that will take time."

"Don't you just have to draw what you find on some graph paper?" I asked.

Hugo turned his head towards me and gave me a pitying look. "It's not that simple, Aunt Marley."

"Did your Aunt Wendy tell you to call me that?" I asked.

"Yeah," Hugo said with a wide grin. "She said that the sheriff said to call you Aunt Marley because you would like it."

"Can we focus on the situation at hand, please?" said Jimmy, a note of panic in his voice.

"You know, it's not like there are roving bands of dinosaur pirates with access to helicopters just waiting around to swoop down and steal these bones," I told him.

"Would you walk away and leave a million bucks lying out on the ground where everyone could see it?" Jimmy asked.

I forced myself to take a breath before I answered. "You don't even know if this bone you found really is valuable. These arrowheads might actually be the most important things in this hole."

"I don't care about the arrowheads," Jimmy said, grabbing a shovel. "If I didn't have scruples I'd just toss them out of the hole before I started documenting my dig."

"So what are you going to do, for the time being?" I asked.

"I'm going to throw a bunch of dirt over the site so nobody can see what's out here." He scooped a few shovelfuls of soil and tossed them over the hole.

"That's a great idea," I said sarcastically.

"Anyway," Hugo said. He scooted closer to me and held up an illustration of the arrowheads. "These are Clovis points. You can tell by the shape. Pretty cool, huh?"

"What else does it say about them?" I asked. The illustration was a crude pencil drawing, and not very helpful.

"Just that this type of arrowhead is usually made out of something called chert."

"Does it say how much they are worth?" I was ashamed of myself the moment I said it.

Hugo closed the field guide and stuffed it in his backpack. "It's not that kind of book, Aunt Marley. And anyway, you'd need an expert to tell you that."

I suppressed a groan. When did I become related to this kid?

A cloud of dust hit me in the face, bringing me back to the here and now. I blinked it away and spit out a fragment of rock. "Hugo, why don't we let Jimmy finish up here and go over to my father's place and see if he's got any hot dogs?"

"Hot dogs are full of nitrites," Hugo said.

I forced a smile. "How about some organic, grass-fed free-range hamburger, then?"

"Do you have any Kool-Aid? Mom won't let me have it because she says the Red number 40 makes me hyperactive."

I was starting to wonder if my father had any Old Number 7 Jack Daniel's whiskey. "Maybe he will have a couple bottles of sarsaparilla."

"Could you tell Nathan that I will be down to see him in about a half an hour?" Jimmy asked. He threw another shovelful of dirt, appraising the hole like it was a Picasso.

"I'll tell him." I got to my feet and tapped Hugo on the shoulder. "Let's leave him to his work."

"Can we come back tomorrow?" He gave me his best pleading child expression and his big brown eyes sliced through my resolve with little resistance.

"We can come back," I said, feeling like a pushover.

"Look, I don't want to tell you what you can and cannot do on your own land," Jimmy said. "But it might be better if you didn't come up here and draw any more attention to this place than is absolutely necessary."

"Because this road is loaded down with traffic," I said.

My sarcasm was lost on Jimmy.

He took off his hat and slapped it against his leg. A cloud of dust flew into the air. "Don't say I didn't warn you."

"Warn me about what?" I asked.

"People can get a little bit weird when it comes to dinosaurs," he said.

"No kidding." I stared at him.

"People can get greedy," Jimmy said. "And when someone is more interested in what's in it for them than what's right for science, a lot of bad can come of it."

I felt the first cool breeze of evening drift up from the foothills, brought on by the slowly setting sun. Jimmy was watching me, his earnest expression distorted with worry. He seemed genuinely concerned. Maybe I was being too hard on him.

"Alright," I said. "How would you handle this if it was your land?"

He thought for a moment, his eyes drifting over the scrub brush and prairie grass. "I would hire a couple of guys with shotguns to stay up here 24/7 and shoot anyone who tries to come on the land without permission."

"Cool!" Hugo said.

"That's not cool," I said quickly. "Jimmy, don't you think that's overdoing it just a bit?"

The young man leaned against the handle of his shovel and clumsily crammed his hat back on with one hand. "Maybe you should put up a fence, too."

"We already have a fence."

I pointed to the string of barbed wire that lined the ridge not twenty feet from where we were standing. It hugged the tree line, delineating the break between the Dearcorn Ranch and U.S. Forest Service land.

"That's not going to do a thing to keep people out of here," Jimmy said. "You need a chain fence with a lock on the gate."

"And attack dogs!" Hugo said.

"Okay, okay. Everybody just take a deep breath," I said.

"At least let me sleep up here tonight," Jimmy said, watching me carefully.

I was starting to get a bad feeling about this. I was certain that he was worried about nothing, but if there was nothing to worry about why was I getting a bad feeling?

Hugo was getting bored now that the arrowheads were covered up. He wandered over to a fat sagebrush plant and was busy torturing an ant mound with a stick. What was it with boys and ant mounds?

I used the corner of my sleeve to wipe a layer of dust off my mouth. Funny, but being a paleontologist didn't seem all that different from being a landscaper to me, because both jobs left you covered in dirt and blisters. "Come on, Hugo. Let's go get you some politically incorrect supper."

Just before we dipped down the other side of the hill, I glanced back and saw Jimmy crouched on the ground, his hat pushed back off his forehead, frantically trying to get a signal on his cell phone.

CHAPTER 4

"That's all of them." My father plunked a sturdy wooden box down on the kitchen table in front of me.

When I scooted it closer the old carved words on the lid came into focus. "Snipe Tails. I forgot you and Granddad had this."

As I lifted the lid, Hugo leaned across the table to see what was inside. "What are snipe tails?"

"It's an old joke. It means 'fool's errand,'" my father explained.

The box was filled with arrowheads, all shapes, sizes and colors. Some of them were chipped, some in perfect condition.

Hugo leaned against me as he peered inside the old box. "Look at them all."

"There's probably forty years' worth," my father said.

I frowned when I started poking through them. "These don't look anything like the arrowheads we found up on the ridge."

Hugo was torn between the contents of the box and the fat hamburger resting on the plate in front of him. After a moment's hesitation, the hamburger won out and he sat back down so he could eat with both hands.

"These are from all over the ranch," my father said. He sat down beside Hugo and set an open can of root beer in front of the boy.

Hugo slurped from the can, keeping one eye on the box.

The points had the familiar notches in the bottom that would allow them to be fixed to the end of an arrow. They looked like true arrowheads to me, unlike the ones Jimmy had uncovered. Maybe the arrowheads up on the ridge were older, or used for a spear, or something not related to an arrow shaft.

"Just so you know, that grad student will be here any minute and he will start filling your head full of crazy ideas about his dig," I told my father.

"Like how the stuff he found is worth a million dollars?" he asked.

I gave my father a surprised look. "How did you know?"

"Because I've heard it all before." He leaned back in his chair, the old wood creaking.

I snatched a potato chip from the bag on the table. "Jimmy said the ridge hasn't been dug for thirty years."

"Thirty-four years," my father said. "The summer before you were born, a fast-talking devil named Myers who was looking for fossils came on our land and spent the entire months of July and August digging up the whole hillside."

I wasn't entirely sure I wanted to bring up the events from my father's past. It wasn't a story with a happy ending.

I frowned. "Jimmy told me about that guy. He said that Clifton Myers found a couple of rare dinosaur teeth here."

My father popped open his own can of root beer and took a long swig. "Your granddaddy, for whatever reason, took to Myers. But I never liked the man myself. Too shifty."

I looked down at the table, not trusting myself to meet my father's eyes.

Marley Thomas Dearcorn, my grandfather, had been murdered the day I was born. November 1st, 1997. My father hadn't just loved Granddad, he'd practically worshipped him. As a final homage to my grandfather, my father named me, his newborn daughter, Marley as tribute to his memory. To this day my father still couldn't talk about what had happened all those years ago.

My father had been the one who found him. Granddad had been shot in the back, which had somehow seemed significant to my father, but hadn't helped him determine who had done it. The sheriff at the time never had any suspects, and whoever killed my grandfather had never been caught. No one was ever charged with the crime and it became one of Killdeer's great, unsolved mysteries. To my father, however, it was much more than an old story. It was a sharp pain he lived with each and every day.

It wasn't easy, but I was curious about the events leading up to my grandfather's death. "He found the dinosaur teeth the summer before Granddad died?"

"Your granddaddy had given that Clifton Myers permission to look for fossils anywhere on our place he wanted," my father said, recalling the events. "For some reason Myers and your granddaddy liked each other. They'd sit on the porch for hours in the evening and tell lies and drink beer. That guy could have accidentally set fire to the prairie and your granddaddy would have forgiven him. He had free run of the house, even. They were friends, which I never did quite see, because they were so different. Myers left at the end of August. We never heard from him again. But he told us before he left that he would be back. He said he wanted to do a bigger excavation the next summer and that we would be famous. He said the dinosaur bones he found were rare, and we'd be millionaires."

I pulled the bag of potato chips closer to me and snacked on a couple while I thought about what all of that meant. "But why would Clifton Myers go to all that trouble just for two measly teeth?"

My father popped the top on another can of soda and slid it over to me. "Well, I was pretty sure when I met him that the bastard just wanted to be famous for something."

"Dad," I said, glancing at Hugo.

"Sorry," he said.

Hugo looked between my father and me. "It's okay, Mr. Dearcorn. Mom swears all the time when she talks about pot hunters."

"Myers didn't care what he found, as long as it was special, and he was hot to trot to get funding for research and kept going on about landing a position at the Smithsonian," my father told me.

"Did he?" I asked.

"Hell if I know," my father said. "We lost track of him after he left."

Someone knocked on the front door. The raps sounded frantic.

"That would be Jimmy Burke," I said.

I went to the door and pulled it open, not surprised to see the young man glancing over his shoulder nervously.

"Come on in, Jimmy," I said.

"Did anyone see you come down from the ridge?" he asked.

"A couple of crows and a porcupine," I said.

Jimmy shot me a look that said he didn't appreciate my sarcasm.

I shut the door behind us and my father was already dragging a fourth chair to the kitchen table before I could sit back down. Hugo had finished his hamburger and was poking through the box of arrowheads with a gleam in his eye.

"Mr. Dearcorn, I strongly suggest that you take steps to protect that site." Jimmy sat down. A thin layer of dust drifted down to the floor beneath him.

"Because it's going to make me a rich man." He grinned at Jimmy. Then he took another drink from his root beer and chuckled.

"It very well could," Jimmy said, his tone sharp. "This site is nothing like I have ever seen before. Now, it's possible that I'm wrong about those arrowheads. But I'm definitely not wrong about the fossil. It's got to have some substantial monetary value."

My father leaned across the table. "Son, you need to settle down and tell me what the blazes are you talking about."

"Didn't she tell you?" Jimmy asked. He looked back and forth between us, his face worried and confused.

I noticed that Hugo had been strangely silent during this inquest. He was sorting the arrowheads into neat rows on the table, scrutinizing each one with care.

Jimmy shook his head, watching my father with a strained expression. "Listen, I called the University of Wyoming and they are going to try to contact the state archaeologist for Montana and see if he can come over to take a look at the arrowheads. In the meantime, my professor told me to map the quarry and, with your permission, Nathan, remove the fossil and not disturb the points."

"Jimmy, this ranch is covered with arrowheads. There's nothing special about them. We've got a whole box full of them and they aren't worth anything," my father said.

Jimmy took another big breath. "I'm not an expert, but it looks like it is some sort of an arrowhead cache. It could be very old, and in fairness, I want the site to be looked at by someone who is an anthropologist."

"That sounds reasonable," I said.

"And I'd like you to sign a consent form to allow me to study the dinosaur fossil, and not sell it right away," Jimmy added.

"Let me get this straight," my father said. He was dressed in old blue jeans and a plain white T-shirt, but suddenly he transformed into an investment banker before my very eyes. "You want me to willingly surrender the right to sell my own property until you have had a chance to study it?"

Make that an attorney.

Jimmy persisted. "That's technically correct. But it's for the science. I'm sensitive about the profit you could stand to gain, but I just need to finish my thesis."

"Do you believe this guy?" my father asked me.

My father's gaze rested on my face and I shrugged. "I believe him. But you should have Boyd read the contract before you sign it."

Boyd Strader was the local free legal expert of Killdeer Valley. He wasn't an attorney, but he'd been on the game show Jeopardy once, and his ranch was riddled with coal bed methane wells that were under joint ownership with him and his two ex-wives. If there was a man in Killdeer who knew how to read a convoluted legal contract, it was Boyd.

My father scratched his chin and let his pale eyes drift over Jimmy, as if he was trying to decide if he was looking at a lamb or a rattlesnake.

"Alright. Bring me a contract and I will take a look at it," he said at last.

Jimmy exhaled so much he deflated with relief, and I almost laughed when the young man grabbed my father's hand and pumped it vigorously. "You won't regret this, Mr. Dearcorn."

"I already do, son."

Hugo had been flipping through his arrowhead book and was reading intently.

"Did you find the type of point that is in the box?" I asked.

"They are Pelican Lake points," he said proudly. "At least, some of them are. One of them looks more like the points that Mr. Jimmy found at the site, except it is broken. And I don't know what this is."

Hugo held up a slender white rod that didn't look anything like an arrowhead. "Maybe it's a tool? I can ask my mom later when I call her."

"I really don't think that's such a good idea," Jimmy said, waving his hands. "We shouldn't tell anyone about this."

"Dad, Jimmy thinks that fossil hunters are going to come on the site and ransack it," I said.

"Does he?" my father replied. "Well, alright. I'll, what did you suggest? I'll take steps to look after it. Will that make you happy?"

"It would indeed, Mr. Dearcorn," Jimmy said.

Hugo was holding up an arrowhead with a particularly pleasing color. It was almost translucent, and it was a pleasing color that made it look like a nice piece of jewelry to me. My father noticed Hugo staring at it, studying the shape like an expert.

"Why don't you take that one back and show it to your Aunt Wendy?" my father said. "Keep it as a souvenir for today."

"Oh, I couldn't separate it from the rest of them," Hugo said. "It's better to keep them all together. It helps preserve the integrity of the find."

My father stared at Hugo for a moment, and then he burst out laughing and scooped all of the arrowheads back into the box. "We will keep them all together, then. Take the box with you and while you are staying with your aunt you can look them all over."

Hugo broke into a surprised smile. "That'd be great! I can describe them to my mom and she can tell me about them."

"Just don't describe anything else to your mom," Jimmy said.

My father downed the last of his root beer and tossed the can into the trash bin beside the kitchen sink. "Don't you worry about the site. By tomorrow morning, I guarantee that nobody will be at all interested in crossing our fence to go have a look at your project."

Jimmy stood up and I got to my feet to show him to the door. He still looked nervous. "I hope you are right, Mr. Dearcorn. The last thing you want is for word of this find to get out."

I let Jimmy out and checked my watch. It was almost dark outside, and I felt a bit guilty for waiting so long to get Hugo a proper supper. He would be awake until midnight, excited and full of root beer. Well, it was summer, after all.

"Dad, don't be too surprised to see us here at the house sometime late tomorrow morning."

I was remembering my promise that I would let Hugo see the dig again.

"That's fine, Kiddo. Just do me a favor and stop by the ranch house before you go up the hill. Alright?"

"Sure. Call me if you see any tomb robbers," I said with a laugh.

My father laughed with me. It was too bad that Jimmy Burke didn't see how ridiculous the whole thing actually was.

I took Hugo back to his aunt's. Loy and Wendy were not home from their date yet, so I went inside with him and we topped off the evening's debauchery with a couple mugs of hot chocolate.

"Aunt Marley, can we go up the hill behind the house here and look for arrowheads? I saw a trail that goes up into the trees."

It didn't do any harm for Hugo to call me his Aunt Marley, so I didn't correct him.

"I don't think we should go on that trail."

"But what if there are paleo artifacts up there? We should try to study them if we can."

I recalled what Loy had told me about Willy, the moose poacher, accessing that trail to reach his illegal bear-baiting trap on the hill behind our ranch, and decided it wouldn't be a smart idea to explore that place until after hunting season.

"At the end of that trail is a steep drop over a cliff. It's easy to get lost up there. Sometimes people who don't want to be found will go up there to hide. I would like it very much if you never went up there by yourself, alright Hugo?"

He looked disappointed, but he didn't argue with me. "Okay. But is there any place else we can go search for artifacts?"

The valley surrounding the town of Killdeer had rolling hills, a dozen different species of game to hunt, a fast-flowing river and excellent locations to camp. If I had been a Paleo-Indian running around Montana several hundred years ago, I'd have wanted to spend time here. I sipped my hot chocolate and ruffled his hair. "I think we might be able to find someplace in these hills that will keep you interested."

As he downed the rest of his hot chocolate, I had an sudden snapshot image in my mind of Hugo huddled beneath the blankets in bed, flashlight in hand, the box of arrowheads sitting in his lap and the identification book clutched in the other hand.

Plus a huge smile plastered across his face.

Sometimes it was good to be reminded about the wonders that existed all around us.

CHAPTER 5

It was nearly nine in the morning by the time Hugo and I pulled up to the ranch house the next day. It promised to be another clear, hot, cloudless sky, and I was glad I'd packed my floppy hat I'd worn during my brief stint as a landscaper. Hugo chatted excitedly about the arrowheads he'd taken home the night before, and I drove down the bumpy dirt road with a smile on my face, enjoying his enthusiasm.

When we pulled into the driveway I saw something that I didn't expect to see. A U.S. Forest Service truck was parked in the spot I usually used, and a flicker of irritation made me lose my smile.

"I wonder what they want?" I asked as we parked beside the truck. It was a massive green pickup with huge off-road tires. The truck bed was enclosed, but I could see through the tinted windows just enough to notice the entire back of the truck was loaded with gear. This was obviously some sort of crew vehicle.

I could see someone standing on the front porch of the house. She turned towards us with a start when I slammed my door, maybe a bit harder than I actually intended.

"Help you?" I asked, using the universal Killdeer expression to indicate that it would be nice to know what the blazes the person you are addressing is currently doing standing on your property.

"I was hoping to get a chance to talk to Nathan Dearcorn? I've knocked but he doesn't appear to be at home," she said.

She was short, maybe five feet tall if her boots had a thick sole. She looked to be in her late fifties, but she might have been sixty, easily. Her hair was bleached from years of abuse from the blazing sun, and it hung in two braids down her shoulders. Her beige uniform shirt flapped in the slight breeze, open at the front and almost concealing her T-shirt, but not quite. The T-shirt image was a stylized painting of an Indian woman kneeling beside a flowing stream, and the woman was holding out both of her hands, offering a drink of water to a white timber wolf that stood before her. Both woman and wolf glowed beneath silvery moonlight. I doubted very much the real Pocahontas ever had such a magical encounter, but each to her own.

The woman positively dripped turquoise jewelry. A huge silver necklace hung nearly to her navel and a bracelet the size of a fist adorned her wrist. She peered at me through a pair of thick glasses. I doubted very much that lipstick or mascara had ever touched this woman's face. She was definitely the back-to-nature, outdoorsy type.

"I just came to see him myself," I said.

She came down from the porch and scanned the area like she was certain my father was hiding close by. "It's rather important that I speak with him as soon as possible."

I extended my hand towards her. "I'm Marley, Nathan's daughter."

"Amelia Snow." Her handshake was like a bear trap.

"Did the Lazy Ox Yoke Ranch Angus get into our upper pasture again?" I asked, flexing my fingers. Usually the only time we ever saw someone from the Forest Service was after an episode of cattle encroachment.

Amelia Snow smiled at me with forced patience. "Ah, no. This has nothing to do with cattle. I need to see him concerning the dig that is currently underway on his property."

"How did you know about the dig?" I asked, surprised.

Hugo started to say something but I put a hand on his shoulder to stop him.

"I received a phone call late last night," she said.

She watched me expectantly, waiting for me to spill my guts.

I thought of Leif, and the expression that his face took on when he was talking to someone who was trying to get information out of him that he didn't feel like sharing. I let my face make that same expression.

Friendly, but firmly silent.

"You don't happen to know how I could get in touch with him?" she asked, prompting me.

"Nope."

Her face flickered with irritation.

"I will let him know you stopped by," I said, verbally indicating that she could feel free to leave now.

She opened her mouth to protest but I was already pulling Hugo back to the SUV.

"But—" Hugo said.

"Thanks for stopping by," I told her.

I started the engine before Hugo could get his seat belt buckled.

"Aunt Marley, she's an archaeologist. I saw her field kit on the front seat of that truck. We should have talked to her," he said.

"Hugo, just because your mom is one of the good guys doesn't mean that every archaeologist is. I think we should respect Jimmy's wishes and not say a word to anyone about the dig until he can get his friends from the University up here to take a look at it."

I drove down the dirt road, frowning at the sight of the Forest Service truck in my rearview mirror. What did she mean, she'd received a late night phone call telling her about Jimmy's dig? Who could have known about it?

Her sudden appearance worried me. Maybe Jimmy Burke was right, and dinosaur fossils did make people a little nuts.

Instead of turning right to go up the ridge, I turned left at the junction and headed back towards Killdeer. "I think that I will drop you off at your Aunt Wendy's shop today. I've got a feeling that things might get complicated out at the dig site."

Hugo frowned. "It's so boring there."

"I know. But until we can have a chat with Jimmy and my father about the Forest Service showing up, I think you should spend the day with your Aunt Wendy."

He considered that, and to my surprise, he nodded agreement. He propped his chin on a clenched fist and leaned against the door. "Okay. But can I at least come out tomorrow?"

"As long as we get this sorted out by then, sure. I don't see why not," I said.

I drove to Wee Wooly's Yarn Shop and we went inside. Wendy looked a little surprised to see us, but she smiled when she saw Hugo and gave him a quick hug.

"Back so soon?" As usual, Wendy was looking beautiful. She'd grown out her blonde hair and each day I saw her she looked more and more like a contestant on America's Next Top Model. The only reason every single man in Killdeer wasn't shamelessly hitting on her was because our local sheriff had taken a very public interest.

"Things might be a bit busy out at the ranch today," I said.

Wendy gave me a questioning look, but I shook my head and glanced at Hugo.

"Well, I think that if Hugo wants to walk over to the library today we could do that," she said brightly.

Hugo looked like he was ready to burst into tears. But to his credit, he sighed and nodded at her. "Sure, Aunt Wendy. The library sounds nice."

It broke my heart to see him so disappointed. I promised myself to make it up to him the next day. I was sure that by then Amelia Snow would be long gone.

I left the yarn shop, and as I drove down Main Street I caught sight of Jimmy Burke's brown University of Wyoming geology van. He was parked at the Stock Market, Killdeer's own kitsch version of a chain grocery store. All of the shopping carts had steer horns glued to the handles, making them look like the ears of livestock, and all of the parking places were painted with lines shaped like lassos. I pulled up beside the van and saw Jimmy just as he was walking out of the store.

He waved at me and hurried to my driver's side window.

"I'm just on my way. I wanted to get some film for my camera." Two heavy bags burdened him.

"That's a lot of film," I said.

"Oh, this? It's bottled water. The tap water at the motel tastes like algae."

"Jimmy, there might be a problem with the site," I said.

His eyes snapped up. "What problem?"

I tried to smile while I delivered the news. "A Forest Service archaeologist came by my father's house this morning wanting to talk to him. She was pretty determined."

Jimmy glanced from side to side like he'd just been caught shoplifting. "This is bad. This is really bad. We need to get up there right away."

"Take a breath, Jimmy. She just wanted to talk to him. It doesn't mean anything. I would guess that she wants to make sure we are not digging on public land. Our property—"

"Sits adjacent to Forest Service land, yes, I know." He was already heading for his van, fumbling with the bags as he opened the door clumsily with one finger.

"I'll follow you up there," I said, convinced he hadn't even heard me.

He threw his bags into the passenger seat and revved the engine before throwing it into gear and lurching from the parking lot.

Jimmy was going to give himself a stroke.

A part of me wanted to turn right around and head towards Lil's café, sit down, have a nice breakfast and chat with Irene. But if my father was not at home, I could guess that Irene was not at her café at the moment. I felt a twinge of disappointment that my father and my best friend were probably spending the morning together. I knew that the relationship was good for both of them, but sometimes, for my own selfish reasons, I still wished I could drop by on either one of them at a moment's notice.

I followed Jimmy down the paved road and cringed when he turned sharp off the asphalt onto the gravel. He barely slowed down. The vehicle rocked from side to side wildly and I had visions of him rolling the geology van into the ditch.

Somehow we made it without a crash, and Jimmy was already scrambling out of his van by the time I parked behind him at the foot of the hill. He crammed two bottles of water inside his old army shoulder bag and dropped a couple rolls of film next to them.

He was already easing himself through the strands of wire on the fence when I had my floppy hat in place and started after him.

"How did they find out?" he asked. "The Forest Service. Who ratted on me?"

I shimmied between the second and third strand of barbed wire and stood up. "She said that she received a phone call last night."

"Last night?" His face was flushed with frustration.

We started walking up the ridge. The hillside was eerily silent.

Not even a bird was singing.

Jimmy scratched his forehead. "I talked to my professor last night, and he said he would get in touch with an anthropologist on staff and see if there was anyone who could come take a look at the site. But he said it would probably take a week, at least."

He marched up the hill and I had to trot just to keep up.

I was already sweaty. "Maybe Amelia Snow got a message from someone else at the University?"

We had almost crested the ridge and I was grateful.

The air was sticky with heat.

"We are at least forty feet from the fence line, easy," Jimmy said. "There is no way they could think we are on public land."

His eyes were fixed on the ground as he walked. He wasn't really listening to me, he was having an internal dialogue and I just happened to be eavesdropping.

"Maybe they think we are using this dig site as an excuse to canvass Forest Service land," he said, trying to puzzle out why a government employee would suddenly have an interest in his operation.

We came to the top of the ridge and when I spotted the site I grabbed Jimmy's arm and jerked him to a standstill.

"Hold it," I said.

I felt my chest grow cold and suddenly every one of my senses was in overdrive.

"What's wrong?"

A portable circular corral had been set up next to the hole. It wasn't the corral that worried me. But what was inside sure did.

A small Jersey cow stood in the enclosure, mouthing a wedge of hay. She looked up at us with a bored expression.

"Oh my god," I said. "It's Suzy-Q."

"What's wrong?" Jimmy asked.

"Jimmy, when I say run, you run. Get inside that corral as fast as you can," I said.

"Who's Suzy-Q?"

"Run!"

I started sprinting for the corral and Jimmy tore after me. A sound like a freight train rushed up from behind and I ran for all I was worth.

"Don't look back just run!" I shouted.

Jimmy was fast but I beat him to the corral by two strides. We hit the rungs and climbed.

Both of us pitched over the top bar and fell inside, hitting the ground with a cloud of dust.

A spray of thick liquid sloshed across the back of my shirt and I heard a bellow of rage as I managed to push myself up.

Jimmy scrambled to his feet. "Holy cow!"

"Yeah. Something like that."

The liquid that had splashed my shirt was a combination of snot and mouth foam. It had sprayed both of us in our retreat, and I could see from Jimmy's face that he was fully aware precisely how close we had just come to dying.

"Jimmy, meet Lewis Pritchett's homicidal prize Holstein bull, Rufus."

A black bull the size of a fire truck paced outside the corral furiously. Foam dripped from his mouth as he trudged back and forth around the bars, frantic to get to us, and bellowed a low moan of anger. One white blaze snaked down his forehead, making him look like he'd been splattered with a dollop of paint. But the rest of Rufus was black as a raven and stout as a bomb shelter.

Jimmy backed away from the bars and bumped into the small Jersey cow standing placidly behind us. She blinked at him and continued to nose her wedge of hay. He yelped and stepped back.

"This, this isn't a bull too, is it?" he said.

"That's Suzy-Q. She's Lewis's prize Jersey milk cow. Rufus has a crush on her," I explained.

"Is this Nathan's idea of securing the site, by turning a two-thousand-pound dog loose in the pasture?" he asked. His face had lost all color.

The huge black bull bellowed with rage and another spray of snot splashed at our feet. He was big, but too stupid to know that if he just put his head down and charged he could destroy the entire corral in about five seconds. As long as we stayed inside the bars, we could expect to keep breathing.

I wiped dirt off my knees. "Rufus will kill anything that comes within fifty feet of Suzy-Q. As long as she is here, he will be too. I'd say this place is pretty secure."

Jimmy stared at me with stunned amazement. "How are we supposed to get out of here?"

"I don't suppose you have a cell phone?" I asked.

Jimmy swallowed. "Ah, I left it in the van."

The reality of the situation settled in and Jimmy slumped to the ground with his back pressed against the bars. "Great. This is just great."

I looked around the corral carefully and didn't see a water barrel. That was good news.

"At some point today my father will stop by to bring Suzy-Q a drink," I said. "But it could take a while."

Jimmy groaned and dropped his head into his hands. "I don't have time for this."

"It was your idea that we post a guard out here," I said.

Jimmy shot me a glare and then dropped his head in his hands again. "So, now what do we do?"

"We wait," I told him.

Rufus had finally stopped pacing the bars and had eased back from infuriated into merely irritated. He stood as close to Suzy-Q as the bars would allow, watching her with an attentive eye. She ignored him.

Jimmy pulled a bottle of water from his pack and handed it to me.

"Thanks," I said, taking it gratefully. I was suddenly very glad I'd asked Hugo to stay with his aunt today.

Jimmy let out a deep sigh, spread his legs flat and crossed his ankles, settling in for the long haul. He slid the water bottle back inside his pack after I handed it over, and took out his notebook. He used his outstretched legs like a table and began flipping through the pages.

"I called my professor at the University. Then I called my girlfriend," he said, thinking.

"So you didn't exactly keep your site a total secret."

He grimaced. "Good point. God help us if anyone else besides that Forest Service lady finds out."

I sat down beside him in the dirt and pressed my back to the bars.

There was no sense in standing for the next few hours.

"Jimmy," I said, looking at him sideways. "What did you mean when you said that people can get weird when it comes to fossils?"

He shrugged and rubbed his eyes. He didn't look like he had gotten much sleep.

"I've seen people go bonkers over bones," he told me. "Dinosaurs are worth a lot of money, if they are rare and complete. People are really passionate about historical things."

Something was starting to trouble me. It felt like an itch that I couldn't quite scratch right between my shoulder blades. "Are people like that about arrowheads, too?"

"You thinking that some likely pot hunter will come to rob the site and save us from Rufus?" he asked.

"More like wondering how many casualties Rufus will inflict before this is all over. Are pot hunters just as bad as dinosaur fanatics?" I asked.

"Probably. I would say they could be just as bad when it comes to artifacts that are valuable, or historically important."

I looked through the bars at the site, covered by a thin layer of shoveled dirt, and thought about the odd coincidence between my grandfather's death and the discovery of two rare fossil teeth by the elusive Clifton Myers all those years ago.

"So, would you say that a site with both fossils and artifacts would be something that could make people go bonkers?" I asked.

Jimmy looked at me and laughed. "Are you kidding?"

"My grandfather was killed on the day I was born," I said suddenly.

My admission surprised even me. But that itch between my shoulders wouldn't let up and I needed to puzzle out the thoughts that buzzed around in my skull.

"That's terrible," Jimmy said.

"It was thirty-four years ago. Exactly."

Jimmy ticked his index finger against the fingers of his left hand. He was doing math in his head. "That would have been 1977?"

"Yes," I said.

"That's the year Clifton Myers found the Megalosaurus teeth here," he said, his eyebrows bunched together.

I gave him a sharp look. "My father mentioned it."

"Sort of odd, isn't it?"

"Who is Clifton Myers, anyway?" I asked, not sure why I was suddenly so troubled.

Jimmy obviously knew a lot more about the man who had first come here looking for fossils, and maybe he had some insight that I didn't.

"He's not exactly what you would call a scientist," he said. "Myers is more like a rock star."

"So, he's famous?" I asked.

"He started out as a paleontologist, according to his book. Then he went off and did something totally insane."

"Rob a bank?" I asked.

"Worse. He became an anthropologist."

I laughed. "Why is that worse?"

"Because of the loss to paleontology. Dr. Clifton Myers found a very prominent mammoth kill site in South Dakota after his work here on your ranch. The South Dakota discovery was a spectacular find. According to his book, Ancient Footsteps, the stone tools at the site helped rewrite history, and after that he gave up dinosaurs and never looked back."

"And you think that is a loss to your science?"

"It's huge. Imagine what a man of his talent could have brought to my field of study."

I smiled and patted his shoulder. "Maybe. But, you have got to admit, it's a funny thing that with all that digging Dr. Clifton Myers supposedly did on our land thirty-four years ago, he didn't turn up the stuff that you just found."

Jimmy glanced over at the hole.

"Yeah," he said with a frown. "That does seem funny."

CHAPTER 6

Jimmy and I were imprisoned inside the corral for almost three hours.

My father came bouncing over the hill at last in his battered pickup truck, not bothering with the rough road and simply driving straight across the field. He shook his head at us when he parked beside the corral.

He stayed inside the truck, choosing to roll down the window to talk to us. "I see you met Rufus, Mr. Burke."

Jimmy stood up and wrapped both hands around the top bar. He gave my father a sour look. "He introduced himself."

"I did recommend to you both that you stop by the house before you came up here today."

"You weren't home," I said.

"I was getting the stock tank loaded up," he told me.

"Dad, you could have warned us about the bull," I said, getting to my feet.

"Well, I didn't know Lewis would let me borrow him. I didn't want to get Mr. Burke's hopes up."

Jimmy put one foot on the bottom rung of the corral. "So . . . how does this work? Do we just jump into the back of the truck? And how am I supposed to work out here with him around trying to kill me?"

My father glanced at Rufus. "I figured I could put another corral around your hole in the ground sometime this afternoon."

Jimmy thought that over while Rufus dribbled froth from his mouth. The big bull was pawing the dirt and trying to decide if the pickup truck was a rival for Suzy-Q's affections or simply an inanimate object.

"Can we get that second corral up right away? I've only got two weeks for fieldwork this summer, and I've got a lot of digging ahead of me," Jimmy said.

"Sure, sure," my father said. "Let me get you two out of here and put out the water barrel."

"How are you going to put up that second corral with Rufus out here?" I asked.

"Marley, I've got a whole bucket of cattle cake in the back. You know he can't keep his nose out of it," he told me.

"You think you can get the corral set up before he finishes his treat?" I asked my father.

"If Mr. Burke knows how to hustle, I can," he said.

Jimmy sighed and started to climb up the bars. It was clear from his weary expression he was already dealing with a lot more than he'd bargained for. The last thing he'd probably expected was getting drafted as a cowboy.

I swung a leg over the top rung and hopped into the back of the pickup with Jimmy close behind.

Rufus menaced the truck to the top of the ridge and halfway down the other side. When we were almost to the fence, the black bull gave up, tossed his head dismissively, then turned and ambled back up the hill towards the dig site, giving us all a view of his impressive backside.

At the bottom of the hill I could see a third vehicle parked just off the road next to my SUV. Someone was standing at the gate watching us as we approached. I didn't recognize the man, or the vehicle.

"What is this guy doing here?" Jimmy asked.

The vehicle was a basic white, generic four-door with government license plates. An upside down triangle with the BLM logo marked the door.

"Bureau of Land Management," I said.

Jimmy looked worried. "I told you this would happen."

"Hello," said the man at the gate. He waved one hand at us as we parked next to the fence. My father stopped his pickup and put it in park, killing the engine.

"Help you?"

The man looked at Jimmy and me as we stood up in the truck bed. He blinked, not quite knowing what to make of the two of us, and gave my father an uneasy smile.

"Are you Mr. Dearcorn?" he asked, slightly mispronouncing our name. He wore a pair of pristine hiking boots and gleaming sunglasses. His gray hair was trimmed military short.

"Yep," my father answered. He was leaning his arm out the window casually, but I could tell by his tone he was expecting trouble.

"I'm Rob Powers? I'm with the BLM office?" He was clearly nervous. Everything he said sounded like he was asking a question.

"What can I do for you?" my father asked.

"I understand you've got a possible artifact cache on your property?"

My father's eyes narrowed. He was studying the man carefully. "So they tell me."

Rob Powers laughed uneasily. "I was hoping I could take a look at it?"

"Hope in one hand and sh—"

"Dad," I said.

My father rubbed his chin. "Why?"

"Well, I'm a site steward as well as being an employee with the Bureau."

Rob Powers waited for his words to sink in.

My father didn't say anything in response, and the awkward silence drew out until I couldn't take it any longer.

"What does a site steward do?" I asked.

"We monitor archaeological sites that might be at risk." He glanced between me and my father, trying to determine who he should address.

"Our site isn't at risk of anything." I kept my tone neutral.

"How did you hear about this dig?" Jimmy asked. The young paleontologist was staring straight at Rob, a glint in his eye that suggested he was on the verge of losing his temper.

"I got a phone call this morning, quite early I might add, from the Killdeer chapter of the Montana Historical Society, indicating that you have a cache of points associated with bone fragments." He gulped after he said the word bone.

"Historical Society," my father echoed. He looked back at me and shook his head. "Lewis must have said something to Rebecca. That man can't keep his mouth shut about nothing when it comes to her."

"Who's Rebecca?" Jimmy demanded.

"She is the granddaughter of the president of the local Historical Society," I told him. "Lewis has been sweet on her for years. I can imagine he would be excited to tell her about this."

The grad student whipped off his hat and beat it against his leg. "Son of a—"

"Jimmy," I said, interrupting him.

I gave Mr. Powers a friendly smile. "I'm wondering what this has to do with the BLM?"

"As you know," Rob began. He cleared his throat dramatically. "As you know, any artifacts associated with human remains are not technically the property of the landowner, even if they are on private land. If human remains are associated with the artifacts, they, technically, belong to the state . . . er . . . the local Native population that can claim relation, that is."

"Who the hell said we had human remains on my land?" my father asked.

"Well, I assumed that bone fragments found with points would be human," Rob said quickly.

"And just why would you think that?" my father asked.

"It is only logical." Rob brushed an imaginary fly from the back of his neck. His upper lip was starting to accumulate sweat.

"This is a paleo site," Jimmy said.

"A Paleo-Indian site? Good gracious. You people need to contact the state archaeologist immediately," Rob said. "And the county coroner."

"As in paleontology," Jimmy said, his tone stern. "It's a dinosaur site. There are no human remains associated with the arrowheads."

Rob's mouth opened, then closed, then opened again. He thought about what he had just heard, trying to make sense of it.

"You have dinosaur material associated with points?" Rob asked.

"That's right," Jimmy told him. "So, unless the law concerning ownership of fossils on private land changed since last night, there is really nothing here for you to look at."

Rob Powers carefully folded his hands behind his back. "I don't suppose I could take a look? Just to satisfy my own curiosity?"

"You think I'm lying to you?" Jimmy asked.

Rob held up both hands. "Now, young man. There is no need to lose your temper."

Jimmy jumped out of the back of the pickup, climbed through the fence, snagging his shirt three times on the barbed wire, and finally managed to wiggle through. He stomped to his geology van and started rummaging around the back.

The van rocked from side to side from the flurry of activity.

My father let his eyes drift back to Rob. "I guess you have your answer."

"I really don't understand how you could possibly have anything but human bones associated with a cache of this size," Rob said.

Jimmy's head appeared around the corner of the back of the van. "How do you know how big the cache is?"

The BLM man swallowed. "I was told it consists of at least a dozen points."

Jimmy stared at the man for a moment, then shook his head and started swearing. He resumed his search for whatever it was he was hoping to find in the back of the van.

"I trust Jimmy when he says that there are no human remains up there," I said.

Rob smirked and looked at me over the top of his sunglasses. "I suppose you went home and Googled the word artifact last night."

"Maybe you should Google the word trespass," I told him.

"There is no reason to get personal. I simply need to see the site," he repeated.

"Why not?" my father asked. "Rufus could use the exercise."

"Dad."

"Mr. Dearborn," Rob began.

"It's Dearcorn," I said.

Rob Powers mumbled an apology and put one foot on the bottom string of barbed wire like he was contemplating making a run for the hill.

At that moment, Jimmy slammed the back door of the van and marched towards us. He took a stack of papers from a folder and sifted through them until he found the one he was looking for.

"Nathan," he said, handing over the papers. "Here is that agreement I was hoping I could get you to sign. Take your time, read it carefully. It states that you will be willing to allow me access to the fossil remains I recover from your property for a period of not less than six months. I'd like it for a year, but at this point I think that is asking a little too much. I'm not even sure yet if it's Megalosaurus or not. If it is, maybe we could talk about extending the time period of study."

"You want him to extend your study time?" Rob scanned Jimmy like a bank officer scans an unemployed ex-con who has just applied for a big loan.

"Jimmy, you don't need me to sign that. I'll let you study it for as long as you want it," my father said.

"Even if it's worth a million bucks?" I asked.

My father swiveled his head around to stare at me. "What's worth a million bucks?"

"The dinosaur," I said.

"Come on, Kiddo. You don't really believe that hokum, do you?" my father said, his expression patronizing.

"Mr. Dearcorn, do you realize that your property touches section thirty-four of the township? This apparent fossil is less than two hundred yards away from BLM land," Rob said.

My father was still looking at me and completely ignored Rob. "I know Mr. Burke here thinks it's worth something," he said. "But like I told you, I've heard that story before."

"Mr. Dearcorn," Rob said, more forcefully.

"Can you hang on one dang minute?" my father said.

Jimmy held up the paper and my father snatched it from him. "Fine. Where do I sign this thing?"

"Let me read it first," I said quickly.

Things were happening too fast.

"I'm not going to read it. I trust Mr. Burke. Gimmee a pen, will you?" my father said.

Jimmy patted his shirt. His face fell. "I . . . I don't have a pen."

"Mr. Dearcorn. I simply want to see the site to verify that there are no human remains associated with the find," Rob said.

"I don't have a pen, Dad. Sorry." I was still standing in the back of the pickup like an idiot.

"Does anyone have a pen?" my father demanded.

Slowly, Rob Powers reached for his shirt and pulled out a ballpoint. He held it up. "If you let me just take a quick look, I will let you borrow this."

My father struggled with his pride for a moment. He could see that Jimmy was mortified by the request.

"I'll agree if you tell me one thing," my father said.

"Certainly," Rob said.

"What sort of expertise have you got?"

Rob Powers chuckled, obviously convinced that he was surrounded by dumb yokels, and was finally in a position to brag about his credentials.

"I've taken human osteology as part of my continuing education. I majored in rangeland management, but we've stumbled across human remains from time to time. If I see a human bone, I'll know it," he said.

Jimmy snorted. "Yeah, right."

My father held out his hand. "Alright. You can take a look."

Rob handed him the pen with a smug look.

"I think that's a mistake, Nathan," Jimmy said.

"Could we all agree on one thing here?" I said.

The three of them turned towards me.

"Could everyone just promise to keep their mouths shut about this from now on?" Not that I believed for one second it would do a bit of good to ask. Word was already spreading at an alarming rate around the valley.

"Fine," my father said. "Not a peep."

"I can agree to that," Rob said.

"I promise I won't tell anyone else," said Jimmy hastily.

I searched their faces, doing the best I could to believe them.

"But it might not make any difference if we say anything about the site or not," Rob said.

I folded my arms. "Why is that?"

He glanced to the side and cleared his throat again. "Well, the woman who called from the

Montana Historical Society said that they have had a dry spell when it comes to publicity."

I felt my heart sink. "And what, exactly, did she mean by that?"

"She asked me if it would be alright if she was kept in the loop about what was found here," Rob said.

Jimmy shook his head. "Here we go."

Rob tried to shine up the bad news with a cheerful tone. "Well, she also said that in the past, the more exposure a site gets, the less likely it is to be vandalized."

"That seems backwards, somehow," I said.

"What does that mean?" my father asked. "More exposure?"

"She said that it would be fun if a camera crew could come down here and document the dig," Rob said with excitement.

I thought Jimmy's head would explode. His face turned so red he looked like a giant beet. "She said what?"

Rob cast an apologetic look at us. "She said it would be possible to have a reporter down here by tomorrow."

"Nathan," Jimmy said. "How many more bulls does your friend own?"

"About a dozen," my father said.

Jimmy pushed his hat back off his forehead and rubbed his eyes so hard I thought they would pop out the back of his skull. "You better go get them."

CHAPTER 7

Irene poured me a cup of coffee and slid it across the countertop. I mechanically filled it with sugar and a generous amount of creamer until it turned a shade slightly lighter than tar. Saying Irene's coffee was stout was like saying a wolverine is feisty.

"So what do you say?" I asked. "Will you fill me in on what you remember?"

"Where's the kid?" she asked.

I assumed she meant Hugo and not the grad student.

"With his aunt." I set my spoon aside. "Look, can't you just give me the highlights? All this activity on our land is bringing up some old ghosts from the past. I would sort of like to know what happened back then."

She sipped her own cup of steaming coffee and shrugged. "I heard you. What makes you think I know something that you don't?"

"I thought you were the keeper of all Killdeer's great secrets."

It was accurate to say Irene knew more about the goings on around town than all the local politicians and law enforcement agents combined.

She smiled at my remark. Irene had been smiling a lot more lately. I was pretty sure it had something to do with the wild affair she was currently conducting with my father.

She stared at me for a moment over the top of her mug. "Okay. I will tell you what I heard. Your father really hasn't talked to you about this?" she asked.

"Not much. I always thought that it was too painful for him to go over the details."

She shook her head. "He doesn't have much to tell. There was so much about the day your grandfather died that they never found out. Nathan never talked about it because he didn't ever find out what really happened."

I grimaced and stared at the counter. "It's because he was at the hospital. I was busy being born and my grandfather was alone at the ranch. I think he still believes if he had been there he could have stopped it."

Irene set her mug down and pulled a little stool out from beneath the counter. She propped her hip on it and gave me a quiet smile.

"I think that if he had been there he would have been killed, too," I said.

Irene nodded. "So do I. But it doesn't stop him from blaming himself."

I wasn't even sure why I was bringing it up. After all, it was ancient history and it had been a painful experience for my father. But after talking to Jimmy while we were stranded in the corral, my curiosity was getting the better of me.

I looked up with resolve. "Alright, tell me what you heard."

She took a long breath. "It was a typical November day." Irene studied her own coffee. She seemed to run out of words and grew quiet.

"Was there a lot of snow on the ground?" I prompted.

"I don't remember," she said. "I was only nine years old. And I got this version from Sadie, Mother's hairdresser, years after the fact. But she was married to Sheriff Larson, so it's probably pretty legit."

I nodded that she should continue.

"Marley, this isn't easy to talk about," she said.

"You think this is easy for me to hear?" I asked. "Other than when Mom died, this was my father's worst day on earth."

She rubbed her forehead and lowered her eyes, scanning the floor of her café. I could see she was trying to decide how much to tell me. She seemed to come to some sort of internal agreement, squared her shoulders and plowed on.

"Your father was excited because he said he woke up that morning knowing you were going to be born that day."

"How did he know?" I asked.

"Your mother told him." Her tone was a little impatient, and I scolded myself for interrupting her.

"Anyway," she said, gathering her thoughts again. "He took your mom to the hospital late that morning. Everything was going perfect, your mom was doing fine and the doctor said it looked like you would be born that afternoon. So, your father called the ranch to tell your granddaddy that he should wrap up work for the day and head to the hospital over in Parkman."

I was trying to imagine it all in my head as she told the story.

I could see my father on the pay phone in the hallway of the Parkman hospital, standing there in his cowboy boots that were most likely covered in muck, urging my grandfather to drop what he was doing.

Not an easy thing for a rancher to do.

"Your grandfather answered the phone—I guess your father said it was just after lunch—maybe one o'clock? At any rate, Nathan told him to come to the hospital because he was going to be a grandfather. Your granddad said he would be right there, that he had to get the battery charger off of the pickup."

Irene paused. Her pale eyes looked glassy.

"He never showed at the hospital, did he?" I asked.

She sipped her coffee, frowned at it and dumped it in the little sink behind her.

It had cooled from lava hot to normal coffee temperature, which was too cold for Irene.

"Your father stayed at the hospital until dark, wondering what was going on. Then he drove back out to the ranch. He's the one who found your granddaddy, and it was pretty clear that he had been dead for several hours."

"All I know is that he had been shot in the back," I said. "I think Dad mentioned once that he was behind the house. Like he was heading to the garage."

She considered that. "I think your father doesn't talk about it with you because he still wants to protect his little girl from all the bad stuff that happened to your family."

"I'm not a little girl," I said.

"It doesn't matter how old you are, you will always be his little girl."

I couldn't argue with that.

"All this digging on our property, all this talk about fossils and university people must be a horrible déjà vu for my father," I said.

"It wasn't like a whole school was working on your place," Irene said. "It was just the one guy."

"Did he ever talk about Clifton Myers?" I asked.

She nodded, her brows creased with the effort to recall the conversation. "Your granddaddy and Clifton would sit out on the porch together in the evenings and carry on like a couple of old women, tell jokes and get smashed."

"But Myers would have been about my father's age. He was young enough to be my Grandfather's son, so what could they have possibly had in common?" I asked.

"Your father said Clifton had a way of charming folks. Your granddaddy included."

"He told my father he would come back to finish the dig someday," I said. "But he never did."

Irene gave a little cough and her eyes drifted over my shoulder slowly.

I turned my head to follow her gaze and saw Finn standing in the doorway.

As usual, his sunglasses obscured his eyes, but I could practically feel him looking at me.

He was dressed in black head to toe, despite the heat from the midafternoon sun. His blond hair was swept off his forehead and he was tanned bronze from hours spent outside. He wore no jacket, so his pistol was plain to see inside its shoulder holster. Wearing a gun openly in public might have been a big deal in a city, but in Killdeer nobody even looked twice.

Finn and I had been involved in a brief, but intense fling the previous winter. Even though I was firmly and happily in a relationship with Leif Gable, I still felt a sharp pang each time I saw Finn. Regret for what could have been.

He was the security chief for a new weather station built recently in the mountains above Killdeer. It wasn't really a weather station, and was actually a SETI institute project, but everyone in town played along with the story nonetheless since the people there tried so hard to keep a low profile. I knew in his past he'd worked as a bodyguard, a profession that colored everything about him. Finn had a very difficult time separating his job from his emotions, and that had contributed greatly to our breakup. He'd become so protective of me that he had embarrassed me on more than one occasion in public by overreacting to loud noises or unexpected situations. But the real reason we ended up separating was the simple fact that Finn couldn't bring himself to truly commit. Most likely, that was due to his troubled past, which he hardly ever spoke about. Whatever nightmare from his past had caused him to become hyper vigilant had also contributed to the end of our relationship. I doubted that he would ever be able to have a truly normal life.

I managed to give him a polite smile as he strolled by and took a seat in a booth at the window. He gave me his secret-agent-man nod in acknowledgment and sat down.

I turned back to Irene. She was still watching him over the rim of her freshly poured mug of coffee.

"He's still looking at me, isn't he?" I asked.

Irene laughed. "He's undressing you with his eyes."

"Have I mentioned you are a dirty old woman?"

"He's fiddling with his gun," she said. "It's some sort of Freudian thing, I'm sure."

I very deliberately and pointedly turned my back to him and put money on the counter.

"You don't want any lunch?" Irene asked.

"I need to get back out to the ranch and make sure that Rufus hasn't stomped Jimmy Burke into a pile of mush."

I stood up and Irene reached out suddenly and squeezed my hand. "Listen, Honey, about your granddaddy. Your father is a long way from ever letting this go."

I must have looked a little surprised, because she hastily dropped my hand and leaned forward, propping both hands on the countertop and fixing me with a pointed gaze. "It might be better to leave the subject alone."

I watched her expression, feeling a mixture of curiosity and worry. "Wouldn't it be a good thing if we could find out who killed my grandfather?"

Irene struggled with her response. "I wouldn't even bring it up."

I felt my face harden.

Irene watched me and her eyes narrowed. "Now that I have told you not to do something, you will immediately rush out to give it a try, won't you?"

I knew my cheeks were flushing as she spoke, but I met her gaze anyway. "I'll tell you what. I won't talk to my father about it unless I absolutely have to."

"Marley, I know you have sort of a knack for finding things out," she said. "But this is different."

"How is it different?" I asked.

"This is your family. Please, don't do anything that's going to upset Nathan."

I turned to see if Finn was still watching me from his seat by the window. He was.

I gave Irene a tense smile. "I will do my best."

She shoved her stool back under the counter and snapped her fingers at her newest waitress. The girl was busy working a stick of gum like it had vital information she could beat out of it, and had failed to see that Finn was still waiting for his menu. When Irene caught her eye, the girl jumped to get Finn his menu so fast her ponytail swung around in a circle.

I waited while Finn ordered his usual mushroom and Swiss burger, and then I surprised myself and sat down at his booth.

"Why would you shoot someone in the back?" I asked.

He set his sunglasses aside. "It's good to see you too, Marley. How are you?"

"Sorry," I said. "I need your professional opinion."

"I wouldn't shoot someone in the back." He was wearing that lopsided smirk that had always gotten under my skin.

"Not you, personally," I told him. "But in general. Why shoot someone in the back?"

He took a moment to ponder my question. Whether he was really thinking it over or trying to figure out why I was suddenly sitting across from him, I couldn't judge.

"I guess I could think of a couple reasons," he said.

His South African accent hadn't eased up a bit since he'd moved to Killdeer.

Finn was exotic, to say the least, and every time he opened his mouth it was painfully clear he was not from Montana. But his presence in our small town had gradually become a part of the landscape, and it was rare that anyone gave him a second look these days.

He brushed his blond hair out of his eyes. "First of all, I would only do something like that if I was a coward."

He took a sip from his water glass and set it back on the table carefully.

"Why would being a coward make any difference?" I asked.

"It's not an easy thing, to kill a bloke," Finn said. "At least, if you're a regular person. You might not want to look at them when you pulled the trigger."

"And the other reason?" I asked.

The smirk spread wider across his face. "Why are you asking me this?"

"It's personal." I could feel Irene's eyes boring into me from behind. I knew she was dying to know what I was talking to him about.

"Personal," he echoed.

I did my best to get past my private irritation with him and stick to business. "What if it's broad daylight? You are in a place where it's possible that someone could see you, but you have some privacy because it's behind a house and you can't be seen from the road?"

"So, anyone driving up to the front of the house could witness the event, or at the very least see you leaving the scene?" he asked.

I nodded. "Probably. You'd have a little bit of warning if you could hear the car approach. But not very much."

He considered that.

I felt like a fool talking to him. But I wanted him to see that I was an adult, and I could handle a normal friendship with someone I'd once been in a relationship with.

Finn ran a thumb across his jaw. "Right. In that situation, the only thing I can think of that would force me to take a risk like that would be desperation. If I was trying to stop someone from doing something that they were intent to do, and I couldn't talk them out of it, that could prompt me want to shoot them. And if they were walking away from me, or if I surprised them, I might be inclined to take advantage."

I leaned back, thinking. "Stop them from doing something?"

He waved a hand. "Maybe . . . they are moving to retrieve a weapon that I believe they might use against me. Maybe they are about to make a phone call to tell someone something I don't want them to reveal. I don't know, Marley. You haven't given me very much to go on."

"I don't have very much to go on," I said.

His eyes narrowed into a glare. "What are you into this time?" he asked dangerously.

I glanced up. "Nothing. I mean, nothing risky. This is ancient history."

The new waitress plunked Finn's rare mushroom and Swiss on the table in front of him and set a bottle of ketchup beside the plate.

He didn't seem to notice his lunch arrive.

"Marley . . ." he said, his voice dark.

"It's what happened to my grandfather," I explained, "thirty-four years ago. All the activity on our ranch with the grad student from the university is bringing up some old memories, that's all. It nothing risky."

Why was I explaining this to him? For that matter, why was I even discussing this with him?

Finn leaned towards me. "Nothing risky? You think that someone who killed another bloke thirty-four years ago, what, wouldn't do it again today because they weren't in the mood? What are you thinking, doll?"

I blinked and stared at him. "Don't call me doll."

He sat back and poured ketchup on his burger. "Right. I would guess Leif wouldn't like it much."

I ignored his remark. "Can you think of any other reason to shoot someone in the back?"

"One." He took a bite of his burger and chewed, staring at me with an unreadable expression.

"Only one?" I asked.

"Listen. If you are desperate enough to shoot someone in a location where you could possibly be discovered, then I'm going to say you are not necessarily a coward. So there is only one other reason you would shoot a person in the back instead of facing them."

"Fear?" I asked.

"Hardly. It's guilt," he said, taking another bite.

"I don't understand," I said.

"It means you know the person, and you don't want to shoot them. At least, that is my professional opinion."

I felt a heavy dread settle in my stomach. "So, whoever killed my grandfather was a friend of his?"

Finn shrugged. "Or I could be completely wrong. The smart thing for you would be to forget about it."

"Finn. When have I ever done the smart thing?"

His lips pressed into a thin line. "Indeed."

CHAPTER 8

The sun was dipping low, piercing the windshield at that annoying angle just between the visor and the horizon.

I had to shelter my eyes from the glare, even though sunset was still almost four hours away.

It was a hot day for June, and filled with new flies and humid air that made working outside miserable.

I was already feeling pretty miserable.

The road next to our fence was crammed with vehicles and unhappy people.

I parked behind Jimmy Burke's University of Wyoming geology van and got out. I took a deep breath, and braced myself for impact.

Jimmy stood beside his van, his face rigid with anger.

Amelia Snow had parked her Forest Service truck practically in the middle of the road, and behind it was Rob Powers's BLM vehicle.

The three of them had already reached the shouting stage of the conversation, and as I approached they paused long enough to draw breath. I could see each one of them was working out how to get me on their side.

"Marley, tell these idiots there are no human remains associated with this site," Jimmy said, his face a mask of frustration.

Rob lifted his chin. "I saw them myself, not four hours ago when Mr. Dearcorn finally allowed me access. It was obvious to me what they were the moment I saw them. Human finger bones."

He was looking at the ground, affecting a humble expression, but I could tell from his tone he was determined.

Jimmy scowled. "You didn't even get out of the back of the truck. How can you say you know what you were looking at from forty feet away? What you saw was the top of the supraoccipital crest of a carnosaur skull. Moron."

"Maybe I could take a look, Mr. Burke," Amelia suggested, her tone soft but insistent.

The fat lenses of Amelia's glasses magnified her wide eyes, making her look like a surprised hoot owl. She was ignoring Rob completely and doing her best to wheedle Jimmy into cooperating.

I noticed she was wearing a pair of moccasins today. Her hair was still braided down her shoulders in two loose plaits and topped off with a leather bandana she had wrapped snugly around her forehead. Her pale, Nordic complexion belied her attempt to look Indian.

At that moment, Rufus decided that we were all making too much of a ruckus for his taste and bellowed out a challenge.

He paced the fence, snorting and sloshing foam on the ground. Rob Powers jumped, gave the bull a wary glance and moved a few paces away from the fence.

Rufus tossed his head with satisfaction.

"Was it really necessary to put that thing in the pasture?" Rob asked, looking at Rufus sideways, not wanting to stare directly at the bull and perhaps draw attention.

"I am starting to think it's pretty necessary," I said. "I think Rufus is the only one up here with his head screwed on straight."

The three of them looked at me. Then they all started talking at once.

"I clearly saw human remains," Rob insisted.

"He's smoking some kind of crack," Jimmy said.

"If I could see them, maybe I could make a determination," Amelia said.

"Did you get your degree from an online university from the Province of Puerto Rico?" Jimmy asked.

"I'll have you know I am an alumni of the University of San Diego," Rob said.

"I think you mean alumnus," Amelia pointed out.

"California?" Jimmy said, his tone incredulous. Saying the word California to a man from Wyoming was like waving a rodeo clown in front of a Brahma bull.

"I have been studying human remains for thirty years," Amelia offered quietly.

"How could you possibly think those fragments you saw were human?" Jimmy demanded.

"The morphology of the specimen is obviously human," Rob said.

"Oh, sure. If he happens to stand fourteen feet tall," Jimmy said.

"Mr. Burke. I daresay you are not qualified to work this site!" Rob shouted.

Rufus bellowed again and a spray of churned mouth foam landed at our feet.

I looked at Rob. "Maybe you ought to keep your voice down."

"I could straighten this all out if you give me five minutes," Amelia said, her voice deceptively soft. Her jaw muscle twitched.

Jimmy waved a hand dismissively. "We have had too many people at the site already."

"Not to mention livestock. You should simply remove that animal altogether," Rob told me.

"Why? So you can come in here in the middle of the night and steal the so-called human remains?" Jimmy said.

"Okay, okay. Everyone settle down," I told them.

Amelia let out a heavy sigh and fingered her turquoise necklace. "Might I remind everyone that the Native American Graves Protection and Repatriation Act clearly states that any and all identifiable cultural items must be turned over to lineal descendants of local Native American tribes for reburial, and failure to comply with that federal law can result in prosecution."

"Section 106 of the National Historical Preservation Act gives a site steward authority to inspect a location to see if it qualifies for protection by the National Park Service," Rob told her.

"That's for buildings," Jimmy said with a growl.

Amelia folded her arms. "The 1906 Antiquities Act supersedes any other legislation."

"The Antiquities Act is intended for areas the size of the Grand Canyon," Jimmy said.

Amelia leaned forward and balanced on the balls of her feet to give herself an extra inch of height. "According to the 1979 Archaeological Resources Protection Act, you can be fined up to twenty thousand dollars and imprisoned for up to one year for illegally removing or disturbing, selling or transporting antiquities."

"A year in prison?" I asked, feeling a sudden wave of shock.

"For removing them from public lands," Jimmy explained.

"Has anyone thought to call the county coroner in to examine the find?" Rob asked.

Jimmy threw his head back with exasperation. "For the last time, people. It's a dinosaur."

"Exactly what is your degree in, Mr. Burke?" Amelia asked.

"I did my undergraduate work in geology, after I changed my major," Jimmy said quietly.

"I see," Rob said with a dismissive tone. "And your graduate degree?"

Jimmy's face darkened. "I'm working towards my master's in paleontology."

Amelia looked stricken. "You are a graduate student?"

"Well, that explains a great deal," Rob said with a sneer.

Amelia balled both hands into fists. She heaved a massive sigh and her face darkened with surprising fury. "They should be left alone. At the very least, everything should be repatriated to the local Crow tribe. Haven't we done enough to these people?"

I stared at her with surprise.

Rob waved his hands like he was trying to shoo away an angry bee. "No one has suggested repatriation."

The sound of tires on gravel made all of us look up. I saw a cardinal red utility van with a cheerful yellow logo painted on the side coming down the road. The van was moving slowly, and affixed to the roof was a heavy antenna and small satellite dish.

"Oh, no." Jimmy's face flushed with frustration.

Amelia Snow took one look at the red van and turned away from us without another word. She kept her head down as she walked off, climbed inside her Forest Service truck and started the engine. When the red van pulled to a stop behind my SUV and parked, Amelia was already bugging out. She obviously knew a television camera crew when she saw one.

I noticed Rob puff out his chest importantly and step forward when a determined-looking young woman stepped out of the van.

A scruffy camera operator was already jumping out and checking his camera as he followed the young woman.

She looked like a reporter from the Weather Channel rather than the local broadcast station. Her dark hair was pulled back in a casual ponytail and she wore a pair of hikers, khaki pants and a ridiculously tight Ralph Lauren T-shirt that showed off her considerable upper assets. For a television reporter she had surprisingly little makeup on her face. Even without lipstick, it was still a perky, attractive face.

I noticed that Jimmy had broken into a hot blush.

Rob stepped forward and introduced himself.

"I'm Rob Powers from the Bureau of Land Management office in Parkman."

"Hello." The reporter checked the direction of the sun and pivoted so that it was to her back. A halo of light glowed around her from behind;

softening her features and making her skin look flawless. "I'm Casey Chastity, from KSQU. I was hoping I could see the dinosaur?"

She beamed at Jimmy and Rob, not bothering to even flick a glance in my direction.

Casey Chastity? I felt my mouth hang open a bit as I watched her working the two men like they were judges at a Miss Teen America pageant.

Rob was already primping his hair.

"I'm Marley Dearcorn," I stepped forward and extended my hand.

She mechanically shook it. Her grip was so strong I felt like my hand had been slammed in a car door. What was it with women and mean handshakes these days?

Casey shrugged a backpack off of her shoulder and drew out a wireless microphone. While she fiddled with the control of the microphone, I thought it would be best if I slowed her down now before she could get her hopes up.

"This is my father's ranch," I explained. "We can't allow anyone who is not associated with the dig site to go up on the ridge at this time."

Casey's eyes locked on me and I was suddenly the absolute focus of her undivided attention.

"What do I have to do to get permission?" She jerked her chin at her cameraman, who dutifully lifted his lens and pointed it straight at me.

"I'm sorry, but we can't give anyone access to the site at this time. It's still being studied." I was fairly certain my father would have said the same thing.

Jimmy coughed. "There really isn't that much to see."

"Only a cache of arrowheads associated with human remains," said Rob.

The lens pivoted.

Casey lifted the microphone and held it towards Rob. "Could you repeat that?"

"I have seen this site." Rob spread his legs and propped both hands on his hips in his best gunslinger stance.

I felt my stomach churn.

"A cache of arrowheads?" Casey repeated. "How many have you discovered?"

"It's my dig site," Jimmy said, doing his best to brush a layer of dust off of his shirt.

Casey didn't miss a beat. She practically shoved Rob aside and headed for Jimmy. "So, could you take us up to see the site? Maybe get some shots of you beside the arrowheads?"

"As I said," I told her. "We can't allow anyone up on the ridge until Jimmy has had a chance to map the area."

Casey glanced at me, apparently trying to determine how much of a hindrance I was going to be.

"They don't want you to see the site because it also contains dinosaur bones," Rob told Casey, tilting his head back defiantly.

Casey backpedaled and shoved the microphone back in Rob's face. "Dinosaur bones and human bones in the same place?"

Rob shot Jimmy a superior look. "That's right. They don't want you to see it because it will blow the lid off of paleontology as we know it today."

Jimmy started sputtering and waving his arms. "There are no human remains."

Casey held the microphone up, her eyes gleaming. "But I thought you said that there were arrowheads?"

Jimmy stammered. "Well, um, arrowheads, sure."

"Look, we are not allowing anyone to go up there," I said, feeling my patience wearing out.

She ignored me.

"Tell me what you saw," she said to Rob.

He looked up at the sky with a stargazer expression. "It's remarkable, really."

Jimmy dropped his hands and looked at me helplessly. "Can't you do something?"

"What do you want me to do?" I asked.

Jimmy walked away, shaking his head.

Rob leaned into the microphone and hooked his thumbs in his belt like John Wayne.

"The cache contains approximately a dozen arrowheads, all in pristine condition. Associated with the cache is a very-well-preserved human hand. You can actually see the finger bones."

Jimmy was pulling open the door of his van and I could see him searching for something.

"Go on," Casey said, rapt and smiling.

"It's quite fantastic," Rob said. "Like having contact with the far distant past."

I actually laughed.

"Listen, Miss Chastity," I had to force myself to say the reporter's name with a straight face. "There are no human remains. It's true there are arrowheads beside dinosaur bones, but it's simply something paleontologists call reworking. It has a perfectly logical explanation."

It was clear Casey was not interested in logical at this point. She blinked at me once, no doubt debating internally on how to proceed. Reasonable and logical didn't sell. When in doubt, go for the most sensational version.

Apparently it was the day to throw caution to the wind and she turned her back to me, practically purring for Rob to continue describing the site.

I shook my head and walked away and went to stand beside Jimmy, who was just closing his cell phone and looking absolutely dejected.

"What's wrong?" I asked.

He looked at me with disbelief. "I managed to get my cell phone messages. My professor said he can't come."

I shrugged. "You can handle this. It's not that difficult."

"Not that difficult?" he asked, his tone close to panic.

"Isn't there someone else who can come give you a hand?"

"My professor said he's going to call in some favors, ask around to some of the other university department heads who have an anthropologist who isn't away in Guatemala, or the desert southwest, or somewhere for the field season and see who can send someone to take a look."

"Who do you think they can find on such short notice?" I asked.

"I don't know." He dropped to the ground, propped his back against the tire of the van and rubbed his face with dusty hands. "Marley, I am so sorry about this."

I looked back at Casey and Rob. They were so cozy I thought the reporter would be asking Rob if he wanted a back rub any second.

Jimmy looked up at me. "You have no idea what's coming next."

I frowned. "Have you seen this type of situation before?"

He nodded. "Yeah, over in the Black Hills area. Listen. If Powers can convince the state that there really are human remains here, you and your father will be swarmed with people. Human remains trump everything. Your land won't belong to you until they are finished. If there are human remains that could possibly be Native American, then the landowner loses all legal rights to the site, and all associated material."

"You said that the only bones up there are dinosaur bones."

"It won't make a bit of difference," he told me. "They will strip this area until they can come up with something. If they don't find anything, they will tie up the fossil for months with paperwork. My dig will essentially be destroyed."

I sank down to the ground beside him. "All of your hard work for your thesis? You could lose it?"

He grimaced. "This is my worst nightmare."

I listened to Rob and Casey massage the truth from the other side of the van, and I sighed.

"Jimmy, have you photographed everything? I mean, have you really documented everything as much as you can?"

He shrugged. "I took about a hundred pictures. I marked everything with GPS coordinates and I sketched the quarry map. So what?"

"Would the photographs be enough to support your thesis?"

He turned to look at me. "If I had the skull back at the lab in Wyoming, I suppose I could prep the dinosaur and determine species. Then I could establish the stratigraphy and write my thesis independently of any associated material and not include the arrowheads, or simply mention them as an aside."

I toed the dirt and thought about my date with Leif later that evening. We were going to make up for lost time and have a nice dinner together. But after that . . .

"I will be busy until about nine tonight," I said.

"Is it with a reporter?" Jimmy asked, heavy on the sarcasm.

"I could meet you here, up at the dig, at nine thirty," I said.

"Why?" he asked, his voice laced with frustration. "You want to steal the stuff?"

"It's not stealing if it belongs to me," I said.

Jimmy looked at me, incredulous. "You want to dig it up tonight?"

"Why not?"

"Seriously, we could get into a lot of trouble," he said.

I chewed the inside of my cheek, trying to think of something that would light a fire underneath Jimmy.

"What else do you want to do? Sit around and wait for some archaeologist to come in here from California and take over your dig?" I asked.

Jimmy's jaw clenched. I may as well have just said Remember the Alamo to a Texan. At the mention of his site being commandeered, Jimmy transformed before my eyes.

He squared his shoulders and lifted his chin with defiance. "All right. We'll do it. But I need a favor first."

"Sure," I said.

He stood up and a cloud of dirt drifted to the ground at his feet. "Do you have about ten pounds of burlap and lots and lots of toilet paper?"

CHAPTER 9

Leif poked at his dinner, eyeing the fish on his plate suspiciously.

"You seem quiet tonight," I said, digging in to my steak.

He gave me a jealous smile. "I'm coveting your rib eye. This," he said, pointing to his plate, "is not sea bass."

"How can you tell the difference?"

He poked the white, rubbery thing that was buried beneath a half pound of spiced couscous. "I've spearfished sea bass off the coast of Puerto Santo Tomas. This looks more like tilapia to me."

I laughed. "You are just like James Bond."

He gave me a questioning smile. "James Bond?"

"You spearfish. You travel all over the world doing who knows what. You drink martinis."

"But I don't make a habit of seducing every beautiful woman I come across," he told me, ignoring the fish and concentrating on the couscous. He grimaced when he took a bite of the side dish, and gave his plate a disappointed look.

I cut my steak in half and held up the plate. "You're killing me, here, Gable. Take the steak."

He hesitated for only a moment. Wordlessly he scooped half of my steak onto his own plate and gave me a smile. "Thanks."

We had come into Parkman to enjoy a nice dinner at the newest restaurant in town. I gave the bistro a careful examination. It was tasteful. The interior had been remodeled with a modern look. No dead animal heads gracing the walls. No peanut shells on the floor. Instead it was Tuscan red with steel light fixtures and beige leather booths. Snazzy.

"Well, the food might be questionable, but whoever redesigned this place knew what they were doing," I said.

The building had been in Parkman for generations. It had originally been a dentist's office, back in the 1940's.

Leif took a bite of the steak and pointed at me with his fork. "Now, that's a good rib eye."

"And I suppose you would know because you used to own a cattle ranch."

"Sure. I had a ranch, once," he said with a shrug.

I shook my head. "You know, the amazing thing about you is that you don't think that there is anything amazing about you."

He took a sip of wine. "What does that mean, Marley?"

"You think that you are just an ordinary guy, Leif. There is nothing ordinary about you, but you don't see yourself as anything special. That's what makes you so special."

He gave a casual laugh and I realized that I'd gotten into the habit of trying to make him laugh simply because I loved to hear the sound of him feeling happy.

Leif finished his half of the steak, took another sip of wine and reached across the table for my hand. He squeezed my fingers once and looked at me pointedly.

"Marley, we need to talk about when you would like to get married."

If I hadn't been sitting down I would have dropped like a stone. "What?"

"I'm going to Panama in a week, and I'll be gone for fourteen days. How about we look at a calendar when I get back and we can pick a time that works for both of us?"

"Married?" I gasped.

He arched an eyebrow. "Unless that's too soon?"

"We've only been dating for six months!"

"We've been living together for six months," he said, his tone easy.

"But . . . but . . ."

"I want you to think about it," he said, still holding on to my hand.

"Are you sure about this?" I could feel my face flushing.

"If I wasn't sure I wouldn't have brought it up." He leaned back in his chair and folded his arms with a smooth gesture.

"But you have only been divorced for—"

"Seven months. I know. I realize that it may seem to you as if I am rushing this, or that I may not be thinking clearly. But ask yourself this, Marley. Have you been happy since you and I started living together?"

I folded my napkin on the table. "I've been very happy."

"So what do you think getting married would change between us? Do you think you would suddenly become unhappy?"

I thought about the fact that I had just ended my own unstable, torrid love affair only a few months ago. How qualified was I to make a choice like this so soon after having my heart crushed?

"Another thing," he said, not giving me a second to backpedal. "Would you agree that getting married is a symbol of a real desire to make a commitment? Would you agree that it demonstrates a willingness to dedicate oneself to a relationship wholeheartedly?"

"Can't you do that without tying the knot?" I asked, perhaps a bit desperately.

"Certainly. But in my case, I would have to say I have a very clear vision of what I want for my life. I know exactly how I feel about you. I know where I would like us to be in five years, ten years. If you know how you feel about me and you can see yourself making that sort of commitment to us, I don't understand wanting to wait."

"Well, Leif, you have simply stunned me stupid here. Give me a minute, would you?" I realized my palms were sweating like a fire hose and I wiped them on my slacks.

He was wearing his most patient smile, studying me with his sharp blue eyes carefully, looking as relaxed as if he was discussing the likelihood that we might get rain showers.

I suddenly remembered that I was scheduled to commit a felony later that evening. If Leif knew that I was going to be hiding a hot dinosaur in our garage in a few hours maybe he wouldn't be so keen to marry me.

"Do you think you know enough about me to make a call like this?" I asked.

He chuckled. "I should be asking you that question. I have no illusions about the fact that we have a lot of ground to cover in terms of our personal histories. There are a great many things about me that you don't know, and probably will never know. You have seen a glimpse of the life that I lead, and so far you don't seem terribly shocked by it."

"I'm not shocked by too many things, Leif," I said with wholehearted sincerity.

"Which is why I fell in love with you in the first place," he replied.

I swallowed. When I met his eyes I saw only genuine affection and calm sincerity. He wasn't worried. He wasn't afraid. Any average man would have been jumping out of his skin with terror. But Leif Gable was not an average man. I allowed myself a moment to really contemplate a future with him.

And then I remembered something that my father had once told me. He'd said that I wouldn't have to worry about finding a qualified suitor. He had said that a qualified man would find me.

"I understand, all too well, what I am asking you to do," he said, all trace of humor gone. "I know that I am essentially asking you to step out over the void and trust that I am going to be there to catch you."

"I'm not the only one who would be taking a big risk," I said.

"But if we don't take a risk we can't possibly hope to have any sort of reward in the end," he said. "And if I don't snatch you up now, some cowboy will come riding across the prairie and sweep you off your feet."

I laughed and shook my head. "Not very likely."

He polished off the last of his wine and sat back in his chair, looking totally relaxed.

"Leif, this is pretty darn sudden," I said, finally letting myself say what I was feeling.

His eyes actually twinkled. "Yes. But it could be pretty darn fun."

I shook my head and stared at my hands. They were rough and scratched from digging in the hard soil at Jimmy's site. I had a few old calluses that were still peeling off of my palms. I didn't know the first thing about throwing a cocktail party. I wasn't exactly what could be called dainty. Weren't wives of company presidents supposed to wear pearls and high heels every day and do things like go to personal trainers and have their teeth bleached?

"I have a lot of flaws," I said.

"And if I expected you to be perfect, Marley, you should run in the opposite direction as fast as you can. Nobody is perfect and I believe it is an impossible standard. However, I know that you have enough character and self-reliance to put up with me. I don't have a conventional life, not by any means. I have spent my entire adult life trying desperately to protect the women who love me from the person I truly am, and I realized that I can't do that any longer and hope to ever have a good marriage."

"You think I have a lot of character?" I asked.

"Maybe a little too much, sometimes. But you don't hide from the truth, no matter how painful it is. And you don't fall apart when a situation deteriorates."

He reached across the table again and took my hand.

His palms were cool and dry.

He smiled. "There are some things in my life that I will need to keep from you, simply because it will be prudent to do so. But the things that I can show you, I will, and I won't apologize for them or try to contrive it so that you will be sheltered from the truth. Can you live with that?"

"You don't do anything illegal, do you?" I asked, feeling foolish. It sounded like a question a six-year-old would ask.

He laughed. "Quite the opposite. I work for the government from time to time. And my work occasionally puts me in situations with some risk. We can get you up to speed on how to keep our lives private."

"What does that mean, situations with some risk?" I asked.

"It means that sometimes powerful people go to jail because of my efforts. I am very good at finding missing money. And, not too surprisingly, the people who steal it are not always keen to give it back."

I thought about this revelation. It squared with the things I had seen of his life to this point.

It was not unusual to find pistols resting in various drawers around the house. They were always loaded.

He paused and scrutinized me. "I can see from your face that you are concerned."

I didn't trust myself to say something that wasn't childish, so I simply nodded. Leif Gable was a complicated man, and I had always felt like I was simply a placeholder in his life until a woman with enough sophistication and charm school came along to fill the void. But I'd been wrong all this time. He didn't seem to want a socialite. He wanted me.

The speed of his proposal was a shock, but he looked so confident there didn't appear to be a doubt in his mind about it.

He plunged on, undeterred. "Let me reassure you that here in Killdeer our lives will be relatively safe. Your personal risk is very low. I can at least do that for you. But to maintain that security, I will inevitably need to shelter you from certain areas of my life. I will gradually tell you what I am doing, as we move forward with our marriage. But in the beginning the best thing is that I not communicate all of my daily activities. Can you live with that?"

My brain wasn't quick enough to process everything he had said. I was still stumbling over my emotions. What had just happened?

Had I just gotten engaged?

Leif leaned towards me. "Sweetheart, I do not want you to feel like I am pushing you. I want you to feel good about this, and trust that I know what best for us. So we can talk about it when I get back from Panama. How does that sound?"

My mouth was so dry my voice came out with a raspy squeak. "Yes?"

He lifted my hand and gave it a kiss. "At least you didn't run screaming from the restaurant. So I take that as a good sign."

I laughed and wiped my palms on my slacks again. Was it possible for a person to perspire this much?

A nod from Leif brought our waiter to the table and the check for the meal. He slid a credit card into the folder and handed it back without a glance.

As the waiter vanished I saw someone familiar come through the door. Loy Shucraft stopped at the hostess station, both hands propped on his gun belt. He was scanning the restaurant intently. His hand shifted so that his palm rested on the butt of his pistol.

Something was wrong.

I stood up and caught his eye. He headed for our table the moment he saw me.

"Loy? Is everything alright?" I asked.

"Leif. Good to see you," he said, shaking Leif's hand hard. He glanced down at me with a hard expression. "Can I borrow our girl here for a minute?"

Leif stood up. "Certainly. I'll settle up with the waiter and meet you outside."

I followed the sheriff to the door and we squeezed by a gaggle of office girls waiting for a table.

The moment we stepped outside, Loy put a hand on my shoulder. "Hun, somebody shot Lewis Pritchett's bull in your dad's pasture. Your dad's fine, but pretty upset."

"Someone shot Rufus?" I asked, incredulous.

Loy looked apologetic. "I would have called out here but this place is so new they don't have a phone number listed yet."

"Was anyone up there when it happened?"

Loy's face looked bleak. "Your dad heard shots about eight o'clock. When he got up there to take a look the wires on the fence were down. Somebody cut them and tried to drive up to that dig site."

"Oh my gosh."

Loy pushed his baseball cap off his forehead and gave his hairline a good scratching. "That's when he saw Lewis's bull."

I could feel the blood drain from my face and put a hand on the brick wall just to feel something solid. "Did he see anything else?"

"I'm getting there," Loy said, trying to be patient and not doing a very good job.

"What about Jimmy Burke? Is he alright?" I asked.

"Will you hit your pause button for a second, Marley?" Loy said.

I tried to swallow but my mouth was dry. "Sorry."

Loy shook my shoulder with his big paw, reassuring me. "Jimmy Burke is fine. He was working up there when he heard someone shooting down by the road, and when he saw a vehicle come over the hill towards him he pulled out his cell phone and yelled out that he was calling the sheriff. Which is a damn lie, because everybody knows you can't get a signal up there half the time—"

"And whoever it was panicked and drove off," I said.

Loy sighed. "That's about the size of it. His University of Wyoming geology van was parked up the hill. Jimmy drove it up there so he wouldn't have to contend with the bull on foot, so from the road it must have looked like nobody was around. Whoever it was, they must have been pretty desperate. But when they rolled up the rise and saw Jimmy they threw it in reverse and got the hell out of there."

"Did he get a description of the vehicle?" I asked.

"You want I should deputize you and put you to work on this, Marley?" Loy asked.

Leif came through the restaurant doors and saw the sheriff and me squared off. He gave us both a cautious look and took my hand.

"Nathan is beside himself," Loy said. "I think it would do him a world of good if you went back to the ranch and sat with him for a while."

I started to ask another question, but Leif steered me off the sidewalk in the direction of the car and opened the door for me.

"You can explain it to me on the way," Leif said.

As we drove out of Parkman and headed towards Killdeer, I remembered what Jimmy had told me about the effect fossils could have on people. He'd said that, sometimes, historical artifacts could make people do crazy things. I was starting to believe he was onto something.

We turned off pavement onto gravel just as the last streaks of sunlight melted away over the peak of the mountain.

I'd told Leif the situation, and as we bounced down the rutted road towards the ranch I saw the porch light from Wendy's little house burning brightly.

"We should stop and let Wendy and Hugo know what all the ruckus is about," I said.

My feet climbed the stairs, but my heart wasn't in it. I had no idea what I was going to say to Wendy that wouldn't upset Hugo. She pulled open the door before I even had a chance to knock.

"What's going on over there?" she asked, not bothering with a greeting.

I saw Hugo hovering behind her, his eyes wide and questioning.

Before blurting out what had happened, I managed to get ahold of my mouth and rein it in long enough to think about my answer.

"Everything is alright, isn't it?" Wendy asked with concern. "We've seen a dozen cars come and go in the last half hour. And the sheriff's truck was over there for a long time."

"Wendy, I don't want you and Hugo to worry. But someone shot the bull over in my father's pasture."

Her eyes bulged. "You don't want us to worry?"

I wanted to reassure her and said the first thing that popped into my head. "Listen. Sometimes spotlight poachers will go out and shoot in the dark at eye shine. Maybe somebody thought Rufus was a deer."

"Then why was your dad out there with a flashlight stringing barbwire?" she asked.

"He was repairing a hole, that's all. Whoever it was is long gone."

Hugo peeked around the edge of the door. "There was a hole in the fence?"

"It was probably an accident. But lock your doors tonight, would you?" I said.

I didn't believe for one second that it was a deer poacher, but the goal was to avoid upsetting Hugo and it was the best story I could come up with.

Wendy crossed her arms. "It doesn't sound like we've got nothing to worry about to me."

"Trust me," I said. "If that changes you will be the first to know."

Wendy closed the door and I heard the lock turn. The last thing I saw before we drove away was Hugo's face pressed to the windowpane, his hands shading the glass so he could see outside into the darkness.

His expression surprised me. Hugo didn't look frightened or worried. He looked angry.

That was not exactly the response I'd expected, but I didn't have time to ponder his reaction at the moment.

I had a dinosaur to steal.

CHAPTER 10

"This is never going to work."

My flashlight flickered. Had I changed the batteries in it recently?

"Don't be such a pessimist," I said.

Jimmy slapped his hand down on the huge plaster jacket that covered the fossil. "Do you know how much this thing weighs?"

"Eighty pounds or so?" I asked hopefully.

"Two hundred pounds. Easy," he said.

"Why didn't you say something before?" I asked.

"I thought it would be incomplete," he told me as he slumped to the ground.

It was close to eleven o'clock. A cricket played its happy song a few yards from where Jimmy sat on the ground and he scowled at it.

"Can't we roll it into the van?" I asked.

"The jacket is shaped like a giant mushroom. It's flat on the bottom and round on the top. There's no way we can roll it, and even if we could, how would we ever pick it up?"

Our plan to steal the fossil was falling apart rapidly.

I shook my flashlight, hoping the light would continue to glow from the dim bulb, and dropped to the ground beside Jimmy.

"I thought you were going to have this all ready to go by the time I got up here," I said.

"I've been at it since you left this afternoon," he said defensively. "Honestly, I didn't expect the skull to be complete and I prepped it as fast as I could. It is much bigger than I initially thought."

"If it really does weigh two hundred pounds, there is no way that you and I are going to be able to do this."

Jimmy rubbed his face. It was so covered in dirt his hand made a rasping sound as it slid across his forehead. "Is there someone you know who would be willing to help us out?"

"At eleven at night?" I asked.

Jimmy's flashlight was so powerful it lit up the entire dig site. It said Shockwave on the side, and the big yellow housing was wide enough that the flashlight remained standing without anything holding it. The two of us stared in silence at the huge white plaster jacket in the center of the hole. The beams of light shimmered as tiny tufts of dust drifted through them.

"Please don't tell me I spent seven hours putting a field jacket on that thing and two hours carving out the bottom, just so it can sit here while the State of Montana rounds up a team of armed men to confiscate it."

I wasn't exactly sure why, but my heart felt heavy on his behalf. Jimmy Burke didn't just want to study the fossil. It was plain to see that he was fiercely protective of it. He wanted to keep it safe. More than that, he wanted it to stay with my family.

His determination was touching, and even though it was probably a huge mistake, I wanted to do everything I could to help him out. That meant swallowing my pride. Something I had never been very good at.

"We need to go for a short drive," I said, getting to my feet and offering him a hand up.

"You know where we can get a backhoe?" he asked.

"Well, yeah, but that would make a lot of noise. I know someone who might be willing to give us a hand."

"Can they keep their mouth shut?" he asked as he scooped up his flashlight.

I sighed. "He's a pro at that."

I'd parked my SUV at the bottom of the hill and we climbed inside. We left Jimmy's geology van conspicuously on the road so it would be visible to anyone who drove up.

If the person who had shot Rufus came back they would see the van and hopefully be discouraged enough to leave.

I drove past my father's ranch house, dimming the headlights as we went by. If anyone asked him, he would honestly be able to say that he hadn't seen anyone.

I knew the gravel roadway so well I could practically navigate just from the position of the potholes, but the running lights on the SUV gave me enough light to see where we were going.

When we passed the ranch house I flipped the lights back on and headed towards Killdeer. As we approached the long straight stretch of road that trailed beside a thick stand of aspen trees, I flipped a U-turn and parked beside the ditch. I killed the engine and left the headlights burning.

Jimmy looked at me sideways. "Listen, I've got a girlfriend."

I spared him an incredulous laugh. "I'm not parking here so we can make out."

"Okay. Maybe you want to tell me what we are really doing?"

It was complicated, but since we more than likely had at least a half an hour to wait I figured there was time to fill him in.

"At the top of this hill there is a weather station," I said.

"The weather station that's not really a weather station," Jimmy said.

"You know about it?" I asked.

"Your father told me a little bit, but he didn't say what it really was. Only that everyone in the valley called it Area 49—"

"Because it doesn't quite rate up there with Area 51," I said, finishing his sentence. "It's really a SETI monitoring station, but they try to keep a low profile and everyone who works there calls it a weather station instead. All the dishes up there are pointed at a certain place in the sky, and their only job is to listen to radio waves in case—"

"In case we get a phone call from the little green men," he finished for me.

"Right. I dated the security chief from the station, and he was so secretive that he never even gave me his phone number so I could call him. If I wanted to get in touch, the only way I could track him down was to drive over here and park on the road. I know it sounds crazy, but somehow the people who work up there can see who is in the area."

The glow of headlights splashed across the trees, telling me that someone was coming down the hill towards us. "That was fast."

"Apparently the security chief has fond memories of the two of you," Jimmy said.

I was glad it was dark, or Jimmy would have seen me blushing.

Whenever I saw Finn my emotions were a jumble. Asking him for help wasn't the smartest thing in the world but I knew one thing for certain; Finn could definitely keep his mouth shut.

The familiar black Jeep rolled down the road towards us and pulled to a stop alongside.

I rolled down my window and tried to smile.

Finn didn't bother to shut off his engine and simply got out of his Jeep. He stood beside my window with a frosty expression.

He started to speak, but then caught sight of Jimmy sitting beside me and he paused.

"Hey, Finn," I said. "You know Jimmy Burke? He's the graduate student working up at my father's ranch."

Finn's expression remained stony. "Mr. Burke."

"Hello," Jimmy said gamely, reaching across me to extend his hand.

Finn ignored it. "Car trouble?"

"We need your help," I said. "The dinosaur fossil that Jimmy is working on is ready to be moved, but it's too heavy for us. It will take at least three people to lift it into the van."

His lip twitched, but otherwise it was as if I hadn't even spoken. He didn't say a word.

"I was hoping you could meet us at the site and help load it up," I said.

"I'm missing Letterman." He was clearly irritated.

"It will only take a half hour," I said.

Finn rolled his head from side to side, cracking his neck loudly. "It's a little late in the evening for this, don't you think?"

"Look, Mr. Finn," Jimmy said in a rush. "If I don't move the fossil by tomorrow, the State of Montana will probably confiscate it because some idiot who works for the BLM is telling everyone that the bones are human remains. It will take months to get it all sorted out, and I need this fossil for my graduate degree. Can't you help us out a little?"

"Not Mr. Just Finn."

"There is no one else we can go to," I said.

"Leif must be in bed, wondering where you are," Finn said caustically.

Why was he being so awful?

"Please?" I asked, my voice plaintive. "It's important."

He studied me for a moment, his eyes forlorn. Finally he dropped his chin on his chest and spun away. "Fine. But let's make this quick."

He already had his Jeep in gear before I could get my SUV started and rolling. He followed us back to the dig site riding my bumper. To my surprise, when I dimmed my headlights as we drove by my father's ranch house, Finn did the same.

I parked on the road when we got to the bottom of the ridge and I pulled open the barbwire gate and tossed it to the side so we could drive back down the hill in a hurry. Finn stood beside me, waiting.

Jimmy hopped out and headed for his van. "I'll park as close to the jacket as I can get."

He tore past us through the gate, the brown van rocking and creaking in protest.

My old flashlight flickered and dimmed as Finn and I climbed the hill on foot. Halfway to the dig site it sputtered out completely, and Finn made an exasperated sound as he pulled out his own small flashlight to illuminate the way up.

"Have you thought about where you plan to hide the thing?" he asked as we trudged along.

"Who said we need to hide it?"

He glanced at me. "You are not relocating this fossil in the middle of the night because you want to beat the heat."

"My father's barn," I said a bit sheepishly.

"Not a very secure location," he said.

I stopped. It took him a moment to notice, but he pulled up and turned towards me, shining the light in my eyes.

"It would be the first place they would look for it," I said, realizing my mistake. Putting the fossil anywhere on our property was out of the question. Why hadn't that occurred to me?

"You didn't think about this very carefully, did ya doll?"

I felt a moment of panic. "This is a problem."

"I'm not taking it to the weather station," Finn said, cutting the air with one hand, his tone firm. "So don't even ask."

"Where else can we put it? If I take it to Leif's, it won't take them very long to figure out what happened to it."

Some of Finn's icy veneer started to melt. He lowered the flashlight and snagged my elbow, pulling me towards the ridgeline. "It sounds like a doff action, but it's true that nobody thinks to look for something when you hide it in plain sight."

"Doff action means mistake, doesn't it?" I asked.

Finn had grown up in Johannesburg, South Africa, and he'd done a stint with the surfing mob there. Sometimes his slang was less than American.

"Right. You want to hide it good, hide it in public," he said as we crested the ridge.

"First we have to get it loaded," I told him.

Jimmy maneuvered the van as close to the white plaster jacket as he could get without crushing the arrowheads that still lay beneath the soil. He propped open the back doors and was frantically shoving buckets, shovels and burlap out of the way to give us room.

We navigated the scrub brush, side by side. The heavy darkness seemed to muffle every sound.

Wads of burlap and toilet paper littered the hole.

I caught Finn frowning down at the mess and explained, "Jimmy said it's to make a barrier between the plaster and the bones."

He studied the mess for a moment wordlessly. Jimmy was still organizing the back of his van and was far out of earshot.

Finn looked up at me. "Marley, are you happy?"

I was so startled my feet snagged an errant stand of sagebrush and I nearly fell flat on my face. Finn's hand darted out and he pulled me upright before I could make a fool out of myself.

After I had my balance back he let go of my arm, but continued to watch me.

"Am I happy?" I asked, stunned by such a question. "Of course I am."

He gave a cough and looked away hurriedly. "Good. That's good."

Before I could blink he was gone, walking fast towards Jimmy, and I had to scramble to keep pace.

Any emotion he may have felt seemed buried instantly when we reached the fossil, and when I gave Finn a questioning look he simply turned his back on me.

Not for the first time I found myself confused and frustrated with his behavior, but there were more important things to deal with at the moment and I turned my attention to the heavy load sitting on the ground at my feet.

"Okay, let's push the field jacket from this side," Jimmy said, kneeling in the dirt. "When it falls over it will be a couple feet closer to the van."

"Two feet isn't going to make that much difference," Finn pointed out.

"It will after you feel how heavy it is," Jimmy told him.

The three of us knelt shoulder to shoulder and did what we could to brace ourselves in the loose soil. The plaster jacket was at least three feet tall, but it was nearly four feet long and almost every inch of it was rock and dirt on the inside. The plaster encased the fossil like a protective cocoon, and I noticed that Jimmy had put a triangle of two-by-four boards along the top of the field jacket and coated them with plaster, to serve as a support base after we flipped it over. Hopefully the boards would keep the jacket together when we lifted it off the ground.

"One, two—"

Finn didn't wait for three and simply dug in with both heels and put his shoulders into it. The field jacket tilted off its base and rolled to the ground without any effort from either Jimmy or me.

Finn stood up and examined the plaster jacket to see if it had survived the fall. Satisfied it was still in one piece, he stepped back and noticed Jimmy staring at him.

"I work out," Finn said with a shrug.

"Let's get it loaded," Jimmy instructed, looking at Finn with an impressed expression.

It took all three of us to lift it, but we managed to struggle our way to the van and slide it in the back without any injuries. Jimmy cussed a blue streak when he realized the two-by-fours were too long and the van doors wouldn't close properly, but Finn and I helped him tie bungee cords across the handles to keep them shut.

"So where to?" Finn asked.

"Lil's," I said.

"The café?" Jimmy asked with a squeak in his voice. "Are you nuts?"

"Nobody, and I mean nobody, will think to look there," I said.

Jimmy's mouth opened and closed a few times, but it was obvious we lacked any other alternatives, and the logic of it, no matter how twisted it seemed, won out.

He relented at last. "I'll drive us."

We climbed inside the van and the three of us bounced down the hillside, Finn and I clinging to both sides of the field jacket in the back of the van to keep it stable.

The dim glow from the dashboard lit his face, but Finn didn't look at me once the entire drive into Killdeer. I was starting to think I had imagined his concern over my happiness.

We pulled up behind Lil's café, the street deserted in both directions, and Jimmy slowly backed the van towards the kitchen door.

One lonely streetlight illuminated the parking lot. Somewhere off in the distance a dog barked.

"Wait here," I said when Jimmy came to open the back door of the van.

"Where are you going?" he asked.

"To get the key."

My friend Irene, like most people in Killdeer, had a hide-a-key stashed for her café just in case she ever lost her set and needed to get inside in a hurry.

Jimmy and Finn probably thought it was strange when I disappeared around the corner of the building and walked across the street. It might have looked odd, but I knew what I was doing. The old streetlight overhead gave off just enough light for me to make my way to the other side of the street to the old coin shop.

The coin shop had been closed for more than fifteen years, but the owner never bothered to liquidate the inventory or sell the property. It still housed long display cases filled with old coins and pieces of pawned jewelry. But nobody ever opened the place for business. A rusty hulk of ancient farm machinery squatted in front of the coin shop, looking generally abused and abandoned. The rusted machine had once been a hay rake built to be pulled by a team of horses. Now it was an eyesore. But along the main shaft of the rake a row of twisted hooks remained intact, and on one of those hooks hung a steel key.

I lifted the key off the hook and squeezed it in my palm. Irene didn't feel comfortable leaving her hide-a-key anywhere on her café property because she said kids could find it too easily. Instead, she left it across the street at the coin shop because she said it would be a stretch for anyone to associate the two.

I unlocked the back door to Irene's café and slid the key inside my jeans pocket.

"Are you sure this is alright?" Jimmy asked.

"There is a metal cart back here they use for hauling in the delivery pallets," I said. "I'll pull it up and we can wheel the jacket in."

Finn's eyes darted around the quiet parking lot, and Jimmy rubbed his hands nervously.

I flipped on a light switch so I wouldn't fall over a case of ketchup, and hurried to locate the cart. I didn't see it where Irene usually kept it. Irritated, I finally checked inside the walk-in cooler and saw the cart nosed against the wall, weighted down with heavy crates of cream and butter.

"Dammit," I said under my breath. "It's Wednesday."

Thursday morning Irene's baker would make pies for the week. It took me five minutes to horse the cream, the butter and the boxes of condiments to the floor.

The cart rolled smoothly when I got it emptied. It would be a snap to load the field jacket and store the cart, skull and all, inside the cooler.

I'd explain everything to Irene in the morning.

As I shoved the cart through the back door it jerked to a halt, and no matter how hard I shoved, it wouldn't budge. The wheels were caught on the rim.

"Give me a hand, would you?" I asked.

Neither Jimmy nor Finn came to help me.

"Hey, it's not going to move itself," I said. "Why are you two standing there with your arms up?"

"Hold it, Marley."

I blinked and turned to stare at the talking shadow hovering beside the door.

Deputy Sheriff Nick Wilcox pointed his sidearm straight at me. He jerked his pistol sideways. "Come on out. Keep your hands where I can see them."

I stayed right where I was. "You have got to be kidding me."

"Move. Over here. Make it slow," he said, his voice as sharp as a razor.

Nick and I had never gotten along, but I'd never expected to see inside the barrel of his pistol.

"You know I am not burglarizing the place," I said.

"You two, put your hands on the side of the van," Nick said to Jimmy and Finn.

Finn lowered his hands and took a step.

"Keep your hands up!" Nick shouted.

Finn's voice was casual. "You want me to keep them up? Or put them on the van, Deputy?"

"Just move it," Nick said.

Nick was dressed in jeans and a polo shirt. He wasn't on duty and must have just come back to Killdeer from somewhere, just in time to see us breaking into the cafe.

What lousy timing.

Jimmy had assumed the position next to the van. Both his eyes were shut tight. It was plain to see he was mortified.

"Deputy, I'm going to walk back inside the café and get the cordless telephone," I said.

He gave a toothy grin. "You are going to come out here and line up."

It must have felt like Christmas and his birthday all rolled up in one to get the chance to arrest Marley Dearcorn.

"I'll only be a second," I said, not giving him a chance.

I walked away and left the deputy standing in the lot huffing and puffing with frustration.

I could hear him trying to scramble through the door, but the cart was well and truly stuck and he was forced to clamber over it. He caught his toes on the handle and tumbled face-first on the floor with a thud.

By the time he managed to regain his feet I was already dialing Irene's house.

The phone rang once, twice, three times . . .

"I told you not to move," Nick said, one vein pulsing on his forehead.

"Come on, pick up," I said to the phone.

After a dozen rings it was painfully clear that Irene wasn't at home. I could try her cell but I had a sinking feeling she wouldn't answer it. Of all the rotten times she could have picked to spend the night with my father . . .

"Take it easy, Nick," I said. "I'm supposed to be here."

"Doing what?" he asked. "It's midnight."

"I'm making a delivery," I lied.

"Out of the back of a University of Wyoming geology van?" he asked. "Pull the other leg, Marley."

At least he'd holstered his pistol.

"Jimmy is doing me a favor," I said.

"You are digging yourself deeper and deeper the more you keep talking," Nick said. "I'm not stupid. You're trying to stash that thing sitting in the back of the van, aren't you? Everyone in town's been talking about it."

He grabbed my arm and started dragging me towards the back door.

That's when the smell hit me. I stared at him with disbelief.

"You been drinking, Deputy?" I asked.

Nick froze where he stood and dropped my arm. "Drinking?"

"You smell like a brewery," I said. "How many beers have you had tonight?"

"One," he said, backing away from me. "I had one beer. I'm not impaired."

I followed him, pinning him against the metal shelving. "One, or two? I'll bet Loy would love it if he got a phone call to come down to the station and deal with his deputy who has been drinking and driving."

"We don't need to call the sheriff," Nick said hotly. "I could pass any sobriety test."

"Do you know how this looks?"

119

A drunk driver had killed my mother when I was nine years old. If there was one thing that made me madder, I didn't know what it was. My jaw was clenched so tight when I spoke my words came out with a hiss.

"You make me sick. Of all the people who should know better," I said, letting my anger take hold.

The deputy licked his dry lips and held up both hands. "Okay, okay. Let's talk about this."

"Word of this gets out and I'd lay money your career here in Killdeer will be cut pretty damn short."

"We don't need it to go that far," Nick said desperately.

"It's a little late for that, Deputy."

He took two steps away from me, his shoulders drooping. "I know what you are doing here tonight, but if I keep my mouth shut about it, will you do likewise?"

We watched each other like two angry cats. The air crackled with tension.

It stuck in my throat, but after a long, furious pause, I managed to respond. "You drive the two blocks to the sheriff's station and stay there till you sober up, or I'm calling Loy."

Nick opened and closed his mouth, on the verge of arguing with me. "That's not—alright. Fine. But you had better by-God take that fossil, whatever it is, and put in right back where you got it. If I find out it's missing tomorrow, I'll squawk until everyone knows who took it."

My stomach lurched with disappointment. But I wasn't in any position to negotiate. "We'll take it back. But Jimmy had nothing to do with this, and neither did Finn, so you lay off those two."

"Not any more than I normally would," Nick told me, defiant. "Now, clear on out of here and don't come back. I know I screwed up, but dammit, Marley, I'm just trying to do my job."

The deputy actually helped me get the cart back inside the cooler before pulling out of the lot and driving ten miles an hour over to the sheriff's station. I felt a measure of satisfaction when he disappeared inside, giving every impression he was keeping his word.

Jimmy was crestfallen when I told him we had blown it and wouldn't be able to hide the fossil. But he was so relieved not to be going to jail he gushed with gratitude that I'd managed to talk us out of being arrested.

Finn seemed slightly amused by the whole incident.

I felt like a fool.

After all the work we had put in, we ended up turning right around and putting the dinosaur back where we had gotten it in the first place. It was not my finest hour.

CHAPTER 11

"You know what's wrong with this country?" asked Irene.

I glanced sideways at Hugo, who was busy working his breakfast like he was a hungry wolf cub.

"Doesn't your mother let you have bacon at home?" I asked.

"She says it has too many hormones and antibiotics," he told me, his mouth full.

Irene refilled Hugo's orange juice.

I gave her a sideways smile. "Okay, Irene. What's wrong with this country?"

"Spoiled. We are all spoiled, rotten brats. And lazy."

I sipped my coffee. Lil's was packed this morning. Everyone in town wanted to get the latest word on the murder of Lewis's bull and they had decided congregating at the café was the best way to accomplish that.

"Why are we all spoiled?" I asked.

"My cellular phone company just sent me a letter telling me that from now on whenever I am close to going over my minutes, they will warn me about it with a text message or an e-mail or some other stupid thing. Can you believe that?" she asked.

"It sounds like a courtesy," I said.

"I have a cell phone," Hugo informed us.

When I glanced down at him, he pointed to the cornbread pancake that sat untouched on my plate.

"Are you going to eat that, Aunt Marley?"

"Where's the personal accountability?" Irene asked, waving the orange juice carafe wildly.

"What ever happened to good, old-fashioned common sense? Can't people even do math these days?"

I slid my plate in front of Hugo and passed him the maple syrup. "It's all yours."

"Is this what we have come to?" Irene went on. "A phone company has to tie our shoes for us? It's ridiculous. If someone is too lazy to sit down with a calculator and figure out how many minutes they have used on their cell phone, then they deserve to get a six-hundred-dollar bill."

Hugo chewed his pancake thoughtfully while she ranted. He seemed to be taking in every word.

"So that's what's wrong with our country?" I asked.

"I could point out a few other things people do that rub me the wrong way," Irene said, finally setting the orange juice safely back on the counter.

"I'll bet," I said.

"If I don't clean my room, Mom says I can't go with her to the museum on Saturdays," Hugo confessed.

"That's a good thing, Hugo," Irene said, staring at me with a rigid expression. "It shows that your mother is bringing you up right. She is teaching you that it's important to take care of things. It's important to pick up after yourself when you make a mess, to be responsible."

I wordlessly slid her back door key across the counter.

She looked at it and snorted. "I should have known."

Irene snatched the key, opened the cash register and dropped it inside before slamming the drawer shut. "Now I have to find a new hiding place for it. Really, Marley. The cooler was an absolute mess this morning. Did you think I wouldn't notice?"

"I'll tell you the whole story later." I wished desperately for an antacid.

"Did someone really shoot Rufus?" Hugo asked.

Irene and I looked at each other and argued silently with twitching facial expressions over who would field this whopper.

I answered with as little detail as possible.

"Yes. They did."

"Why?" he asked.

I didn't have a good explanation and was grateful that Irene chose that moment to jump in.

"Hugo, sometimes people do things that are not very nice."

"I know. In 1519, the Spanish conquistador Hernán Cortés marched on the Aztec city of Cholula and killed three thousand people," Hugo told us. "He was looking for gold."

"His mother is an archaeologist," I told Irene.

"Anthropologist," Hugo corrected.

"We don't know why someone shot Rufus," I said.

"Maybe they knew there was something really valuable up at Mr. Jimmy's dig and they wanted to steal it," he said.

"The only thing valuable up on the ridge was that bull," Irene said.

I groaned. "You know that bull was worth eight thousand bucks?"

Irene's eyes slid over Hugo to see how the boy was taking it. He was mopping up the last of the maple syrup with the final bite of pancake.

I felt a lump in my chest. I hated talking about it in front of Hugo.

"Loy called the game warden from our district to come out and help him with the autopsy," I said.

"I guess a game warden would know how to look for bullets in a big animal," Irene said. She pulled her small stool from beneath the counter and sat down, looking grim.

"They used a metal detector, and Loy said he recovered a slug that looked like someone used a hunting rifle."

"A hunting rifle?" Irene shook her head. "So that narrows it down to about half the population of Montana."

The front door opened, letting in a burst of warm wind, and Irene nudged me with one hand. "It's your geologist fella."

Jimmy Burke collapsed on the stool beside me and nodded gratefully when Irene handed him a menu. He looked like he had neither bathed nor slept for days. He mumbled as he carefully studied the specials, then set the menu aside and shrugged. "Surprise me."

Irene took the menu and called into the kitchen through the pickup window. "Steak and eggs. Knock the horns off and put it to bed smothered."

Jimmy's expression shifted from tired to startled.

I patted him on the shoulder. "It's just steak and eggs rare on a bed of hash browns with gravy."

He relaxed a bit and slumped at the counter. "What a night. I don't think I got more than a half hour of sleep."

"You didn't stay up at the site, did you?" I asked.

"I had to." He gulped down an entire glass of water that Irene had set in front of him.

"You shouldn't have done that," I said.

"What was I supposed to do? Sit on my butt in my hotel room while someone went up there and looted my site?"

"Nobody went up there, did they Mr. Jimmy?" Hugo asked. He looked more upset by the idea of pot hunters than when he heard about Rufus.

"No, the site is fine. I asked that toad, Rob from the BLM, to keep an eye on it while I came into town to clean up a little."

"You trust him?" I asked.

Jimmy laughed. "Not really. But I didn't have any other choice. He was hovering around like a vulture so I asked him if he could loiter at the gate and look official for a few hours."

I waited a couple heartbeats before I asked the questions that had been brewing in my head since yesterday. Jimmy looked fragile as hell and I wanted to move slowly so I didn't push him over the edge.

We had been a little bit busy the night before and it hadn't seemed like a good time to bring it up, but now I wanted to know what he had witnessed when the bull had been killed.

"Loy told me you were there when it happened yesterday," I said, keeping my voice even. "Did you hear the shots?"

Jimmy ran a hand through his hair. Flakes of dirt drifted down to the counter. "I thought it must have been deer hunters or something. But then I remembered it's June."

"So you thought it was deer poachers," I said.

He gave a nervous laugh. "I knew right away that I was in serious trouble when the person tried to drive up the hill. I sort of panicked."

"Did you see the make of the car?" I asked.

"Are you kidding? I couldn't even tell what color the thing was, or if it was a truck or an SUV or what, and I was looking right at it but all I could see were headlights."

"Did you get a look at the driver?" I asked.

"Didn't you just hear the part where I said all I could see were headlights?" He spared me a desperate look. "Anyway, I wasn't concentrating on the car. All I could think about is that someone was driving up the hill, that they had a gun, and that I was in their way."

Irene filled him a glass of orange juice and he drank half of it in four gulps.

"I'm sorry, Jimmy. That must have been pretty scary," I said. "Don't feel bad about not getting a better look at the car."

He shrugged. But then he paused and looked away. "It's probably nothing, but . . ."

"What's probably nothing?" I asked.

He rubbed the back of his neck with one grimy hand, pondering. "Something that seemed funny to me."

I gave him an encouraging look. "If it was something that stood out it might be useful."

He fingered his orange juice glass. "There was one thing that seemed strange when the car drove off. I heard a high whistling sound."

I felt my eyebrows crease. "A whistle? Like a person whistling?"

127

"Not really like a person. It was too loud. It was sort of like a starter's whistle. You know, a coach's whistle. But I could have imagined the whole thing. It seemed so out of place I remembered it."

"Order up!"

Irene turned at the call from the cook and scooped the plate of steak and eggs from the pickup window. She set it before Jimmy with a flourish and when he saw the dish he scrambled for his silverware.

He took a bite and beamed at Irene. "Are you married, ma'am?"

"I'm too old for you, Mr. Burke."

"I think you should let me be the judge of that." He tore into his breakfast.

Irene gave me a proud smirk. "See that, Marley? That's how you snag a man. Feed him. Now, if you fed Leif Gable half as well as I feed your father, he'd propose."

My face must have turned six shades of pale. I felt my eyes widen so far I thought my forehead would pop off. Irene took one look at my stunned expression and stood up from her stool so fast it tipped over.

"He didn't," she said. "Leif proposed to you!"

Before she could reach across the counter and grab me I practically fell off the back of my stool to escape. "Can we talk about this later?"

"Marley Dearcorn, you get back over here this minute," she snapped.

Irene darted around the counter after me, when a wolf whistle from one of the other diners made everyone in the café stop.

Harvey Wilson, clad in his usual bib overalls and sporting the same sweat-stained John Deere tractor ball cap he'd worn since 1987, was leaning over one of the tables and staring out the window at the parking lot, transfixed.

Everyone turned to see what had caught his attention.

Harvey chewed his bottom lip. "Would ya look at that?"

Irene paused in her pursuit long enough to go to the window and peer outside. She wheezed a laugh and shook her head. "Oh my God. It's General George Armstrong Custer himself."

I looked through the glass out at the parking lot and saw a row of gleaming black Suburbans lined up bumper to bumper like a caravan. All three vehicles sported tinted windows, heavy luggage racks on the roof packed with gear, and personalized license plates from Colorado. I could see one of the license plates from where I stood: DIGGER 1.

Irene was staring at the man sitting behind the wheel of the first SUV. It was impossible not to notice his flowing blond hair, even from across the lot.

The door of the vehicle opened. A pair of shiny Tony Lama cowboy boots hit the pavement and the man inside unfolded from the front seat with a flourish worthy of a bullfighter.

He was tall and lean, with striking features and a smile that could cut glass. His suede leather jacket dripped fringe, sparkling with beads and sterling buttons.

Irene stared shamelessly. "Now he's a long, cool drink of water."

Hugo came to stand beside me, shamelessly pressing his nose against the window. "Who's that?"

Three women emerged from the other Suburbans, appraised their surroundings with disdain and sashayed towards the blond man like a pride of lionesses. They hovered languidly beside him, their tanned skin glowing in the morning sunshine. One of them wore her thick red hair so long it brushed her belt loops. A second wore hers cut in a jet-black pageboy style, and the third woman, a curvy blonde, was girl-next-door pretty. You couldn't have slid a length of dental floss between these women and their pants. Their khakis were so tight if they had been wearing any underwear I could have read the cleaning instructions on the tags.

The women's uniforms consisted of khakis, white sleeveless tank tops and brown waterproof Crocodile Dundee field hats. It looked like Vanity Fair magazine was doing a cover shoot featuring shabby-chic designer jungle wear.

The redhead was laughing at something the tall blond man had said. She ran a hand through her long hair and pivoted to the side, showing a perfect profile of dangerous curves. Her tight tank top was size small, but her bust was size vadda-voom. Both nipples were so hard it looked like a couple of marbles had been dropped down the front of her shirt. She wasn't wearing a bra.

"Hugo, go back and sit at the counter before you accidentally enter puberty," Irene said.

Hugo trudged away from the window obediently.

Two men climbed out of their long Suburban and stood with the group, but they were a stark contrast to the others. One man was muscled and swarthy with the look of a rock climber who studied Latin for amusement. The other man was dressed head to toe in black, his bare shoulders covered with tattoos.

The blond man, who was clearly the undisputed leader, held out his arms with a broad gesture and enthusiastic expression as he addressed his group. They followed his every move, nodding at practically every word he said.

"Here comes Nathan," Harvey Wilson announced to the café. He was chewing his toothpick so hard it broke in half.

I was more than a little surprised to see my father pull into the parking lot in his battered pickup truck and stop beside the black convoy. He slammed his door and with a forced smile strode towards the tall blond man with outstretched hand.

They shook hands but all I could see was the back of my father's head. I couldn't tell if he was happy to see the man or not.

"The one and only Dr. Clifton Myers," said Jimmy, his voice flat. "My professor called me and let me know to expect someone from Colorado, but I sure didn't expect to see him."

He held his plate in one hand and stood beside me to watch the sideshow, eating as he talked.

"The tall guy?" I asked.

"I remember him from the mug shot on his book. The world famous archaeologist and regular guest on the History Channel. He's got to be in his late fifties, but you sure wouldn't know it by looking at him." Jimmy's tone suggested he wasn't too impressed.

"Who are the sexed-up vampires with him?" Irene asked.

Her eyes were locked on the redhead, who happened to be standing precariously close to my father, flashing him a winning smile.

"Anthropology students working on summer credits, probably. One of them might be a teaching assistant." He shoved another bite of hash browns into his mouth, chewed for a moment, and resumed his seat at the counter.

Jimmy spoke to his plate as he speared another mouthful of steak. "I guess it used to be his dig site. But I'm a little surprised he came all the way out here to Killdeer to look at a spot he abandoned thirty years ago."

Hugo was at my side once again. He hopped from foot to foot. "Can we go?"

"Hugo, the bathroom is at the end of the café," I said.

"I don't need to go to the bathroom." His jaw was clenched.

I watched the congregation in the parking lot as they regrouped. Some arrangement had been made and the Colorado contingent drifted back towards their Suburbans. My father pointed down the street in the direction of our ranch and shook Clifton Myers's hand once more before turning back to his truck.

"They must be going to the site," I said. "Jimmy, you better finish that steak because the Coco Chanel spring fashion collection is about to hit the catwalk."

Jimmy tossed money on the counter and got to his feet as he gulped the rest of his water. "I'm coming, I'm coming."

Hugo poked my arm to get my attention. "Aunt Marley, can we go?"

"Sure. I think it would be alright if we watched them while they work."

"I don't mean to the site. Can we go back to my Aunt Wendy's yarn shop?" he asked.

"Hugo, are you feeling alright?" I asked.

He swallowed and studied his toes. "I guess. I just don't really want to go up there right now."

Irene nudged him with her hip. "I'm sure that Rufus isn't up there anymore. I think that Lewis went and got him. It'll be alright."

Some inner turmoil tugged at the boy, but as he watched the caravan speed out of the parking lot, he seemed to come to a decision.

"Okay, I guess," he said.

I expected a lot more enthusiasm from him, because it wasn't every day one got to rub elbows with a "world famous" archaeologist. Still, it had been a busy couple of days, and maybe Hugo was simply feeling a bit overwhelmed.

I knew exactly how he felt.

"We can watch them take some pictures and then if you still want to leave we can go back to your Aunt Wendy's. How does that sound?"

He murmured something and went back to the counter to retrieve his backpack.

I was fumbling for my wallet when Irene grabbed my arm and hissed in my ear like an angry goose.

"And when you are finished up there, you are going to get your skinny butt back down here and tell me all about the situation between you and Mr. Leif Gable."

I grinned at her. "I have to work at the library this afternoon. Sorry."

"You are not sorry, you weasel," she said.

"There isn't that much to tell, honestly. We talked about it, but we haven't made any plans."

Her lips twitched to the side, but she nodded. "My middle name is Susan, just so you know."

I gave her a quizzical look.

"In case you are looking for baby names," she said.

"Let's go, Hugo," I said, rolling my eyes.

As we walked to the car I noticed that Hugo was clutching his backpack so tight his little fingers were turning white and his skin was waxy.

As someone who grew up on a ranch, I never imagined that some people might be upset by something like a dead bull. I'd seen death regularly when I was a kid. But the only death that most city kids were exposed to these days came in the form of wrapped packages of beef in the grocery store. Maybe I was pushing him too hard?

As I buckled my seat belt I gave him a reassuring smile. "We don't have to go, if you don't want to."

"No. It's okay. But can I wait in the car?"

I started the engine. "Sure you can. And if you get bored and want to leave, you can honk the horn and we'll come back to Killdeer. How does that sound?"

He buckled his seat belt, looking a little more relaxed. "That sounds good."

As we drove towards the ranch, Hugo sat beside me staring straight ahead, not making a sound the entire way.

CHAPTER 12

As Hugo and I drove around the corner, we both sat up straight in our seats to get a better look at the circus that had just come to town.

"Who are all these people?" I asked.

At least a dozen cars lined the road beside our pasture. I saw the University of Colorado Suburbans lined up like a blockade in front of the gate on either side of Jimmy's van. Several other cars that I didn't recognize were squeezed tightly end to end along the ditch.

Rob Powers stood beside his BLM vehicle with a smug look.

Amelia Snow had just parked on the opposite side of the road. She stepped out of her Forest Service truck, looking dismayed, and trotted across the gravel towards my father.

My father stood with his back to the pasture, arms folded. He nodded to Amelia as she approached and stopped beside him. He didn't say a word and continued to stare straight ahead, red-faced and glaring at the line of cars helplessly.

I maneuvered my way through the throng and managed to squeeze in between two of the Colorado Suburbans. I had to park nose in, and my back bumper stuck out in the road.

Hugo immediately scrunched down into his seat. "Let's just go. I don't want to be here. Can we go?"

I gave him a worried glance as I stepped out. "It looks like that reporter from the local news station must have run her piece on the site. Don't worry, Hugo. You can wait in the car. I need to talk to my father for a minute to see what is going on."

Jimmy stood directly in front of the gate. Two women I didn't recognize were harassing him. It was all he could do to fend them off. He waved his arms and kept repeating, over and over, "I understand, ladies. I understand. But . . ."

I was greatly relieved the red television van was nowhere in sight.

Clifton Myers, man of the hour, sat in the driver's seat of the lead SUV talking on a huge cell phone. Either he was using ancient technology from the nineties, or he was actually talking on a satellite phone. In any case, I was grateful he wasn't in the middle of the chaos adding to it.

As I made my way towards my father, Clifton glanced over at me and eased his head from behind the windshield as I walked past him. He mumbled something into the phone, unfolded his lean frame from his Suburban and tossed the satellite phone onto the seat. He gave me a smile and headed me off before I could reach my father's side.

"Hello, I'm Dr. Myers." His voice dripped like warm honey.

He held out his hand and I shook it purely by polite reflex. "I'm Marley Dearcorn."

His eyes drifted up my frame and came to a sudden stop on my face. "Marley . . . Dearcorn? I beg your pardon, young woman, but you look nothing like the Marley Dearcorn that I knew and loved."

"He was my grandfather," I said, a bite to my voice. I instantly felt intense irritation that this man had known my grandfather, but I had never had that privilege.

"But of course he was." Clifton gave a slight bow of his head. "I can't tell you how devastated I was to hear of his passing."

He still hadn't released my hand, so I relaxed my grip and as politely as possible took a step back. He finally let me go and I tried to edge my way around him as I headed up the slope.

One stride with those long legs and he blocked me. "As I understand it, there happens to be a discussion going on concerning the site. Something to do with human remains?"

Jimmy was still pinned down at the gate by the two excited women. Clifton obviously hadn't spoken to him.

I reluctantly answered as I tried to edge away from him. "Someone made a mistake."

He watched me intently. "Even I make mistakes. From time to time."

Talking to Clifton Myers was like being scrutinized by a curious mountain lion. I got the distinct impression that he was excessively friendly with people, but only if he wanted something.

"I'm sure that Mr. Burke can fill you in as soon as he's done with the firing squad over there," I said, easing past him.

He chuckled and followed me up the slope. "I'm sure he can. But in the meantime, perhaps you would like to join us, with your father of course, and we can make a preliminary examination of what has been uncovered thus far."

I stopped dead where I was and gave him a surprised look. Why in the world would Clifton Myers want me to go with them to the site?

He watched me with a faint smile, his lips parted slightly.

I glanced over his shoulder and saw the red-haired anthropology student glaring at me like I'd just backed over her Pomeranian with a Humvee.

"I'd just be in the way." I walked around him deliberately and felt a wave of dismay when he followed practically on my heels.

I stopped beside my father and we shared a tortured look. Clifton planted next to me, sparing a nod for my father.

I overcame my intense irritation with General Custer long enough to introduce him to Amelia Snow.

"Amelia, this is Dr. Myers from the University of Colorado."

She sniffed. "Hello, Clifton."

His easy smile faded when he saw her. "Oh. It's good to see you again Miss Snow."

She avoided his gaze and mumbled at the ground, her fingers fiddling with her long necklace. "Likewise."

I glanced back and forth between them. The mutual dislike was obvious.

How in the world did these two know each other?

"So, Nathan," Clifton said, rubbing his hands together with enthusiasm. "Let's go take a look at what you've got for us."

"This is Jimmy Burke's dig," my father said.

Clifton blinked. "Ah . . ."

My father stared straight at Clifton. "And you are just the hired help."

Myers hesitated for a tenth of a second. "Now, Nathan. I think we can agree that a graduate student is hardly qualified to assess a find of this magnitude."

"I signed a contract, Cliff."

Dr. Myers's eye twitched. "I'd prefer it if you didn't refer to me as 'Cliff,' Nathan."

"If you want to see the bones, you talk to Jimmy," my father said.

"Jimmy Burke is a student, Nathan."

Rob Powers, proud representative of the BLM, chose that moment to horn in on the conversation.

"Dr. Myers, it's a genuine pleasure to meet you," he said, grabbing Clifton's hand and pumping it.

"And you are?" Myers asked, his veneer of grace peeling off rapidly.

"I'm Rob Powers, site steward for the local BLM office. I identified the bones as human. I think this is going to be a great day for science."

"Fine, fine. Can you just stand over there for a moment please?" Clifton said, pointing back to the ditch.

Jimmy managed to disengage from the two women interrogating him. He stomped towards us. "Can we get this over with now?"

"Why not?" Clifton said. "Let me assemble my team."

"Nope. No team. Just you," my father said.

"Now, Nathan—"

"No team. No BLM. No Forest Service. Just Burke, Cliff, and my daughter. Nobody else."

Rob Powers looked back and forth between Clifton and Jimmy, a confused expression spreading across his face. "But Casey Chastity said the story about the burial ran on TV last night. She wants me to do a follow-up interview later this afternoon. I have to be included."

If Jimmy had been standing close enough to Rob he would have punched the man in the nose.

Amelia Snow sputtered and stepped forward. "Mr. Dearcorn, I have been more than patient. But I think you have handled this situation like an amateur. These remains deserve a lot more respect than you have given them, and I insist that I have a chance to look at the burial."

Jimmy threw out his arms. "For the last goddamn time, this is not a burial!"

Everyone stared at him awkwardly. No one said a word.

I took the opportunity to engage in a little crowd control.

"Dad, why don't you stay down here with Hugo? I think he isn't feeling too great about Rufus getting shot and he could really use a buddy right now. Jimmy, if you could walk Dr. Myers and me up to the site and show us what you have, I am sure this whole thing will be cleared up in no time."

"Someone was shot?" Clifton asked.

"Lewis Pritchett's Holstein bull was the victim of would-be tomb raiders," Rob said.

Clifton surveyed the vandalized fence and let his eyes roam over the rugged countryside. He shook his head. "Thirty years and this place hasn't changed a bit."

"The three of you can take lots of pretty pictures to show to the rest of us," my father said, urging us on with a wave. "Now, run along. Daylight's a-burnin'."

Amelia Snow sputtered in protest, flapping her arms like a goose. "Mr. Dearcorn. Your daughter is hardly qualified to participate in this evaluation."

"If by qualified you mean she doesn't have a degree in some sort of college discipline that encourages her to jump to the conclusion that aliens built the pyramids, then I guess I'd have to agree with you there, Miss Snow."

"She's not even a trained field technician," Amelia said.

"You know, there is some evidence that the tool markings on the pyramids closely resemble what you would find if a plasma torch had been used," said Rob.

"Please, shut up, Powers," Amelia told him.

"Now look, everyone," I said, raising my voice. "Can we all agree that Dr. Myers here has a pretty good handle on fossils and artifacts?"

"He's a world authority on plains Indian paleo sites," Rob said. "He's written a best-selling book, traveled the world and I follow him on Facebook."

Clifton stared at Rob with a slight frown.

Amelia looked up the ridge towards the site, her expression bleak with intense longing. "This isn't fair."

I rubbed my temples with both hands and suddenly wished that I had gone with Hugo back to the yarn store. "If Dr. Myers sees the site and determines that there are no human remains, will everyone be satisfied?"

Jimmy stared at me. "Sure. All of these huge egos will settle down and see reason any minute now, no problem. And I saw Bigfoot riding a unicorn across the field this morning."

From the look on my father's face I could tell it was time to go.

I pulled Jimmy towards the gate. Clifton Myers hurried to catch up to us, and I could almost feel the glares from all the unhappy souls left behind.

Myers squared his shoulders and looked like he was about to summit Mount Everest.

Jimmy trudged up the hillside, grumbling the entire way.

It wasn't easy to keep my expression neutral when I saw the plaster field jacket we had attempted to steal the night before. The bottom of the skull was only just visible. Still, for someone as experienced as Myers it wouldn't take long to identify the bones.

Suzie-Q had left behind a few well-placed cow pies and Dr. Myers minced around them, protecting his expensive boots as he followed Jimmy into the hole. "Gads, I hate those things," he muttered.

"I spent yesterday prepping it for the field jacket," Jimmy said, his cheeks flushed. "I was going to load it this morning, but then you guys showed up."

"I'm not interested in your dinosaur, Mr. Burke. Where are these human remains supposedly buried?"

Jimmy shrugged. "You're looking at 'em."

"Excuse me?"

Jimmy knelt over the field jacket and pointed at the partially exposed bones. "These are the remains that Rob Powers identified as human."

Clifton stared at the fossil. "Obviously, the man is an idiot. What did he use as his touchstone for making that observation?"

Jimmy shook his head. "I'm sorry, what?"

Clifton sighed and rolled his eyes dramatically. "What bones did he look at that he said looked human?"

"The upper arch of a supraoccipital crest."

Clifton squatted down and traced the exposed bone with one finger. His hands looked baby soft. The fringe on his leather jacket brushed the ground as he stroked the black fossil. He turned his attention away from the skull and scrutinized the soil.

"Did he not see the formation is clearly Jurassic?"

"He must have thought they were Pleistocene," Jimmy said.

"You must be joking."

"Do I look like I'm joking?" Jimmy asked.

Clifton stood up and theatrically slapped the dirt from his knees. "Alright. Show me the arrowheads."

Jimmy carefully moved to the area where we had discovered the arrowheads and used a hand brush to start removing the dirt.

"You know," Clifton said as he watched Jimmy work. "The irony of this situation is not lost on me."

"Irony?" I asked.

Clifton waved a hand where Jimmy worked. "A scant ten yards separated my original find from those points. Had my funding been sufficient, I would have been able to return here the following summer as I'd intended, and more than likely I would have discovered them."

Jimmy brushed for what seemed like a very, very long time. "They should be right here."

"I'm waiting, Mr. Burke," Clifton said.

Jimmy began brushing faster. He scanned the ground, looking alarmed. He threw the brush aside and began feeling along the ground with his bare hands.

"Marley, isn't this the spot?" he asked me, looking up from his crouch with a desperate expression.

"It's exactly the spot," I said.

He crept along the ground systematically, feeling every inch of the place with his hands.

"That's impossible," he said.

Clifton was watching with a stern expression. "Where are the points, Mr. Burke?"

Jimmy felt something with his left hand and eagerly grabbed his brush again. He carefully cleaned the spot and when he removed the dirt his face fell.

A perfect stone point had left an impression in the hard soil. There was only one problem. The impression was all that remained.

The arrowhead was gone.

Jimmy brushed frantically until he had uncovered the entire area. He managed to find two more impressions in the soil indicating that an arrowhead had once been there, but wasn't any longer.

Jimmy stood up and looked like he was about to be sick. "Are you kidding me?"

Clifton clenched and unclenched his fists. "You need to explain yourself, Mr. Burke. Where, exactly, are the arrowheads?"

Jimmy sat down hard on the lip of the hole, letting his face fall into his hands. "I was gone for an hour. One lousy hour!"

My heart caught in my throat. I was just as guilty as Jimmy. We had been so focused on the dinosaur we hadn't bothered to think about the arrowheads for one second last night when we left the site unguarded.

Clifton Myers was staring at Jimmy with a murderous expression. "Are you telling me that you have no idea where the points are, Mr. Burke?"

"It's impossible," Jimmy said, frantically running his hand through the loose soil.

All I could do was stand by helplessly and watch. After he had uncovered the entire area and exposed at least a dozen point impressions in the ground, it was painfully obvious what had happened.

Every last one of the arrowheads had vanished into thin air.

CHAPTER 13

The moment we descended the hill Clifton summoned his team of diggers and pulled them into a tight circle.

"The site," Clifton said, his words heavy with grief, "has been compromised."

The redhead gasped. She covered her mouth and gave every impression she'd just been told of a death in the family. Had there been a fainting couch close at hand I had no doubt she would have dropped onto it like a Southern belle.

The two men shook their heads, not missing the chance to shoot disgusted looks towards Jimmy.

For his part, Jimmy was doing what he could to quietly inform my father what had happened, but it wasn't long before everyone else within earshot got wind of the theft.

It wouldn't take long for the indignant shouting to begin.

As I walked towards my father Clifton darted over and seized my arm.

"Miss Dearcorn, please impress upon your father the importance of allowing me to take charge of this dig."

I looked down at his hand. "Because you did such a bang-up job with it thirty-four years ago?"

He dropped my arm and turned his back on me, barely managing to keep his temper.

"Elise," he said, staring intently at the redhead. "Take Max and Troy and go back up to the site. Take the Total Station, set it up and get the GPS coordinates from that Burke person. Try to determine if he was at least competent enough to get that right. Start a grid search, and map everything that you see. It's possible he missed something."

He turned to the young woman with jet-black pageboy hair. "Pauley, I would very much like you and Megan to go back into Killdeer and check us all into a motel. I don't have a preference for accommodations. Anything will do, but we are staying here for a bit longer than I had originally anticipated."

The two women from the Historical Society were already shouting at my father and I went to his rescue.

"Dad, it sounds like Clifton wants to go up and take charge of the dig."

"Over my dead body," he said.

I could see by his face that he wasn't kidding. "You had better let him know that, because in about sixty seconds the hill will be swarming with anthropology students."

My father stormed off to confront Dr. Myers, and for the time being, it seemed that Jimmy would still be the only one with unfettered access to the dig. Where had Jimmy gotten to?

I hurried past the cluster of people in search of the grad student. Rob Powers stood beside Amelia, his jaw slack and his eyes wide. Amelia looked stricken. Nothing traveled like bad news.

I found Jimmy sitting in the driver's seat of his van. He was staring straight ahead, looking at nothing.

147

"They are trying to take over your dig," I told him.

I rested a hand on the open door of the van. He didn't even glance in my direction.

"Maybe that's for the best. At least until I can shoot myself," he said.

"Don't worry," I told him. "I doubt very much the Colorado people will be allowed to go up there."

"What a nightmare," Jimmy told me. "How could this have happened?"

"I think this isn't going to be that hard to figure out," I said. "It may take some time, but eventually the person who took the arrowheads will show the cache to the wrong person, or the points will end up on the Internet. Something. Don't let this discourage you. Your site got vandalized, but the fossil is still in one piece."

"You forget that I just made myself look like a complete fool in front of Dr. Clifton Myers," he said, scowling.

"So?" I asked, a bit of an edge to my tone. "You still have a job. You think it stings a bit when you make a mistake? Try having your own boss accuse you of a crime, getting fired from a job you love because of the accusation, and then having to slink home to your father because you are flat broke and don't have any friends left."

He scrutinized me. "Sorry, what?"

"Never mind. Just don't let this setback get you down. Alright?"

A horn honked, three times.

I looked around.

The horn sounded again.

I saw Hugo in the front seat of my SUV, waving.

"I have to go now, but tomorrow if you still need someone to help you load up the field jacket, I would be glad to come back."

Jimmy nodded his head once. "Thanks. I'll take all the help I can get."

Hugo leaned on the horn again. I waved at him and he settled back into his seat. I squeezed Jimmy's shoulder hard. "I will be here first thing in the morning."

He gave me a grateful smile. At least he had one person here who was firmly on his side.

I headed back towards my SUV, giving the shouting group of archaeologists, state officials and Historical Society folks a wide berth. As I put my hand on the door I heard the crunch of tires on gravel and turned to see a black Jeep rumble fast down the road, then skid to a stop behind my vehicle. A cloud of dust shot into the air.

Finn practically jumped out of the driver's seat and slammed his door. He stood looking at me, his mirrored sunglasses steamed from sweat.

"Hi, Finn," I said, feeling my stomach drop.

He didn't speak. I could feel his eyes boring through me.

"So, what brings you up this way?" I asked, hiding my concern. What was he so angry about?

"You cannot marry Leif Gable." He enunciated each word with extreme precision.

"Dammit, Irene," I said.

"She didn't say anything. Harvey Wilson was telling anyone who would listen over at Lil's about your engagement. He said that you had finally met a man who could handle you. What does that mean, Marley? A man who can handle you?"

I looked over my shoulder at Hugo. He was squirming in his seat so much the car was rocking. I heard my father shout something at Clifton Myers, and one of the Historical Society women was crying like a dishonored television evangelist.

"Can we talk about this later? I really, really have to get out of here," I said.

"Are you listening to me?" he said.

I dropped my hands at my sides helplessly and tried to control my temper. "You told me that you believe Leif is a good man. I thought you were fine with moving on and being friends."

"I was . . . I am. But think about this, would you? You're moving too fast."

My palms started to sting and I realized my fingernails were digging into them. I gave Finn a scathing glare. Who did he think he was, telling me what to do with my life? He was the one who had slithered out of our relationship.

"It's really none of your business," I said.

His upper lip was sweating. "As your friend it's my job to point it out when I see you doing something reckless."

"Reckless. Oh, as opposed to dating a guy who disappears for days on end with no explanation, refuses to tell me his real first name and vanishes after sex like a horny politician stepping outside his marriage? Right, Finn. I was much better off with you than I am with Leif."

He looked blindsided by my words, but shook them off and grabbed my shoulders with both hands. "Listen to me, Marley. Please. You cannot marry him. You have no idea what you are doing. Will you let go of your damn stupid pride for one moment and just listen to me?"

I actually felt my temper snap. Without a word I threw off his hands, turned my back on him and climbed inside my SUV. I slammed the door so hard the windows vibrated. When I started the engine Finn stayed where he was in the road, his Jeep directly behind me, blocking my path of escape.

I was so mad I could hardly see straight.

"Hugo, put on your seat belt," I said, my voice soft.

Hugo buckled up and gave me a pleading look. "Can we please get out of here now?"

"Yes," I said. "We sure can."

I reached down and pushed the four-wheel drive button on the console, I carefully put the SUV in reverse, checked my rearview mirror, and hit the gas pedal with both feet.

We shot backwards and crashed into Finn's Jeep with all four tires digging in for traction. I heard the grind of metal on metal as I pushed the accelerator down as hard as I could. The SUV groaned with effort but Finn's Jeep slid across the road sideways with the front tires bouncing.

Finn watched from the safety of the ditch, his face twisted up with disbelief.

When I had pushed the Jeep back far enough to have an avenue of escape, I threw the SUV into drive, flipped a U-turn and pulled up beside Finn. I slammed on the brakes when we were eye to eye.

My window rolled down with a gentle purr and I looked straight at his mirrored sunglasses. "Don't call me stupid, Finn."

I hit the gas and left him in a cloud of dust in the middle of the road. I caught a glimpse of the crowd stationed around my father. Every last one of them was staring at me. I didn't care one whit.

I looked over at Hugo, only now realizing what I had just done, and took a breath to slow down my heartbeat.

"I really hope I didn't just scare you, Hugo," I said.

He was laughing. "Are you kidding? That was awesome!"

"Your Aunt Wendy won't ever let you hang out with me again if she finds out I drove like a stock car racer with you in the car."

"Not if we don't tell her about it," he replied.

"You know, Hugo, you are a pretty brave kid," I told him.

"Yeah. There's nothing that scares me."

"Even seeing Rufus after he'd been shot?" I asked, suddenly suspicious.

"Nah. That's nothing. I see dead stuff all the time when my mom takes me in the prep room at the museum."

I watched him for a moment. He was his usual bouncy self once more. His squeamishness had evaporated as soon as we left the dig site, and if what he said about not being bothered by dead things was true, it wasn't Rufus that had caused Hugo to be nervous.

"It's too bad about all those arrowheads going missing," I said, as casually as I could.

He looked out the window and fiddled with his backpack. It hadn't been out of his grasp since we'd left the diner. "Yeah. That was too bad."

I put both hands on the wheel and looked straight ahead so he wouldn't see the look on my face. Hugo had been in the car the entire time when Clifton, Jimmy and I had come back down the hill. I hadn't seen him so much as poke his head outside the window.

It was a safe bet that he hadn't spoken to a soul the entire time we were at the site, so it was impossible for him to know that the arrowheads were missing. Unless, of course, he'd known they were gone even before we got there.

The last thing I had any right to do was lecture a ten-year-old boy about stealing artifacts. There wasn't a doubt in my mind that Hugo's intentions were pure even if his methods weren't. The arrowheads were undoubtedly safe and snug inside his backpack at that very moment. So I had a little bit of time to sort out the mess before finding a diplomatic way to return them to Jimmy without Dr. Clifton Myers finding out about it.

As I watched Hugo clutching his backpack to his chest ferociously, it occurred to me that getting him to give them up might require a degree of finesse that I lacked. It was possible that, for this situation, I would need professional help.

CHAPTER 14

I dropped Hugo off at his Aunt Wendy's yarn store and made sure he was careful about where he put his backpack, but managed to keep it casual enough he wouldn't suspect I knew what he had been up to the night before.

Wendy and I had come to an agreement about Hugo. It probably surprised her, but it seemed that for the duration of Hugo's stay in Killdeer, he would indeed have two aunts looking after him. I mentioned to Wendy that I might want to take the boy for a road trip later that afternoon when my shift at the library was over. It surprised me to realize that I actually liked the kid, in spite of the current trouble he was causing.

The morning had been a complete disaster. Between the circus at the dig site, Finn's abrupt appearance and subsequent proclamation that I wasn't qualified to run my own life, and the fact that I was mostly responsible for a ten-year-old boy carrying around a sack of hot artifacts, I was starting to feel like an innocent bystander at a crime scene. Since I only had to work half a day at the library up in Fable, and didn't need to clock in until noon, I decided to stop at Lil's and fill Irene in on all the chaos that had occurred that morning.

When I got to Lil's, I was floored.

The three University of Colorado Suburbans were crammed in the small parking lot. True to his word, my father must have drawn a line in the sand and flat refused to let Clifton and his anthropology students on the property. They were having a powwow at the café because the two motels they had to choose from in Killdeer didn't allow early check-in. The Colorado vehicles were parked crossways of the lines, forcing the other cars to accommodate them.

They weren't the only vehicles displaying out-of-state license plates.

Three white utility vans, all painted with black logos on the doors that said Church of St. Augustine, were haphazardly parked in the lot alongside the Colorado contingent. The license plates on the vans indicated they were from somewhere in Nebraska. Since Killdeer wasn't exactly a popular tourist destination, the appearance of so many out-of-state vehicles was an event.

I walked inside the café and instantly knew something was brewing.

I caught Irene's eye and took my usual seat at the counter. She came from behind the soda station and leaned down until both elbows were resting flat.

"It's the last gunfight." Her voice was low and she kept her eyes on the customers.

"Between who?" It was practically silent in the busy café, but you could feel the crackle of tension in the room.

"The Creationists and the University Students," she said.

She wordlessly poured me a cup of coffee and jerked her chin towards the back of the café. "General Custer has his troops holding the high ground in the north, while the Church of St.

Augustine has taken up flanking positions on the west and the south."

"Creationists?" I asked. "What are they doing here?"

She looked amused. "The reporter ran the news broadcast about your property on television and it's made us famous. The good people of St. Augustine want to go see the place that proves mankind walked with dinosaurs. It's a pilgrimage."

Three groups of churchgoers were seated at the tables.

Clifton Myers and his students occupied two booths towards the back. Neither group was speaking to the other, but I could see from the angry expressions on everyone's faces that before I had arrived somebody had said something wrong to someone.

"Oh, boy." I felt lucky I'd managed to get a seat at all. The usual crowd had converged on the café to see the showdown.

"Oh boy is right. Remember that time when Congress wanted to change the name of French fries into freedom fries? I'm thinking of changing the name of the smothered fries platter to Truth Platter. What do you think?"

I stared at her. "Have I ever talked to you about your shameless marketing strategies, Irene?"

"It's brilliant. They'd both be all over themselves to order the Truth Platter before the other guys could order it. I could jack it up two bucks for each and nobody would say a word."

"That's not very Christian of you, Irene," I said.

She sighed and started filling water glasses for her two frantic waitresses. "I try to be a good person, but sometimes all the idiots around me make it practically impossible."

"So why is everyone looking so unhappy over there?" I asked.

"Okay, first, the University Students walked in and, well, just look at them," she said.

I obediently turned my stool so that I was in position to stare blatantly at the anthropology students. Clifton stood out right away. Who could miss him? He was seated in a chair that he had snagged from one of the tables.

The angry redhead who had shot daggers from her eyes at me earlier sat against the window, her finger toying with a strand of hair as she listened to Clifton. Her mouth was set in a permanent pucker.

Although the other two women lacked the shock appeal that the red-haired student possessed, they certainly did draw attention. The blonde girl looked like she should be in a women's magazine selling baby products. She was strikingly beautiful, in an innocent and angelic way. Her long wavy hair and enthusiastic expression made me feel dumpy by comparison.

The angelic blonde's two booth-mates were polar opposites of her sun-kissed look. I'd seen them in the parking lot earlier when they had all arrived, but this was the first chance I'd had to get a good look at them up close.

A man and a woman, Goth pale and striking, sat beside her. Both of them had hair so black it had to have been dyed. The young man had more tattoos on his arms than some bikers I'd seen. One ear held at least ten earrings that snaked up the lobe and ended at the top of his ear. The young woman beside him had a nose ring and jet-black pageboy haircut, but the sleeves of a black shirt covered her arms and I couldn't see any tattoos, but I imagined them.

The last anthropology student had thick wavy brown hair, a swarthy complexion and bore a disdainful expression. He sat alone in the second booth, his hands lingering over a pack of cigarettes he'd set on the tabletop. He scanned the tables across from his booth with a scowl, looking like he was about to commit a felony.

The church group, by contrast, was made up mostly of women. Since I was staring at them without reservation I counted them. Fifteen. There were only three men with the group, and one of them was obviously a driver and nothing more, as he sat apart from the women slightly, his head bent down reading a newspaper. He seemed to be ignoring everyone and looked to me like a man who was on his break.

Irene's waitresses were flying. The two girls nearly collided several times as they dashed between tables, taking orders, bringing drinks and rounding up extra place settings. It wasn't long before plates of food appeared, and that only added to the chaos.

Not more than three minutes after I'd sat down, I found myself handed a BLT with avocado.

I gave Irene a questioning look as she plunked the plate before me. "I didn't order anything. Hugo and I just had breakfast a couple hours ago."

"They wanted no mayo. That stuff's impossible to scrape off."

I made a show of laying my napkin across my lap, rubbed both hands together and dug in. Already I could hear the murmurs of discontent and the barbs and insults being quietly exchanged between the two groups behind me, and I wanted to have my early lunch finished before the show started.

"Has anyone said anything yet?" I asked.

Irene snorted. "Oh yeah. The church ladies have been going on about the miracle of man walking with the dinosaurs, and Clifton is so mad about your father kicking him out it looks like his head is about to launch off his neck."

The girl with jet-black pageboy hair sported a shirt with a walking fish embossed on the front with the word evolve written across the bottom.

One of the church women laughed out loud and made a comment I missed.

The anthropology students paused in their discussion. The swarthy student said something sharp to Clifton, baring his teeth like a barracuda.

"I'm sorry, what did you just say?" asked Clifton with a haughty tone.

He had turned sideways in his chair, but wasn't about to give them the benefit of his direct attention and asked the question with his back still partially turned to the group.

"I said, you must be here for the same reason that we are," said the church woman.

"Excuse me ladies, but do you know who I am?" Clifton asked, still turned sideways.

"I don't have the faintest idea," she replied.

"Irene, can't you do something?" I asked. "I'm not finished eating yet."

"Sorry, the curtain goes up promptly at eleven. I can't help it if you aren't in your seat yet."

The woman speaking to Clifton was in her mid-fifties, wearing a pair of slacks and a button-up pale blue shirt.

Pretty much the look and uniform of all the other women sitting around the other tables.

"I'm Dr. Clifton Myers. Perhaps you have seen me on the History Channel discussing the early migration routes of ancient man?"

"We don't watch the History Channel," the woman said. "The shows they broadcast are nothing but lies and propaganda."

"I'd have to agree with that," I said.

Irene shrugged. "I once saw the History Channel run a daylong special about archaeological evidence proving that space ships from other planets had been visiting the earth for centuries. For once I'd like them to do a show about something that really matters. Like, how is it that all those shopping carts at the grocery store always seem to end up on the sidewalk by the end of the day?"

"In what respect, madam, do you consider the programming on the History Channel to be nothing but lies?" Clifton asked.

"Where should I begin?" she asked.

"I only engaged you in conversation to determine the motivation behind your previous statement. I would like you to clarify what you meant."

"What statement?" she asked.

"The statement that prompted this conversation," Clifton said, his face turning pink with irritation.

"The reason you came to this valley in the first place?" he prompted when the church woman gave him a blank look.

"Oh, you mean about finally finding evidence that shows the truth."

Irene nudged me. "See? See? Truth Platter. I'm telling you, I could have made a mint today."

"And pray tell, what truth are you referring to, exactly?" Clifton asked.

The woman bustled with importance. "Why, the fact that they have found irrefutable evidence dinosaurs and humans lived on the planet at the same time."

THE JADE ARROWHEAD

The tattooed anthropology student actually laughed out loud. He turned his attention away from his clam chowder and stared at the woman. "Evidence of what?"

"It is a well-known fact that humans and dinosaurs lived together," the woman replied. Several murmurs of support came from other church members around the tables.

"And where did you get such a preposterous idea?" Clifton asked.

"In 1990, the University of Arizona Department of Geological Sciences was sent a sample of bone to date using the carbon-14 method. The results came back and it was determined that the bone was no more than sixteen thousand years old. Well, guess what, Dr. Clifford? It was dinosaur bone. The University had just proved that dinosaurs were not as old as everyone says they are."

She sat back in her chair, looking smug.

"Score one for the Saints," Irene said under her breath.

"Rebuttal, Doctor?" I said softly.

"Madam, you obviously do not have a scientific background, otherwise you would know that carbon-14 dating cannot be used to determine the age of a fossil. As the name implies, it uses the radioisotope carbon-14 to estimate the age of organic material. However, the method requires the presence of carbon to determine the decay of the isotope. It is only accurate to approximately sixty thousand years. No more. It's useless in determining the age of fossils."

"Tell that to the University of Arizona," the woman replied.

Clifton bristled. "Didn't you comprehend what I was saying? Fossilized bones do not contain any organic material. Any organic material

161

originally in the bone has been replaced with minerals. And any fossilized material from the Mesozoic is hundreds of thousands of years old. Stratigraphy and context are the only accurate method for determining the age of dinosaur bones."

"You just don't want to admit the truth," she said.

"That mankind walked on the planet at the same time it was populated by dinosaurs? That's simply insane," he said.

The red-haired student leaned forward, letting her lock of hair fall to her shoulders. "Hey. If there were people and dinosaurs running around at the same time, why didn't the dinosaurs eat us? I mean, how are there any humans left? We would have pretty much been a Snickers bar for a T-rex."

"Dinosaurs didn't eat meat," she said earnestly.

"What did they eat then?" the redhead asked.

"They ate grass, and mankind and dinosaurs lived together in peace."

Clifton's mouth dropped open a fraction. His eye actually twitched and he gave every impression that he was going into labor.

I had to force myself not to laugh.

"I have no response to that," he said.

Without another word Clifton stood up from his chair, slid it underneath a table, spun on his heels and walked out of the café trailing a cloud of righteous indignation.

I was shoving the last of my sandwich in my mouth as fast as I could. If this moved out into the parking lot I wanted to be able to scramble after them.

"Have you ever tried to eat a salad with a steak knife?" the redhead asked the church woman.

"I don't see what that has to do with anything," the woman said.

"Naw. I'm sure you don't."

The student with jet-black pageboy hair and pierced nose was watching the group from St. Augustine with a placid look. "What church are you from?" she asked.

The man reading the newspaper glanced over the top of the sports section and answered. "We represent the Nebraska chapter of the Church of Scientific Apologetics."

The pageboy girl persisted. "Are you Christians, then?"

"Of course we are Christians," the woman who had argued with Clifton said defensively.

"Oh. Okay. Thank you," she said, a soft smile on her face.

"You know that there are over thirty-three thousand denominations of Christianity," the tattooed student said, slurping the last of his chocolate milk shake. "Your chances of winning the lottery are better than picking the right faith that will get you a free pass into heaven."

"And I suppose that you belong to none of those denominations," the woman said.

The tattooed student chuckled. "I'm a philosophical Taoist."

"I don't even know what that is," the woman replied.

He grinned. "Know your enemy."

Sudden silence filled the café.

It was like someone had flipped a switch.

Irene and I shared a look.

"Is that it?" I asked.

Irene glanced hopefully from booth to table, but finally she shook her head. "Show's over."

163

"I'm not really clear on who won," I said, searching the faces of the contestants. "Did they decide who was right and who was nuts?"

Irene's eyebrows shot up. "Don't look at me. I'm Catholic. As far as I'm concerned all the people in here are nothing but a bunch of godless heathens."

"It probably wouldn't be very good for our culture if they ever managed to declare a true winner," I said. "What would the cable television shows have to broadcast then?"

I let my eyes drift back to the tattooed student. He had an evil smile on his face as he watched the church ladies. When the apparent leader of the group cast him another angry glance, he winked at her lasciviously. She broke his gaze quickly and stirred her tea with a stiff hand.

I spun around on my stool again. "Can I get a milk shake?"

"Chocolate or strawberry?"

"Got vanilla?"

"Of course I've got vanilla," Irene said.

The great theological debate had officially come to an end. It was time for dessert.

CHAPTER 15

Reluctantly I left the café and headed down Main Street for work. I caught a glimpse of Hugo walking towards his aunt's yarn store and stopped to give him a lift the rest of the way.

"Were you down at the library?" I asked.

"I wanted to see if I could find another reference book about ancient stone tools. But the one I wanted they said I couldn't check out because it's in the special collection."

He looked disappointed and glum.

That, in turn, made me feel disappointed and glum, too. After the sideshow I had just witnessed at Lil's, it was pretty clear to me I needed to get the situation concerning the arrowheads cleared up sooner rather than later. The quicker I could find someone to identity them, the easier it would be to convince Hugo to give them back without a fuss.

"Hugo, do you still have that wooden box my father let you borrow?" I asked.

I pulled over and parked on the street in front of Wee Wooly's Yarn Shop, and Hugo listlessly unbuckled his seat belt. A perfect white cloud breezed across the bright sun, casting a dull shadow.

"They are back at my Aunt Wendy's," he said, his palm on the door handle.

"I know you are interested in finding out what they are, so maybe we could take them to someone who is an expert and have him take a look?" I suggested.

The last thing I wanted to do was spook Hugo into doing something desperate with the arrowheads he'd pilfered from the site. His methods were flawed, but I knew in my heart he had good intentions. Obviously his goal was to protect the artifacts from being stolen by pot hunters, and since I had come up with the same solution for Jimmy's dinosaur skull, I couldn't be too hard on the boy.

It seemed logical to suggest we take the wooden box of arrowheads to an expert, and in so doing, contrive it so the points from the dig site tagged along for the ride inside Hugo's pack. It was a bit sneaky on my part, but it would be easier than forcing him to surrender the points to Jimmy.

"I think Clifton Myers will be able to tell you all about them," I said.

Hugo's face twisted up. "That guy? Did you see his jacket?"

I had to suppress a laugh. "He's very smart and he knows a great deal about artifacts."

"Sure, if the artifacts have a whole pile of government grant money stashed underneath them." His tone was so adult and bitter I imagined that his mother had said something very similar at some point.

"Okay, we don't need to show them to Clifton."

I was feeling foolish about my personal behavior, so I was giving Hugo a great deal of leeway.

Not only had Jimmy and I made asses of ourselves the night before, when Finn had arrived at the pasture and confronted me about getting engaged I'd completely jumped off the deep end. Maybe it was the fact that in a few hours I would have to explain to Leif exactly how my borrowed BMW had gotten a dented bumper, but I was suddenly sympathetic to Hugo's obvious desperation. It would be smart to demand Hugo turn over the stolen points immediately, but my own poor judgment over the last twelve hours was making it difficult.

"Why don't I find someone else who can tell us about them?" I asked.

He tilted his head towards me. "Are there any PhD anthropologists in southern Montana?"

I felt a headache coming on that would drop a quarter horse. "Listen, I have to go to work now. When I get done I will come by here and pick you up. By then I might be able to track someone down who is like your mom and we can go have a word with them. How does that sound?"

"I'll be ready." His face was so adult and serious; it was easy to forget that he was still just a kid. Hugo would win the National Science Award someday. There wasn't a doubt in my mind. If he didn't get arrested first.

I left Hugo in Wendy's care after filling her in on my idea and making plans to pick him up after she closed her yarn store for the day. I managed to make it up to the branch library in Fable before my shift started.

My boss hardly said two words to me as she sprinted from the building. She shouted over her shoulder as she darted out the door that the electricity had been going on and off all day and to expect unreliable power for the duration. She grinned and waved, heading off to enjoy the rest of the day outdoors. A mountain bike was strapped into the rack on top of her Subaru, and a small backpack rested in the front seat. She was headed for the trails.

My boss was gone in a flash and a cloud of dust, and I was relieved she hadn't said anything about the fact that I was wearing my hikers and a pair of jeans to work. I hadn't had time to change after leaving the yarn store.

It was another lovely June day and I suspected that I might have one or two people drift in, but that everyone else was out enjoying the summer and it would be a quiet day.

As it turned out I hardly had a moment to myself the entire afternoon. Everyone wanted a beach book for the coming weekend. It was accurate to say we got slammed by patrons. Still, in between searching for the very last copy of Where Rivers Run North, dealing with the electricity fading in and out and re-shelving a stack of books higher than I was tall, I managed to find enough time to locate an artifact expert I was fairly sure could assist me with my problem.

I'd made a quick phone call to a tiny museum just south of the border in a town called, appropriately enough, Buffalo, Wyoming. The museum, called the Gatchell, housed a remarkable collection of Native American artifacts. The gift shop was originally an old Carnegie library building that had been converted back in the late 1980's, and the museum was a handsome addition that had been added on. I'd been to the museum once before, back in the days when I'd been a determined college student. My college career ended with a two-year degree instead of a bachelor's, but the museum had made an impression on me because of its knowledgeable staff and beautiful collection.

I called the Gatchell museum on the telephone, in between assisting patrons, and they were as helpful as I remembered. I had a hunch that someone who was an expert on Native American artifacts had been a part of identifying the collection. Not only had the Gatchell enlisted the help of an expert, as it turned out that person lived only sixty miles from Killdeer just across the border in northern Wyoming. The Gatchell staff was all too happy to pass along his name and his telephone number. His name was John Taylor and he was apparently an authority on arrowheads. If he was good enough for the Gatchell, he was good enough for me. Hugo and I had an appointment to see him that very evening.

By the time I closed the library for the day I was worn out. I'd scrambled to get the place straightened out before I locked the doors and headed back down to Killdeer.

I stopped at Leif's house just long enough to snag a jacket, and to tell Leif that I would be home late. He smiled and gave me a kiss on my forehead before turning back to the NBA finals. He was the most understanding man I knew. A tiny voice inside my head scoffed at my hesitation when it came to making a commitment to him. There really wasn't a doubt in my mind that he was the best man I had ever met. I told myself as I pulled out of the driveway that as soon as this fiasco was over, I was going to spend serious time thinking about my future with Leif.

I filled the SUV with gas and pulled up in front of Wee Wooly's Yarn Shop, barely tapping the brake, when I saw Hugo dash from the front door and sprint towards me.

He was still clutching his backpack with both hands and I wondered silently if he had let it hit the floor at all since yesterday. It took us only twenty minutes out of our way to swing by Wendy's and pick up the wooden box of arrowheads my father had given Hugo to play with.

As we drove south towards Wyoming Hugo chatted away gamely, but I hardly heard a word he said. I murmured appropriate responses when he asked questions, but for the most part I was lost in my own head.

A disturbing thought kept circling around my skull, gnawing at me and refusing to give me any peace.

What if the person who had shot and killed Lewis's bull knew something about Jimmy's dig site that I didn't? Was it just a coincidence, or had Jimmy found something at the site that someone in Killdeer dearly wished had not been found?

I pondered that question as we drove and couldn't settle on an answer that gave me any satisfaction at all. But as I watched Hugo sitting beside me, gripping his backpack, certain in the knowledge that he carried in his hands a find of immeasurable value, I started to think that maybe the boy was right. What if the arrowheads were not worthless after all, but were in fact very valuable? Valuable enough that someone was willing to kill for them? Of course, they had killed a rambunctious bull, probably a simple act of eliminating a threat that stood between them and the points. But it had been an act of desperation nonetheless. What could be so important that it would drive someone to such violence?

I thought back to the scene earlier by the gate of my father's pasture. Between the bald-faced contempt shown by Amelia Snow, the obvious bitterness felt by Rob Powers at not being taken seriously, and the disdain displayed by Clifton Myers, I didn't have a difficult time believing that someone in that group was angry enough to take matters into their own hands when confronted with the likes of my father, who was probably in their eyes nothing more than an uncooperative landowner.

It sent a chill across my skin when I realized two of the three people associated with this situation had been kicking around Killdeer at the same time my grandfather had been murdered. That thought sparked a flash of worry inside me, but I pushed it away quickly. My grandfather had been killed thirty-four years ago. Whoever had committed that terrible crime was long gone by now.

I was startled back to reality when Hugo bounced up and down in the seat beside me as a huge whitetail deer darted across the road in front of us. A fat buck with budding antlers, he bounded up the slope on the left side of the road and stopped at the crest. He flicked his tail once and turned to look at us as we flew by at sixty-five, and for a moment I saw his black eyes study us intently.

Hugo rattled off a list of twenty or so useful things that prehistoric Native Americans made out of the skin, bones and antlers of deer. He was smiling and enjoying the drive immensely. I decided it was time for me to shake off my gloomy speculations. More than likely, the person who had shot Rufus was simply a greedy pot hunter. Someone desperate to make some quick and easy cash. This was no deep, dark mystery. It was probably a simple case of greed.

I kept my eyes on the faded road signs, and as we approached the turn that took us off the highway I decided it was better not to speculate about the situation too hard. Far better to let the experts tell me what was fact and what was fantasy.

In all probability, the arrowheads in Hugo's possession were not that valuable. The artifact expert I was about to see would most likely tell me that they were interesting, but not worth an excessive amount of money.

If that was the case it gave me a whole new set of worries to consider. If the arrowheads hadn't been what the desperate pot hunter was trying to steal, what had they really been after?

CHAPTER 16

"You must be Marley."

I blinked back surprise. I hadn't even knocked yet, and already a man was standing in the doorway.

"I am," I said, a little surprised. "Are you John Taylor?"

"So they tell me." He ushered Hugo and me inside.

"This is Hugo. He is my partner in crime."

Hugo beamed at the introduction.

"Hello," John said, a smile crinkling the fine lines around his eyes.

The house was remarkable for its simplicity, and nearly invisible from the road. I had almost shot right past it as we drove down the dirt track that forked off the highway. John's detailed directions were all that had saved me. The area was remote, to say the least.

The house blended into the landscape seamlessly. It was a single-level wooden structure with a flat roof and utilitarian feel. As I glanced around the dining area I saw immediately the house was built for comfort and function. John Taylor was not a junk collector. There was no doubt about that. A single table with four chairs, a simple kitchen area with a beautiful granite countertop, and a living area with a leather couch came into view. Nothing fancy, but everything had a place and everything that I could see was useful or beautiful in some way.

A few picture frames decorated the walls, but instead of paintings, the frames housed what looked to me like pieces of very old weavings.

A sideboard, holding a collection of stone tools of various shapes and sizes, stood by a row of tall windows in the living area. A glass case rested in the center. It held a carefully arranged assortment of arrowheads, and Hugo immediately went to peer at it with curiosity.

"Wow. These are great," Hugo announced.

John chuckled as he watched the boy. "I keep a small collection for myself, only the best items I come across."

"Thanks for seeing us on such short notice," I said.

John pulled out one of the chairs at the dining room table and I eased into it.

The moment I sat down my stomach growled so loud even Hugo looked over to see what it was.

I saw John's lower lip twitch with amusement. "Would you two like some dinner? I was about to have a bowl of chili."

"Are you sure that won't be too much trouble?" I asked, mortified that I'd forgotten to feed Hugo before we'd left Killdeer.

"No, it's not any trouble. I've got plenty here for all of us." He set to work pulling down bowls from the open cupboards and retrieving spoons.

In no time at all the three of us sat at the table with hot bowls of chili, a plate of fried flatbread and freshly chopped fruit drizzled with honey and lime juice.

"This is amazing," I said, digging with relish into the chili.

"It's rabbit," he said.

Hugo studied his bowl. "Cool! I've never had rabbit before."

I savored the chili with surprise. It was actually very good. I didn't ask if he had gotten the rabbit from his own backyard, but I had a pretty good idea that he had.

After we finished our fruit and each of us had settled back with a cup of hot tea, I could feel my shoulders finally relax. I hadn't realized just how tense the day had been until I had a moment to sit still.

"So, you mentioned on the phone that you had something that might be very interesting," John said.

I touched Hugo on the shoulder and he jumped from his seat. "Be right back. It's in the car."

The boy darted outside and John watched him with a slight smile. His blues eyes sparkled a bit. Hugo seemed to have jogged some memory.

"Do you have kids?" I asked.

John nodded and leaned back in his chair. "Two boys. Grown, now. But your young friend reminds me of them."

John was not what I had expected. To be honest, I wasn't entirely sure what I had expected from a professional artifact authenticator. After my experiences with Clifton Myers and Amelia Snow, not to mention the awful Rob Powers, I had imagined that John would be some sort of mad, paranoid survivalist. Out of the lot of them, John was by far the most normal person I had come across. He didn't wear a pretentious fringed leather jacket. He wore jeans and a T-shirt. I glanced at his feet. Sneakers.

I looked at his hands and I could see an array of tiny scars. Puzzled, I thought maybe he had been a butcher. They looked like tiny knife wounds, long healed but still visible.

"How did you get all of those cuts on your hands?" I asked.

He held up his left hand and studied it. "Oh who knows? I can't remember most of them. Probably from flint knapping. Or from cutting up a deer. Maybe from my time in Alaska. It's difficult to say."

"Flint knapping?" I asked.

Hugo returned and took his seat beside me, clutching the wooden box of arrowheads, his backpack draped over one shoulder. He gave me a strained look, aghast that I didn't know what flint knapping was. "It's making tools and weapons out of stone, Aunt Marley."

"Well, of course it is," I said.

I heard a rustling sound and searched the house, trying to identify the noise.

John shook his head with irritation. "I've got a pack rat problem at the moment. I've got a few traps set up outside in my garden, but the rats don't seem to be too interested in the bait I am using. I think I'm going to try peanut butter next."

"Why don't you get a cat?" Hugo asked.

"I would, but the coyotes would eat him," John replied.

Hugo's eyebrows quirked up and he set the box on the table, not sure how to respond to that statement.

One thing was certain; John's house was remote enough for that to be a distinct possibility.

"Let's take a look at what you have brought," John suggested.

The box was simple. Leftover oak planks that had been crudely fashioned with leather straps for hinges. But it did the job.

Hugo slid it over to him.

John chuckled when he saw the words carved on the lid. "Snipe tails? I haven't heard of snipe hunting for twenty years."

After he flipped open the lid, all humor was forgotten and he examined the contents of the box carefully, a frown creasing his mouth. "Well, there isn't much here of any value, except this is interesting . . ."

He held up the long, pointed object we had all wondered about back at my father's kitchen table. It was slender, a creamy color, and one side was stained with a red substance. It looked like the broken end of a small broom handle. But I honestly had no clue what it really was.

"This is a beveled bone rod," John said. "Normally these are found in association with Clovis sites. Most of the time they are made from mammoth ivory, and some believe they are used as specialized tools for removing flutes while knapping a point."

"Are they old?" asked Hugo.

"About thirteen thousand years," John said. "This is interesting because it is stained with red ocher. That usually only occurs when an object is used in a burial, or for ceremonial reasons."

"So it's valuable," I said, not certain what his explanation meant.

"They can be. It depends on the condition. This one? It's marginal."

"So it's beat up," I said.

"And so is this Clovis point with it."

John held up a broken arrowhead, or half of one, at least. It was the bottom half of a point that was shaped very differently than the others inside the box. "This used to be a Clovis point, now it's more the suggestion of one. But, still, it's important. I'd keep it separate from these others so that it doesn't get hammered inside the box anymore."

John carefully set it aside and I nudged Hugo. "Why don't you show Mr. Taylor the other points?"

Fear flashed across the boy's face like lightning. His eyes betrayed him and he darted a glance at his backpack.

"It's alright," I said. "We can sort out how you got them later. The important thing right now is getting them identified, right?"

John watched the exchange quietly. Hugo took a moment to study the authenticator, and apparently John passed some sort of test because the boy nodded and pushed the wooden box aside.

Hugo took a deep breath before finally unzipping his backpack. He reverently removed the arrowheads one by one, placing them on the table in front of John. Each one was carefully wrapped in burlap and taped with silver duct tape.

John raised his eyebrows at the strange packaging, but I could also see that he was suddenly intrigued. This was not going to be an average day at the office.

"I had to do it this way," Hugo said, looking embarrassed. "I didn't have a lot of time."

"I don't think we need to bore Mr. Taylor with the details." I didn't think it was a very good idea to tell John that the arrowheads were not exactly supposed to be sitting on his kitchen table at that moment. At least a dozen people would have broken down the door to get a crack at them, but that was information I didn't necessarily want to share.

When I glanced up at John, his sharp blues eyes were watching me carefully. His expression had changed from amused to cautious, and I knew without a doubt at that moment he was already well aware of what was going on. Hugo and I were not giving him the whole story. He made not one move to unwrap the arrowheads, but simply stared at me with a calm expression. He had read me like a book.

I felt my shoulders slump and I decided I needed to tell this man the truth. If I didn't, I had the distinct feeling that he would politely stonewall me. Well, at least I had managed to establish one thing. John was an honest man. He obviously wouldn't deal with me unless I was honest, too.

"My father has a ranch sixty miles north of here in the Killdeer Valley just across the border in Montana. Thirty-four years ago, a famous archaeologist named Clifton Myers found two dinosaur teeth on our land."

"Myers. That's interesting," John said. He was watching me with a perfect poker face. He wouldn't give away a thing until I'd told him the whole story.

"A few days ago a graduate student from the University of Wyoming came back to the site and said he wanted to see if he could find the rest of the dinosaur for his master's thesis. Well, he did."

John's eyes actually twinkled. "And he found a few other things that he didn't expect to see, didn't he?"

"He found all of these," I said, nodding at the wrapped arrowheads.

"And you wanted to see if they are valuable," John said, a bit too casually.

"I know they are valuable. I just don't know why. The Forest Service sent a woman who wanted to check the site and determine that it didn't have

179

any human remains associated with it. Then the BLM sent a man who claimed he was a site steward, or something, and he said he could clearly see human remains in the hole."

John's eyes stopped sparkling. "Were there? Human remains, I mean?"

"No. It was the skull of the dinosaur. But the BLM man kept telling anyone who would listen that it was a burial. So did the Forest Service woman. It's a mess."

"Marley, I appreciate you leveling with me, but you haven't told me anything I didn't already know," he said.

I must have looked surprised, because he chuckled again and leaned forward to explain.

"The artifact business is a very close-knit world. If it's important, and it's going on here in the west, I probably know about it. I have been keeping loose tabs on the dig at the Dearcorn Ranch. If you had lied to me about these arrowheads I would not have been able to work with you. I don't associate myself with people who try to skirt the law. But because you told me the truth, we can work together. I just need to know one thing."

I was obviously out of my league. "Anything."

"How was it left? The site, I mean."

I shifted in my seat. "The hotshot from Colorado, Clifton Myers, took a look at the dig and determined that it's just a dinosaur. No human remains. And then he proceeded to try and bully my father into letting him take over."

John leaned back in his chair and folded his arms. "Clifton Myers."

I heard a note of dissatisfaction in his voice.

"Do you know him?" I asked.

"I met him once at an artifact auction in Chicago. He's a slime ball."

Hugo sat up straighter beside me. "I know, right? Did you see his jacket?"

"Listen, Marley. I don't usually give advice to people unless they ask for it," John told me. "But in this case I will make an exception. You should tell your father not to have a thing to do with that guy."

"We both wish he would leave," I said. "But Dr. Myers seems pretty determined to hang around."

John reached out and lifted one of the burlap-wrapped arrowheads, cradling it with care. "Well, if you can, persuade your father that he should call in somebody else. It's his land."

I had to admit, the idea of kicking Clifton Myers off of our property in favor of another anthropologist did cheer me up considerably.

"Now let's take a look and see what all the fuss is about," John said.

The process to unwrap the arrowheads was painstaking. Hugo had practically mummified the points with burlap, and John was too much of a professional to simply take a pair of scissors to them and slice them open in a hurry. It took us almost a half hour to get them unwrapped and lined up on the table.

John cleared away the dishes and pushed back the chairs. He laid a soft piece of leather over the wooden table and deftly arranged the arrowheads in neat rows on top of the hide.

When he was finished, fourteen pristine arrowheads of various sizes, but similar shapes, lay on the leather in two neat rows.

"At first, I thought they were like the Pelican Lake points," Hugo said.

John glanced over at the boy with surprise.

"You know about arrowheads?"

"I looked it up. My mom studies ancient people."

"Really," John said. "Have you ever been to a dig site she was working on?"

Hugo nodded. "Lots of them. I like to identify things. But I couldn't find a book that would help me with these. The book my Aunt Wendy gave me was for kids."

"I think Mr. Taylor will be able to fill in the blanks," I said.

I took a few steps away from the table, tugging Hugo along with me, to give John room to work.

John didn't say a word as he studied each arrowhead individually.

He never held a point in his hand unless it was directly over the table. One at a time, he carefully transported each point into a small office just off of the dining room. I caught glimpses of him studying them under a powerful microscope. Then he would return the point to the table and lay it in position, seemingly satisfied that he'd come to a conclusion about it.

He turned each point with the tip facing down when he was finished with it, and arranged them all into three groups. I didn't understand it, but to John the three groups represented unique qualities that set them apart, or made them similar in some way. At least, that was my guess.

The points were like jewels.

Each one had its own unique color and sheen. Looking at them all together on the table, I realized they were quite beautiful.

One in particular stood out. It was a lovely smoky green color and it glistened against the tan leather.

Hugo watched every move John made, rapt with the excitement of the moment. The room practically crackled with anticipation.

The sun was close to setting when John finally pulled the chairs back around the table and asked us to sit down.

"These are pretty amazing," he said. "At first blush."

"What does that mean?" I asked.

"Are they valuable? Are they important?" Hugo asked, nearly vibrating with excitement.

"Oh, they're important," John said. "But not valuable."

I suddenly had a very bad feeling.

John folded his arms across his chest and leaned back in his chair. "Do you know anything about arrowheads, Marley?"

I slumped in my seat. "Not really."

To my surprise, John looked at Hugo and began asking him a series of questions that I didn't even begin to understand.

"Did you see these when they were uncovered, Hugo?"

"I was there, sure."

"Do you remember if you could see anything else that was with the arrowheads? Were there any tiny bone shafts, or was there red dirt beside these points?"

"No, there wasn't any red dirt. Do you mean red ocher?" Hugo asked.

"Yes. Red ocher. And were there any of those tiny thumb scrapers?" John asked.

"No. It was just all of these arrowheads," Hugo said.

"Why is that important?" I asked.

"Because if there were any beveled bone rods or if red ocher was associated with these points,

I would suspect that it was actually a burial and that would be trouble."

"Because that would mean human remains," I said.

"Exactly. Where did your father find the beveled bone rod that was inside the box?" John asked.

"All of them, the arrowheads and the bone, were picked up down by the creek," I said. "We never found any up on the ridge."

John set the last point aside and studied his hands for a moment.

I could see he was trying to find a way to deliver some bad news.

"This assortment of arrowheads is exactly what I would expect you to find on the ground, walking around in the fields in your area of Montana," he said, pointing at the wooden Snipe Tails box. "Average quality Pelican Lake points."

"What about these?" I asked, surveying the fourteen points on the table.

"They are called Clovis points," John told me. The way he said it made me think the discovery was significant.

"See I knew it!" Hugo said, pumping his fist with enthusiasm.

"Why is that important?" I asked.

"They were made by Paleo-Indians in the late Pleistocene, and were used to hunt big game, particularly mammoth. Your Clovis points are made of Bighorn chert, and they are probably the best examples of this type of point that I have ever seen."

"Really?"

"Really. They are perfect. Absolutely perfect. The knapper who made these points was extremely skilled. His technique is flawless. I could go on and on about overshot flake scars and reduction strategy, but I don't think that would mean a great deal to you."

"It wouldn't mean anything to me," I confessed.

John was struggling to find the right words. I could see his disappointment. "Well, let me just say that for a minute there, this cache really had me going."

I felt my stomach clench with sudden apprehension. I knew what he was going to say, and in an instant the realization hit me with such force I almost felt dizzy.

"They are all perfect. Except for this," he said.

John reached for one point in particular and lifted it carefully with one hand. He held it in front of me, hefting it for emphasis. It was the lustrous, smoky green arrowhead I'd admired, and it still had a perfect edge.

"It looks just like the others," I said.

"But look at the green color. What does it remind you of?"

"A piece of jade," Hugo said.

"It does look like it's made from jade." I swallowed hard. A lump was forming in my throat even as I spoke.

"And it's fake," John said, letting the bomb drop at last.

"Fake?" Hugo said, his voice coming out in a squeak.

"Are they all fakes?" I managed to ask.

"They are likely all made by the same person," John told me. "And this one is a fake. No question. This cache is a forgery."

I felt the heat rise up my throat and wash over my face as realization dawned. Now I knew why Rufus had been shot and our fence had been cut down. Someone had wanted to steal the arrowheads all right, but not to sell them. They wanted to protect a secret.

"How do you know for certain that this arrowhead is a fake?" I had to be absolutely sure about what he was telling me.

John placed the arrowhead in the center of my palm and closed my fingers around it.

He gave me a sympathetic smile. "Because it's not made out of jade. No point on the face of the earth is made out of jade. It's far too hard to knap."

I opened my palm and studied the arrowhead. All of that trouble for such a tiny little thing.

"What's it made of?" Hugo asked.

John shook his head, a sad look creeping up to his eyes. "If I was going to guess, I'd say it's made out of an old 1950's-vintage ashtray.

I sat back against my chair hard. "Thank you, John. This isn't what I expected to hear, but it clears up a lot."

John leaned forward and tapped the arrowhead where it rested in my hand. "Just because it's fake doesn't mean it's worthless. Marley, somebody went to a lot of trouble to make this look like it was a genuine arrowhead cache."

"What do you think that means?" I asked.

John took the glass arrowhead and placed it back in line with the others. He looked me straight in the eye, his tone dark. "It means, when you get home, I think you should be very careful who you tell about this."

CHAPTER 17

"You know, Dearcorn, there was a time I was surprised by the stuff that comes out of your mouth. Not anymore."

I sat at the desk across from Nick Wilcox at the Killdeer sheriff's station. He was leaning back in the office chair with his feet propped up by the computer keyboard. His eyes were bloodshot and I got the impression he was less than happy about seeing me.

"Does Loy mind it when you sit in his chair?" I asked.

"Shucraft ain't going to be the sheriff in Killdeer forever," he replied.

Since it was only seven in the morning and not even Valerie the office manager was there yet, I decided to give Nick some leeway. After all, he'd agreed to meet me at the station when I hadn't been able to get in touch with Loy, so technically he was doing me a favor.

Neither one of us mentioned our midnight confrontation at the café. I got every impression from the deputy that he never would bring it up again.

"So, what do you think?" I'd told him the whole story concerning the arrowheads, hoping for a sympathetic ear.

"About what? This box of rocks sitting on my desk? I think you have finally pitched over the deep end this time."

"They are arrowheads, Nick. Not rocks. Like I said, somebody went to a lot of trouble to make them look like real artifacts. I'm pretty certain that person was Clifton Myers. I had an expert look at them. Don't you think it's more than a coincidence that he's the one who shows up to take over the dig site from Jimmy Burke all these years later?"

Nick slid his feet off the desk and leaned in. "So let me get this straight—you and this university geek find a pile of Indian bones with a bunch of other crap buried on your dad's place and jump to the wild conclusion that this guy from Colorado faked an artifact find thirty years ago. Do you know how nuts that sounds?"

I bit my tongue. I'd wanted to say something about doing his job for him, but knowing Nick as well as I did, I knew that it would spell the end of this conversation.

"There were no Indian remains at the dig," I said patiently, repeating Jimmy's mantra.

"Whatever. That's not what the hot-looking news lady said on her program. The only crime I'm investigating right now is the killing of Lewis Pritchett's bull and the trespassing that took place on your property Wednesday night. You got any leads on that?"

I shook my head. "Didn't you manage to find any tire tracks?"

"Sure we found tire tracks. Standard Goodyear retreads with a wheelbase matching your average pickup truck. Fat lot of good that does us. You know how many vehicles in Killdeer County have those things in common?"

I decided to try one more time to get Nick to see my point.

"Deputy Wilcox," I said, trying to appeal to his professional side. "The summer following my grandfather's murder, Clifton Myers apparently found a cache of arrowheads in South Dakota that was so important it made him famous. Don't you think that's too much of a coincidence? Doesn't it seem just a little bit odd to you he managed to find such an important site the summer after he was digging on our land?"

"So? It only means that he is a good archaeologist."

"But then it turns out the arrowheads on our property are all fakes?" I said, losing my patience.

"What's your point?" he asked.

"My point is that he planted them. And maybe my grandfather's murder was enough to scare Clifton Myers into abandoning those fake arrowheads on our ranch, even after he'd gone to all the trouble. I mean, who would want the discovery of the century associated with a homicide?"

"And this pertains to my job . . . how?"

I could feel my teeth grind together. "I swear, Nick, you can be such an idjit."

Nick stood up and pointed a finger at my nose. "I think we are done here, Dearcorn."

"You aren't going to at least go talk to him?"

"To who?" Nick asked, gathering up his keys and making it obvious that he was about to head for the door.

"Clifton Myers. Will you at least question him?"

"About what? Listen, I don't know if you understand my job description very well, so I'll explain it to you. I investigate crimes. I don't investigate UFO sightings, or the Virgin Mary burned onto a piece of toast, or people who say that werewolves are running around in the woods behind their house. You see a crime here? Did Clifton Myers try to sell those arrowheads? Did he try to profit from them somehow? No. There's no crime here as far as I can see."

"But if he forged our site, isn't it a safe guess that he faked the site in South Dakota, too?" I asked.

"Who cares? Does my badge say South Dakota Sheriff's Department?"

He hefted his keys and motioned that I should stand up.

I practically growled. "Nick, this guy is a scumbag. It would help a lot if you would question him, maybe spook him enough to leave Killdeer and never come back."

The deputy put both fists in the center of the desk and leaned over it until he was inches away from my nose. "Look. I don't do maybes. If you got a photograph of Clifton Myers holding a smoking gun over the dead body of Lewis's bull, I'm interested. Otherwise, stop wasting my time."

I got to my feet and carefully lifted the wooden box from the desk.

John Taylor had been gracious enough to help Hugo and me repack the fake arrowheads.

It had seemed practical to switch the Pelican Lake points from the wooden box and use it to hold the Clovis forgeries instead, and use Hugo's backpack for the arrowheads my father had picked up.

Hugo had the Pelican Lake points, and I was stuck with the fake Clovis points until I could figure out a place to stash them where Clifton wouldn't get his grubby paws on them.

"Can I leave these here until we get all of this sorted out?" I asked, holding up the wooden box.

"We aren't a damn bank safe deposit. You want to put them someplace secure, it's your problem. Let's go."

We left the station and Nick locked the door behind us. He didn't say a word as he climbed into his truck and pulled out into the street.

I stood in the parking lot for a moment, watching two robins squabble in a chokecherry bush in the grassy area next to the station. The sun was peeking over the trees, warming the air, and everything smelled rich with life. The cheerful summer day did nothing to improve my sour mood.

I shouldn't have been surprised by Nick's reaction. He and I had never gotten along, and I didn't know why I imagined this case would be any different. Still, I did have some small consolation that I'd voiced my suspicions to law enforcement. I didn't think it would make much difference, but it made me feel better.

Even though Nick wasn't about to lift a finger to help me, I'd at least had the common sense to come up with a plan B.

Before I'd left John Taylor's place I'd asked him for a favor. It was a long shot, but if there was anyone kicking around our area who could help me prove Clifton Myers was a fraud, it was John. He'd agreed to do a little snooping on my behalf and hopefully his investigation would be able to find the name of the person who had made those arrowheads thirty-four years ago. Like me, John had a rigid definition of right and wrong, and he saw Clifton Myers's forgery as an affront to his profession. Nothing would give John more pleasure than sniffing out a con man and exposing him. He had agreed to tell me right away if he was able to find any useful information.

At least someone involved with this mess knew what he was doing.

I drove to Lil's, feeling defeated, and saw one of the University of Colorado Suburbans parked in front of the café. I felt my nerves jangle at the thought I might have to see Myers face-to-face. I wasn't completely sure I was capable of having a civil conversation with the man just yet.

Luckily, Clifton wasn't there. Two of his anthropology students sat together at a booth, their heads bent towards each other, and their voices low. It was the red-haired girl and one of the well-muscled diggers.

"They just got here," Irene told me. "I'd pay a hundred bucks to hear what they are talking about. They were yelling at each other in the parking lot a minute ago."

"Irene, I need to talk to you." I placed the wooden box on the counter beside me. I didn't dare let the thing out of my sight.

"What is that?" she asked, looking at the box labeled Snipe Tails.

"My worst nightmare," I said. "Can I ask you something?"

"You can ask me about anything at all." Her expression was like a traffic cop watching the last ten seconds tick off a parking meter. "As long as it's about what colors you want at your engagement party."

I groaned. "Oh, right. Leif and the infamous proposal."

"So he did ask you to marry him," she said.

"Well, not exactly."

"What does that mean, not exactly? Did he or didn't he?"

"We talked about it," I said.

"You need coffee." She poured a cup of brew so strong the steam made my eyes water.

"He's going to Panama in a few days and said we will talk more about it when he gets home."

Irene slammed the coffee carafe back in the brewer. She turned on me ferociously. "If you are about to tell me that when Leif Gable asked you to marry him you said that you would think about it, I'm going to get a doctor to give you a psychological evaluation."

"What's wrong with taking the time to make sure it's the right decision?" I asked.

"Marley, when a man like Leif asks you to marry him, there is only one correct answer and that is 'What time do you want me to be there?'"

I wrapped both hands around my steaming cup. "Irene, I'm far from perfect. What does a man like him see in a little hayseed like me?"

"Listen, you two have years for him to figure out all the things that are wrong with you as a person. Let him have the joy of discovering all of your quirks after the two of you have tied the knot. You don't need to give him a laundry list of your baggage beforehand."

"But shouldn't Leif know what he is getting into before he makes that kind of a commitment to me?" I asked.

"I don't think you are giving him enough credit, Marley. He is a grown man and can make mistakes all by himself without any help from you. If he wants to make you the happiest woman in the world, for Pete's sake, dear, let him."

"Excuse me, but aren't you the woman from the dig site?"

I was so startled I spilled my coffee. As I swiveled my stool to the right I came face-to-face with the exotic red-haired anthropology student. She was wearing a little more clothing than she had been the first time I'd seen her. A University of Colorado sweatshirt covered her ample bosom, but she was wearing a pair of cutoffs so short they may as well have been bikini bottoms. She was perfectly tanned and it must have taken her an hour to do her makeup. Who wore makeup while digging in the dirt?

She slid onto the stool beside me and tossed her long red hair over one shoulder. It smelled faintly of strawberries.

"Clifton mentioned that you might be able to help us," she said, her voice like a purr. "The University of Wyoming student hasn't been very cooperative."

"Help you with what?" I noticed that when she spoke about Dr. Myers she referred to him by his first name. No wonder she had glared at me the day Myers had talked to me just before we'd gone up to the site. From her casual tone, it was clear she considered him her personal property.

"Information about the person who stole the arrowheads." Her big green eyes flicked from my face to the wooden box on the counter. She frowned when she saw the words carved on the cover, and she read them with a question mark expression.

Snipe Tails?

I felt someone drop onto the stool to my right and when I pivoted around I saw the other anthropology student perched beside me. His swarthy complexion and wavy brown hair reminded me of a famous Spanish actor, but his hands were covered with calluses and scratches and his shoulders bulged. He was obviously simply there to move dirt around so that Myers didn't have to get his hands dirty.

I pasted an innocent look on my face. "Listen, if I knew who had those arrowheads I'd be happy to hand them over."

It took all of my strength not to reach for the box on the counter, and I was careful not to look at it.

"What do you think, Max? She telling us a story?" the redhead asked.

Max the swarthy leaned towards Irene, his hair tousled just so and his face sporting a perfect, rugged two-day beard. He smelled like sweat and suntan oil. "Have you got any pie?"

"Peach or apple?"

"Apple." He gradually shifted his gaze over to me. One side of his mouth curled up. "I think she is being straight with us, Elise."

"I don't have to tell you how important those arrowheads are to Clifton," Elise told me.

I mopped up my coffee with a napkin and sipped what was left in my cup. "I wish I could help you out."

Max leaned against my shoulder. "Now she's lying."

Elise slipped a roll of lip balm from her shorts and dabbed it on. Cherry. Of course it was cherry.

"We think that you can help us out," she said, ignoring the box and staring straight at me.

Irene plunked a piece of apple pie on the counter in front of Max. He didn't even glance at his fork, keeping his eyes locked on me as he started to eat the pie slowly. I couldn't help but notice how hairy his knuckles were.

"And how do you think that I can do that?" I asked.

"We think that you know who has them." Unlike her companion, Elise wasn't smiling.

"Really?"

She pressed her lips together. "Clifton says that everyone here knows everybody else. There are no secrets in a town this small."

"God if only that were true," Irene muttered.

"Clifton says that you can settle this whole issue if you just tell us where the arrowheads are." She was smiling now, but it didn't reach her eyes.

If I heard the name Clifton one more time I was going to scream.

"And why does he think that out of all the folks here in Killdeer I'm the one who can settle this?" I asked.

Max took another bite of pie. "Because your father hates his guts."

"Be nice," Elise said.

I laughed. "You think my father stole the arrowheads?"

She tossed her hair but didn't reply.

"We think he may have picked them up and given them to someone he knows for safekeeping," Elise said.

"If he did, do you think for one minute that I'd be stupid enough to tell you about it?" I asked.

"We were hoping for that," Max said, his mouth full. "Sometimes people give things away, even when they don't mean to."

Elise placed one well-manicured hand on the counter only a few inches away from the wooden box. "It's easy to screw up when you are under pressure."

Max ate the last bite of pie and slid the plate away.

With one smooth motion, Irene made a show of draping Max's napkin over his plate, and with the other hand she deftly slid the wooden box underneath the counter.

It happened so fast I hardly saw it myself. Both anthropology students seemed oblivious.

Max turned slowly on his stool to face me. "If your father doesn't have the points, and Jimmy doesn't have the points, then maybe we should go talk to that kid who was up there the day you found them. We asked around and it sounds like that kid was all over the site that day."

Irene froze in the act of retrieving the empty plate and stared at Max. Her eyes pivoted to me. "Marley . . ."

"You don't want to do that." I turned slowly towards him.

He lifted his napkin from the plate, and with painful precision, wiped the crumbs from his mouth. "Oh? Why is that?"

"Hugo has no idea where those arrowheads are."

His smile faded. "Then maybe the person who does know should step forward, and then we won't have to go talk to the kid."

"Max took clinical psych last semester," Elise said as she leaned against my left shoulder. "He knows when people are not being straight with him."

"And you, Missy, are not being straight with me." He leaned so close I could see each and every one of the pores on his face.

"I've got nothing to hide," I said. "Unlike your boss. Why don't you ask him about those arrowheads? Ask him why they are really so important to him."

For a moment Max's expression flickered with uncertainty. Then a grin spread across his face and he jerked his chin at Elise. "Classic misdirection. She knows where they are."

Elise lifted a perfect hand and examined the tips of her fingernails. "Sure she does."

"But maybe that kid does too," Max said smoothly.

"And we could ask him to help us out," Elise said.

"Of course, that won't be necessary if you suddenly get the urge to be cooperative," Max told me with half-hooded eyes.

The redhead tried to slide off the bar stool, but her thighs has glued themselves to the Naugahyde and she was forced to peel herself up.

"Clifton will make it a point to visit the site later in case your father comes to his senses and lets us have access." She looked at me with a catlike stare. "If you can fit it into your busy schedule, you should go talk to him. Get this all cleared up before it gets messy."

I could feel my heart pounding, and had a sudden vision of following them out into the parking lot and giving them both a demonstration of frontier justice.

Max threw a five-dollar bill on the counter and followed Elise to the door, oblivious to my silent fury. They strolled outside with a flourish.

My eyes didn't leave them until the black SUV had disappeared.

"I've seen you like this once before," Irene said. "The day you found out Allen had been cheating on you with that cocktail waitress from Bozeman. It's a good thing you were down here and not up in Helena, or I think you would have killed him."

"I have to go. Thanks for the coffee," I said.

Irene called after me. "Marley. You need to get ahold of yourself. Calm down before you do something you might regret."

The expression on my face must have been brutal. She clamped her mouth shut and took a step back.

"I've already done something I regret."

I headed for the door and decided that it was time I stopped being cautious and started dealing with the situation head-on. My father and I had endured the selfish, crazy horde of onlookers, government lackeys, television reporters and obnoxious university groupies for long enough. I'd finally reached the breaking point.

I didn't even care that I'd walked out of Lil's and left the wooden box of fake arrowheads with Irene. It didn't matter anyway.

I told myself that I never wanted to see those damn things again as long as I lived.

CHAPTER 18

"Fakes." Jimmy froze, his hands covered in plaster and his hat slipping over his eyes. He pushed the brim back, smearing white goo across his forehead. The sun was already beating down on the dig site, making both of us sweat.

I sat down on the lip of the hole. "They probably aren't more than a few decades old."

I was relieved to see that Jimmy was alone at the site. We had the place all to ourselves and I decided it was time to confide in him. A cheerful meadowlark sang from a tuft of tall buffalo grass, oblivious to our human troubles.

Jimmy glanced back at his hands and seemed to remember what he was doing. He dug a strip of burlap out of a pile of the cut cloth and dunked in into the plastic bucket of wet plaster at his feet. He swirled the burlap in the sticky white mess until it was soaked, and then slapped it on the last uncovered bit of the big field jacket. Since Dr. Myers had officially identified the skull, Jimmy could finish encasing it and get it ready for the long drive back to southern Wyoming.

"How, exactly, do you know this?" he asked.

"I went to see an expert."

"Which means that you know where the arrowheads are." He shot me a perturbed look.

"They are in a safe place. Listen, Jimmy. I'm sorry. I should have brought them to you right away, but I've got my reasons."

"Like you wanted to keep Hugo from getting in trouble." He grabbed another strip of burlap and coated it with plaster.

The dinosaur skull was almost completely encased, and after a few hours drying in the hot sun it would be ready to load up. Again.

"Not just that," I told him. "I want to prove that Myers is a fraud."

Jimmy smoothed the last piece of burlap over the skull, leaned down to examine his work, and dropped back on the ground so he could finally rest. "It's done."

"You understand, don't you?" I asked. "I hate it that Clifton used my grandfather the way he did. It's obvious to me now what he was planning to do all along."

He waved his hands in the air, shaking off as much of the wet plaster as he could. Clumps of the white substance rained to the ground. "Maybe you should explain it to me."

"My father told me once that he never liked Clifton because he always got the impression the guy just wanted to be famous. It didn't matter to him how he did it."

Jimmy rubbed his arms. "So thirty years ago, Myers, recent graduate from the University of Wyoming and eager beaver, is out here running around looking for dinosaurs on your grandfather's ranch for an entire summer, and all he finds are two lousy teeth."

"That's not nearly enough to get him the notoriety he wants," I said. "But the two of them spend a lot of time drinking beer on the porch in the evening, and one night they pulled out the box of old arrowheads that my grandfather kept around, and my grandfather asks Clifton if he can identify them."

"And Myers gets the idea that maybe he can be famous for artifacts instead of dinosaurs," Jimmy said. "Well, I guess it would explain why he suddenly gave up paleontology."

I wiped a spot of plaster off my jeans. "Back in the seventies, I would think it wouldn't be that difficult to find someone to fake an arrowhead that would be able to fool just about anyone. So Clifton finds some patsy flint-knapper to forge a cache, he buries it on our property, and he figures that the next summer he will come back and make his world-famous discovery."

"But he didn't come back," Jimmy said.

"Because my grandfather was murdered, that November. I doubt very much that Clifton would want his new discovery associated with a ranch where a homicide had been committed. So he just moved his operation over to South Dakota, and made his discovery there instead."

"You think the site in South Dakota was fake too?" Jimmy asked.

"You bet I do. How else was he going to guarantee his success?"

"What a jerk," Jimmy said.

The white goo on his arms was dry and he started scraping it off with his fingers. I'd noticed before Jimmy's arms didn't have very much hair from the elbows down. Now I could see why. It had all been bikini-waxed off by drying plaster.

I stared at the heavy field jacket on the ground. "No way I am helping you lift that thing again. I'll go down to the ranch house and get my father. He's got a front-end loader on his yard tractor and I'll ask him if we can borrow it."

Jimmy was rubbing his arms, a thoughtful look on his face. "That's a good idea."

I left the site and walked back to the road so I could drive down to my father's. As I stuck one leg inside my SUV, I heard the crunch of tires on gravel and closed my eyes, not wanting to see who was driving down the road this time.

"Not Finn, please don't let it be Finn." I was far from ready to face him again. Maybe in about a hundred years.

I forced myself to look up and saw a green pickup roll into view, a U.S. Forest Service logo on the side.

Amelia Snow parked behind me and killed the engine of her truck.

She stepped out, holding a camera.

I was not as irritated as usual to see her. Maybe it was sheer relief that I wouldn't be forced into another confrontation with Finn. Amelia was annoying, but I could handle her.

"Hello." She lifted her hand with a friendly gesture, clearly wanting me to have the impression she came in peace.

Her long braids were smooth, pinned at the ends with bright silver Conchos, and two feathers dangled from them. Instead of an Indian maiden with a stylized wolf, today her T-shirt showed a bare-chested warrior brave holding a buffalo skull above his head. A bolt of lightning flashed above him.

"Amelia," I said with a curt nod. It wasn't very polite, but I planned to let her do all the talking.

"I was hoping, now that things have quieted down, that I might be able to go up and at least take a look at the fossil."

Her tone was conciliatory. She knew she had acted unprofessionally on the day Clifton had arrived at the dig. She seemed to want to make up for it now.

"Jimmy is up there. He's about to take it out, and you can't see it because he's wrapped it in plaster."

She fiddled with the lens on her camera. "That's alright. Can I have your permission to walk up anyway?"

She didn't seem to have an agenda other than curiosity.

I didn't see what harm it could do now. All the damage had already been done.

"Let him know I said it was alright."

She smiled faintly and closed the door on her truck. As she turned to head for the gate, something occurred to me.

"Amelia. Can I ask you something?"

She stopped and looked back.

I left my hand resting on the door of my vehicle, showing her that I didn't intend to keep her very long.

"How is it that you know Clifton Myers?"

Her mouth twisted up with disgust, but to her credit she answered me anyway.

"I was a new hire with the Forest Service the summer he was digging here. I had just graduated with my master's degree and wanted to get some field experience. I heard about his work. You know how word gets out about something unusual like that. When I came out here to see his site, Clifton was furious. He practically threw me off the land and told me that Mr. Dearcorn would sue me for trespassing if I came back. It was terrible. I was not much more than a kid, only twenty-six at the time, and he scared the daylights out of me. Clifton is a bully. I don't think he is a very good scientist."

"I'd have to agree with you there."

"He doesn't care about the artifacts he finds. All he cares about is what they can help him achieve personally. He uses the sacred past for personal financial gain and I don't have a great deal of respect for that."

"Financial gain," I said. "I thought that all artifacts had to go to the university he works for. How could he get anything out of a discovery other than fame?"

She sneered. "More likely it is the money."

"But he can't sell the artifacts he discovers," I said, not understanding.

"No, but he can apply for grant money. And then there is the prospect of television appearances, paid speaking engagements, book sales and department funding. In the academic community, you need to stand out to compete for funding. I don't think anyone stands out better than Dr. Myers."

I had already made up my mind about the man. I suppose it was simply my own need for validation that had caused me to ask Amelia her opinion. I was gratified that someone other than my father and me thought that Clifton was a snake. The only surprise was the realization that fame probably wasn't the driving force behind the fraud.

Amelia suddenly turned pale. "Marley, I . . . I'm sorry."

I shook my head. "What for?"

Her shoulders hunched up as she spoke. "Back then, I was a mess. I wasn't very mature, and I blame myself for how things got handled with your grandfather."

"I'm not sure I know what you mean," I said.

"I may have said some things that ended up causing a lot of friction between your grandfather and Clifton." She laughed a bit at that remark. "I guess you could call it friction. It was more like combat."

Her laugh faded and she seemed full of remorse.

"Amelia. Did something happen between Clifton and my grandfather that made them have a falling out?"

Clearly, she was ashamed. Nobody could judge us as harshly as we could judge ourselves.

She seemed to be gathering the strength to confess, and I waited quietly for her to tell me what she was on the verge of saying.

"Even back then, with as little experience as I had, I knew the significance of a beveled bone rod stained with red ocher."

My thoughts screeched to a halt and I closed the door on my vehicle. "When did you see something like that?"

She fiddled with her camera, grimacing. "After Clifton shouted me off his dig, I admit I started hounding your grandfather. All I wanted to do was find out what Clifton was working on. Finally your grandfather showed me his box of arrowheads that he kept at the house. He said that he thought maybe Myers was working on something similar. That's when I saw the beveled bone rod stained with red ocher. Those are always associated with a sacred site."

I wanted to explain to Amelia that the bone rod had come from the creek, and not up on the ridge, but it suddenly seemed more important to ask her what she had said to my grandfather.

"Did you tell him that it was from a burial?" A feeling of dread had started to creep over me.

"Of course I told him. My best advice to him was that it was a terrible mistake to let Clifton

Myers work on his property, because more than likely he was desecrating a grave. Your grandfather was livid."

"Did they argue about it?" I asked.

"All I know is that not very long after I told your grandfather what he really had on his property, Clifton Myers disappeared and never came back."

He never came back because my grandfather had caught him in the act of hiding the fake arrowheads. I was absolutely sure of it.

Had my grandfather confronted Clifton about it? Had they argued and things turned ugly?

My knees wobbled slightly. I felt light-headed under the hot sun and held out a hand to rest on the SUV. It scalded me almost at once and I jerked my palm off it quickly.

"Go on up to the dig and take as much time as you like. I'm sure all of this will have a happy ending," I said, not believing my own words one bit.

She seemed to have forgotten the reason she was there. Her hands fiddled with her long necklace, her eyes unfocused, as she seemed to be remembering the past.

After a moment she recovered and gave me a grateful look. "Thank you. I won't be long. You have been very kind."

She turned away and walked towards the gate with a bit more vigor in her step.

As I got into my vehicle Amelia's story replayed over and over in my head.

I forced myself to sit in the hot cab without starting the engine while I thought about what she had told me.

Was it too much of a coincidence that my grandfather had been murdered only a few months after he and Clifton had argued?

My instinct was not to believe in coincidences.

No question, Dr. Myers was a scoundrel and a fraud, but was he a killer too?

Either way, in a few hours I would have to face him and finally have it out about the arrowheads. The blatant threats from Clifton's anthropology students back at the café to harass Hugo if I didn't turn over the points had worked. I fully intended to meet Clifton back up at the dig site later in the day and settle the issue once and for all.

There were new questions that needed answers. Questions about the events leading up to the death of my grandfather. The only problem? How was I going to investigate a murder that had happened over three decades ago on the day I was born?

CHAPTER 19

At noon I drove back out to the dig site. The sun was shining brightly, the birds were singing in the trees and I couldn't help but think the pastoral feel of summer was mocking me somehow.

When I pulled up behind a University of Colorado Suburban and saw Finn's black Jeep parked in front of it, I cut the engine and simply sat there for a moment.

"Can't I ever catch a break?" I said to the windshield.

It took a full five minutes of arguing with myself before I finally got the courage to step out of my vehicle. When I did, I saw Finn standing in front of his Jeep talking to the red-haired graduate student. Max stood off to the side, chain-smoking.

I walked around the front of Finn's Jeep and noticed with a measure of relief that the heavy bumper had absorbed most of the impact. It was bent beyond repair, but the side door was all right and the only other damage I could see was the front quarter panel. It wasn't as bad as it could have been.

He wasn't wearing his sunglasses today. Elise was watching him with a spark in her eyes. Finn was in the process of watching her right back.

For a moment I felt a stab of jealousy, but I tamped it down hard and tried to act casual.

"Hey, Finn. I'm sorry about your Jeep."

He glanced over at me like he hadn't seen me arrive. "No worries. I wanted a new one anyway, and the institute may offer to supply a replacement if the repair bill for this old Jeep is too high. Honestly, doll. Ya should have hit it harder."

"I'll keep that in mind for next time," I said.

"So. You are from South Africa?" Elise said to Finn. "That's hot."

"Only in January," Finn said, quirking a smile at the girl.

She giggled. She actually giggled. I saw Max roll his eyes and draw hard on his cigarette. A butt lay on the ground at his feet and I glared at it until he caught the hint and shoved it in his pants pocket.

"January? But that's the wintertime." She blinked rapidly a few times. "How can it be hot in the winter?"

"South Africa is in the southern hemisphere," Max told her.

She continued blinking.

Finn gave every impression that he was utterly captivated.

I suppressed a groan. "Have you two been able to talk to Jimmy yet?"

"I haven't," Elise said.

"I spoke to him a moment ago." Max flicked the last of the ashes from his current cigarette with one finger until the embers died. He crushed it completely out on his pant leg and shoved the butt in his jeans pocket.

He stared hard at the back of Elise's head. "Jimmy said we can try talking to Mr. Dearcorn again, whenever you are finished with your lunch."

Elise shot him a perturbed look.

"Finn, can I talk to you for a minute?" I asked.

Elise stood where she was with one hip cocked.

I stared at her pointedly. "Alone."

She made a small sound of disappointment, but after a moment's hesitation she sauntered over to the University of Colorado Suburban and rummaged in a huge cooler, drawing out a soda. She popped the top and pressed the cool can against her chest, uttering a sigh.

Since apologizing to someone for wrecking his car was something I'd never done before, words were not coming easily. "Listen. I am really sorry I lost my temper the other day. There is no excuse for what I did."

Finn watched me for a moment, his expression impossible to read. He shrugged with one shoulder. "I won't call you stupid ever again, count on that."

"I just want to know why it is that you seemed so upset. Why did you drive all the way out here to tell me not to marry Leif, when last winter you couldn't get out of our relationship fast enough? Explain that to me, would you?"

He fished his sunglasses out of his khakis and slowly covered his eyes. "I don't know what to tell you, Marley. It was friendly advice. That's all."

I couldn't determine if he was putting me off, or if he was telling the truth.

"You seemed angry," I said, prompting him.

His mouth was a flat, expressionless line.

"Well?" I asked.

"Well, what? You would have done the same thing for me."

"I would?" I was confused.

"If I suddenly said I was gonna marry that kitten over there," he said, jerking his head towards

Elise, "you'd be a good friend and tell me I'd gone crackers."

"You've known her for twenty minutes," I said.

"That's my point."

"I've known Leif long enough to make this call," I said.

"Alright." His eyes were drifting around the pasture as if he was suddenly bored.

"You said that I was being reckless. You said I needed to slow down and think about what I was doing before I made a terrible mistake."

He kicked the ground with one foot. "Did I? Huh."

"Dammit, Finn. What did all of that mean? Were you serious? Because at the time you looked serious to me."

"I seriously wish we were done with this conversation," he said.

I let my head fall back. "Why do I even bother?"

Max and Elise watched me with impatience. Obviously they were expecting me to saunter over and hand them the arrowheads like they had rightful ownership.

My teeth ground together at the thought. I would deal with the two of them in a minute.

"Finn, if you have anything you want to say to me, you better say it now because after this conversation I'm not going to look back."

He let out a sour laugh. "Like you'd listen to me even if I did have a reason."

"I'm not kidding, Finn. This is your last shot."

He shifted his weight from foot to foot, and I could see he was thinking.

"Congratulations on your engagement." His tone was dead.

I crossed my arms and felt a lump fill my throat. "Fine. Thanks a lot. Good luck with the kitten."

I turned my back on him and went straight for Max and Elise.

The redhead was watching Finn with her mouth slightly open.

I rubbed my eyes as I stopped in front of them.

Max shot me a look. "He was staring at your chest the whole time."

I ignored the comment. "Alright, let's get this over with. Where is Dr. Myers?"

Elise chirped as she watched Finn climb back inside his Jeep. "He was amazing."

"Really, Elise? You didn't know that the southern hemisphere experiences summertime in January?" Max asked.

"Of course I did," she said. "Men like to think that they are smarter than girls. I don't mind encouraging that illusion."

"How dumb were you pretending to be?" Max asked.

"Well, he wasn't the brightest bulb on the string, was he?" she said.

I was doing what I could to suppress the urge to strangle them both. "Look. I am supposed to be up at the site helping Jimmy Burke load up the field jacket. Since your boss didn't think it was important enough to come up here and talk to me, could we at least go up there and give him a hand?"

The two students stared at me with dull expressions.

"I don't load field jackets," Elise said.

"And I'm not touching the thing until we have permission from Dr. Myers," Max said.

I grumbled and shook my head. "Then come with me so I can keep an eye on you."

They both looked smug at the invitation and followed me through the gate on foot.

When we finally reached the dig site, Jimmy was squatting in the hole with the plaster cast, checking his watch and rapping the cast with the backs of his knuckles.

"It's almost ready. Maybe another half hour," Jimmy said.

I stepped into the hole beside him and sat down. "My father is bringing the little tractor up in a bit."

Max looked at the cast. "You are absolutely sure it's really a dinosaur."

He and Elise were busy stalking the area, their eyes pinned to the ground. At least they appeared to be cautious where they put their feet.

"Don't tell me you are on the 'human remains' bandwagon, too?" Jimmy asked.

Max knelt down and ran his hands over the loose soil where the arrowheads had once been. A few impressions were still clearly visible in the dirt. "I simply don't have much faith in people. Most of the time they are incompetent."

"Jimmy knows what he is doing." I was feeling so surly I hardly trusted myself to open my mouth.

"Which is why all of the arrowheads are missing," Elise said, a snide expression on her face.

"That was not his fault," I said.

"It doesn't matter anyway," Max said as he stood up.

"Why is that?" Jimmy asked.

"We know where they are," Elise told me. She smiled sweetly.

"You do?" Jimmy asked.

"Don't you?" asked Max, turning to Jimmy.

"And we expect them to show up this afternoon," Elise announced.

Jimmy's eyes bulged and he shot me a look. "Really."

"You should just go get them right now, and stop all this screwing around," Elise said, staring straight at me.

"I don't have them," I told her, my veneer of patience just about exhausted. "They are in good hands at the moment."

"Good hands," Max repeated.

"And until I get a chance to talk to Clifton, they are staying where they are," I said.

The redhead's eyes flashed. "You can't do that."

"Well I'm doing it." The two of them were really starting to push my buttons.

Max casually stepped beside the field jacket, turned his backside to it, and sat on it with a sigh. "We just happen to be in a position to tell you both what you can and cannot do."

Jimmy took a step towards him. I held up my hand and stopped him. "How so?"

"Dr. Myers has the original permit for this quarry," Max informed us. "Anything that comes out of here, anything at all, goes to the academic institution of his choice."

Jimmy sputtered. "Like hell. This is private land. And his quarry permit was destroyed in a fire."

"And Mr. Dearcorn, the elder Mr. Dearcorn, gave Dr. Myers permission to remove anything he discovered on this property," Max said.

"Verbal permission," I said. "More than thirty years ago. It isn't valid anymore."

"I guess we will see what a judge has to say about it," Elise said smugly.

"Did Clifton promise the two of you extra credit if you could alienate every single person in Killdeer?" I asked.

"We are not the ones being unreasonable," Elise snapped. "If you would give him the damn points, he would let your grad student keep his stupid dinosaur."

My blood was nearly boiling. "That's it. Both of you, out of here."

Max started to pull another cigarette from his shirt pocket but before he could I reached out and shoved him off the field jacket.

He nearly fell over backwards and staggered to his feet. "Watch it!"

I had finally reached my breaking point. "Tell Dr. Myers to forget about ever seeing those arrowheads again."

"He will get a court order," Elise said.

"Tell him to give it his best shot," I said. "I was willing to talk to him, but not anymore."

"You are making a huge mistake," Elise said.

"Off my property," I said. "Now."

Max spat on the ground. "Dr. Myers is not going to be very happy."

"Nothing could please me more," I said, staring them down.

The two anthropology students wilted under my glare and finally shuffled away from the site. They headed over the slope, arguing the entire way.

Jimmy stood beside his carefully prepared field jacket, his expression a mask of worry. "Are you sure that was a good idea?"

"I don't even care. I'm too mad to think about things like consequences at the moment," I said.

I sat on the lip of the hole and did what I could to calm down. "Why didn't I listen to you when you said fossils can make people do crazy things?"

Jimmy rubbed his hands on his filthy pants. "I'm pretty sure my permission form that your dad signed will keep them from having any rights to this quarry. But it might not have been a very good idea to piss them off like that."

"I seem to have a knack for finding the wrong thing to say."

Jimmy patted his field jacket protectively. "If I can get this thing to the University, my chances of holding on to it will be a lot better. I think I should leave Killdeer as soon as possible."

"Take me with you," I said, shaking my head.

At last, I heard the sounds of a small John Deere tractor chugging towards us. My father was finally coming to help and soon it would all be over.

As far as I was concerned, the issue was settled. I had no idea what to do with the arrowheads, but one thing was certain, Clifton Myers wasn't ever going to get his greedy hands on them.

An old green tractor nosed over the ridge, puffs of smoke chugging out the exhaust pipe. My father sat at the wheel with a contented smile, face shaded by his old floppy hat. I envied his ignorance concerning the whole affair. After all the trouble and heartache the situation had caused Jimmy, and me I wasn't about to tell my father the whole sordid tale and get him wrapped up in the drama too.

I didn't know how, but I was suddenly determined to find a way out of the mess without involving him, if I could.

My father eased the little tractor forward and lowered the front-end bucket next to the plaster field jacket.

At least we could finally get the skull inside Jimmy's van where it would be under lock and key.

After the fossil was off our property, surely things would calm down and get back to normal.

Back to normal. Right.

CHAPTER 20

It took us two hours to accomplish a task that should have taken two minutes. The little tractor my father had driven up to the site promptly ran out of diesel before we could even load the field jacket in the bucket.

By the time we had driven back to the ranch for diesel, listened to my father answer a phone call from someone wanting him to change his phone company, and driven back up to the site with the old pickup truck hauling a fifty-five-gallon drum of fuel, it was well past two p.m.

Loading the dinosaur skull was a bit of a letdown after all of the work it had taken. My father lowered the bucket into the hole and Jimmy and I tipped the heavy plaster cast inside with three mighty shoves. It took only moments for my father to load it into the van. After the struggles Jimmy and Finn and I had endured the night we'd loaded it by hand, having the operation go smoothly with the tractor made me feel even more foolish.

I thought about all the National Geographic specials I'd seen on television and it was possible my expectations of paleontology were not very realistic. After watching Jimmy for one afternoon the glamour of the profession had dimmed. In truth, the work was backbreaking and tedious. Dirt managed to find its way inside every crack and crevice on your person, and by the end of the day I was convinced that Jimmy's knees had to be a patchwork of bruises.

As we manhandled the fossil into the back of the geology van it occurred to me there really wasn't a thing about the whole ordeal that had been an adventure. So much for Jurassic Park.

After the fossil was locked safely inside, again, my father lowered the bucket of the tractor and killed the engine.

"Just remembered. You got a phone call early this morning, Kiddo," he said, wiping his brow with a ratty bandana.

"I did?"

"Some fella named Taylor. Said to relay you a message."

I pretended that my bootlace had come undone and bent down so my father wouldn't see my expression. I had forgotten I'd given John Taylor my father's phone number to call.

"He said the guy you asked him about is still alive. Northern Cheyenne Indian about a hundred years old, lives up on the reservation east of Crow. He said the guy's named Badger Hand, and he said he remembers that green ashtray really well. Taylor wanted you to know he'd get in touch with you when he got back and fill you in on everything. He's going up there to talk to the old guy soon."

I finally trusted myself to look my father in the eye and I stood up, keeping my face as neutral as possible. "Great. Thanks, Dad."

My father was doing a fine job pretending he wasn't curious about the phone call. I held my breath for a moment, convinced that I was about to be on the receiving end of a battery of questions. But strangely, my father shoved the bandana back inside his jeans pocket and leaned over to start the tractor.

My father waited a moment, probably to see if I would let him in on the reason behind the phone message, but I managed to keep my mouth shut and he finally gave up. He backed the tractor away from the geology van and turned towards the ranch house, bouncing down the hillside, whistling loudly. Obviously he had better things to do than play twenty questions with his daughter.

I almost laughed at the sight of him driving away. The tractor was so loud I could barely hear the tune he whistled. It wasn't long before I couldn't hear the whistling at all.

"Was that from the Movie Bridge over the River Kwai?" Jimmy asked.

"I think so. Too bad that pot hunter who shot Rufus hadn't been whistling something we could recognize when you saw him," I said.

"It was a mechanical whistle that I heard, smart-ass. It wasn't a person."

"Was it a Lady Gaga song?" I asked, poking him on the shoulder. "Is that why you didn't recognize it? You're probably more of an Oak Ridge Boys sort of man."

"Bach." He shoved his field hat back off of his forehead and studied the ground.

"So, what happens next?" I asked.

So, what happens next?" I asked.

Jimmy pulled a half-eaten stick of beef jerky from his shirt pocket and took a bite.

He held up the hand not full of snack food and raised his fingers one at a time. "I go back to Wyoming. I write my paper. I become a doctoral candidate."

"What happens to the dinosaur?"

"Hugo? He goes on the auction block and your dad makes enough money to buy Lewis Pritchett a new prize Holstein bull."

"Hugo?"

"I had to name the fossil something, didn't I?"

I couldn't help but smile. "I think the kid will really love that."

"Where is the kid, anyway?" He swallowed the last of the jerky and carefully folded the wrapper inside his pocket. Almost every time I had seen Jimmy eating he had been standing up. One more thing about being a dinosaur hunter that rubbed the shine off of the profession.

"I would guess he is at the library. Wendy hasn't called me to babysit today. Not that it's really babysitting. More like acting as a personal assistant to the dean of antiquities."

Jimmy nodded and fished a set of keys out of his khakis. "Tell him that I said goodbye. He's probably going to be a professor someday, and I'll be able to say I knew him when."

"You don't think you will see Hugo before you have to leave?"

"I'd like to be back in Wyoming by tomorrow, after I've sorted this out with your father."

"What about the arrowheads?" I asked.

"What about them?"

"I've got a feeling they will be making their debut fairly soon. Don't you want them back?"

"Are you kidding? As far as I'm concerned, you can bury them exactly where we found them in the first place. I don't really care, Marley. Give them to Rob Powers or that Snow woman from the Forest Service. Rob's a boob, but he will know what to do with them and maybe they will get a great display case in some museum."

"Jimmy, didn't you hear me when I told you that they are all fakes?"

"At least a quarter of the arrowheads in museums back east are fakes. It's been a long tradition dating back a hundred years," he said.

"What tradition?"

"Sticking it to the white man."

Jimmy tipped his crusty hat, gave a little bow and climbed inside the battered University of Wyoming geology van. He waved out the window with one hand as he bounced down the rough hillside, following in the tractor tracks.

I was relieved, and sad, to watch Jimmy go. It had been an education all around for me, and he'd certainly gotten more than he had bargained for on this expedition.

But more than anything I was simply glad it was all over.

My boots kicked up tufts of dry dust as I descended the slope. I carefully closed the gate behind me, casting one final look towards the ridgeline before heading back into town.

There was only one thing left to do now.

Find Clifton Myers and tell him that if he didn't stop harassing us, I would personally and cheerfully ruin his career.

The phone call from John couldn't have come at a better time. Not only had John managed to locate the man who was probably responsible for crafting the fake arrowheads, he'd revealed the man's name, and all I would have to do was say it out loud to Clifton's face and that would be the end of it.

Dr. Myers couldn't possibly risk the truth coming out. If I threatened to tell the world about his forgery, his only option would be to leave Killdeer for good.

I wasn't sure how long it had taken the Cheyenne Indian, Badger Hand, to make the arrowheads, but if my math was correct it couldn't have been more than a few days.

It wouldn't have been difficult for Clifton to hide a cache of arrowheads on our land without anyone knowing about it. He had been given free run of the property by my grandfather.

As I drove towards town, the thought of my grandfather's murder damped my spirits once again. Something as horrible as a homicide would not have been good publicity. The last thing Clifton would have wanted was to be associated with a murder. So he had abandoned the Dearcorn Ranch. That is, until Jimmy Burke had come along and pulled the scab off the wound.

Or, maybe Clifton Myers had abandoned his dig on our ranch for an entirely different reason?

Amelia Snow's story about the confrontation between my grandfather and Clifton was seriously troubling. It was possible that my grandfather had confronted Clifton and the two of them had argued. It was even possible that the confrontation had escalated to the point that violence had occurred. Had Myers killed my grandfather in a moment of desperation? It was possible, but how could I ever hope to prove it?

The simple answer was, I couldn't.

As much as it pained me to admit, the only thing I could accomplish was to give Myers a very good reason to leave us alone.

I didn't like feeling so helpless, but under the circumstances, it was the best I could do.

My hands tightened on the steering wheel as I drove past Wee Wooly's Yarn Shop, and I peered through the window hoping to see Hugo, but he wasn't anywhere in sight.

On a whim I stopped and parked across the street from the yarn store. I thought Hugo would be tickled to hear that Jimmy had named the dinosaur after him, and I wanted to see his expression when I told him the news.

"Hey, Wendy. Is Hugo around?" I asked, poking my head inside the yarn store.

She looked up from a catalogue she was reading. "He said he was going to the library. He wanted to look up the Clover people."

"Clovis people?"

"Something like that. He said he would be back in an hour."

I thanked her and decided that my vindictive confrontation with Clifton could wait long enough for me to take a detour to the library. In spite of my trepidation about spending time with Hugo the first day I'd met him, he had really grown on me.

I parked at the library and dashed inside, hoping that I could find Hugo fast and give him the news. I was anxious to find out where the University of Colorado contingent had gotten to. If I were lucky, I'd get the chance to confront Clifton about the "jade arrowhead" in front of all of his students. That would give them all something to talk about during the long drive back home.

"Have you seen Hugo?" I asked the librarian at the front desk.

Killdeer was small enough that most of the kids who came in the library were on a first-name basis with the staff.

She shook her head, her white hair bobbing. "I haven't seen him since he left yesterday."

A tiny alarm bell went off inside my head. I tried to remember exactly what Wendy had told me, and I felt my throat tighten up. "Can you watch for him? If he comes in could you call his Aunt Wendy and tell her to come pick him up?"

She frowned and nodded. "Everything alright?"

"I think so. But there is a lot going on in town right now and I think it's a good idea that Hugo is within arm's reach of his aunt for the time being."

She agreed to call Wendy. I left in a hurry and drove to Lil's, breaking the speed limit and ignoring the stop signs.

I pushed open the door of the café and saw the University of Colorado anthropology students crowding together around one of the tables. They all glanced up as I walked in. Dr. Myers was nowhere to be seen. I stopped at their table.

Max and Elise surveyed me dismissively, then bent their heads back together over a topographical map spread out under their hands.

My heart started thudding in my chest. "Where's your boss?"

Elise tilted her head back and puckered her lips. "He's at the site looking for you."

"I just came from there." My chest was tight with worry.

"Well, then I don't know where he is. Maybe he went to talk to your father about something."

"Did you tell him Hugo has the arrowheads?" I asked.

She rolled her eyes and laughed. "I don't know, Max. Did we?"

Max ran a finger around the rim of his coffee cup with a languid motion. "It's so hard to keep track of all the things we talk about with Dr. Myers."

My worry was quickly turning into anger. "Did you tell him the kid has the arrowheads or not?"

Max smirked up at me. "You are the last person who should expect a straight answer from anybody, considering that it's your policy never to give one yourself."

I didn't have time for them to jerk me around. "Do you know where your boss is, or not?" I demanded.

Max looked around the café with dramatic confusion. "Do you hear someone talking?"

His face was so lackadaisical it pushed me straight over the top of furious.

"We used to run beef cattle on our ranch," I said to Max.

He looked back down at his coffee cup and ignored me.

My hands were clenched into fists. "Sometimes we had to deal with a mean bull that wouldn't load up in the chute. They can weigh fifteen hundred pounds, but there is one thing you can do to a bull that guarantees he will cooperate."

"Really. What's that?" Max asked.

A napkin sat neatly beside his elbow, complete with a spoon and a fork that had not been touched. I smiled as I bent down so I could look him in the eye. I reached beside him slowly and took ahold of his fork in my fist, still smiling, and wrapped my other hand around the back of his neck.

For a moment his face flickered with a suggestive smile.

Then I shoved the tines of the fork up his nostrils like a nose ring and held on.

"Did you," I said, enunciating each word, "tell your boss that the kid has the arrowheads."

"Oh my God!" Elise squealed, leaping away.

Max yelped and tried to grab my hands but the moment he made a move I twisted the fork until he froze. "I asked you a question."

Irene came running from the kitchen, and when she saw what was happening she shouted at me to stop.

Max tried to escape by sliding his butt back in the chair, but he only managed to pin himself tighter against the wall.

"Maybe . . . yea . . . we did."

"Where is he?" I asked.

"I don't know!" Max said, squirming frantically. But just like a bull with a ring in his nose, he was finally cooperating.

"How long has he been gone?"

"An hour, an hour that's all!"

"And what did he say when he left?" I asked, my grip holding firm.

Elise fluttered her hands like she was trying to speed-dry a coat of fingernail polish. "He said he was going to the site, I swear to God. That's all he said."

I stood up and pulled the fork from Max's nose, letting it fall to the floor as I headed for the door.

Irene was yelling at me, but I couldn't seem to understand what it was she was saying.

I jumped into my SUV and left two black lines on the sidewalk as I pulled into the street. I drove past the sheriff's station and it didn't even occur to me to stop.

If there had been a gun in the car I would have been steering with my knees and loading it.

As I reached the end of Main Street I hit the brakes and forced myself to stop and take a breath.

My SUV sat in the middle of the road. I didn't care that I was blocking traffic.

"Come on, Marley. Think, dammit."

A horn honked behind me. I ignored it.

A battered pickup truck eased up beside me, and out of the corner of my eye I saw Harvey Lewis peering in at me.

"You know you're in the middle of the—"

"Yeah?"

He sniffed once and spit out his window. "Just sayin'."

He drove around me and disappeared.

I kept my foot on the brake, my thoughts racing.

I squeezed my eyes closed, trying to recall word for word what I had told Elise back at the dig site. I'd said the arrowheads were in safe hands. She had clearly thought I'd meant they were with Hugo, and obviously Clifton thought that too.

If Clifton had managed to find Hugo alone between the yarn store and the library and Hugo was carrying his backpack, Clifton would have simply taken it from him then and there and would have gone back to the café. Since Myers wasn't at the café, that meant Hugo hadn't been carrying his backpack. It was someplace else.

Where would Hugo leave his backpack when he wasn't carrying it?

"The caretaker's house."

I hit the gas, turned right off of Main and tore for the ranch at top speed.

I was going sixty when I hit the gravel road and felt the front tires slide. Cursing, I eased back on the gas and got the vehicle under control before I rolled the car.

The SUV kicked up a cloud of dust the size of a volcanic eruption as I sped down the gravel road.

When I pulled up in front of Wendy's house I saw a black University of Colorado Suburban parked on the lawn. It was empty, the driver's side door hanging open.

I pulled up beside it and threw open my door, not bothering to shut off the engine.

"Hugo!" The front door of the house stood ajar, and even as I ran inside I knew the house was empty. It didn't take long to check every room. Nothing.

I raced out the back door and my heart was nearly exploding with fear as I stopped on the landing. I couldn't see anything. There was nobody in sight and though I strained with all my might to hear any sound, even the woods behind the little house were ghostly silent.

Then I caught sight of the trail.

I'd told Hugo about it the first day I'd met him. I'd told him that poachers used it sometimes. I'd told him about the silent spring hidden in the forest, that it was a perfect place to hide out when you didn't want to be found.

I hit the ground running.

CHAPTER 21

The trail was steep, hard going and in no time at all I was out of breath and gasping. I wanted to keep running but my body refused to cooperate. Not even halfway to the top my lungs forced me to stop.

I was bent over, sucking in air so loudly I didn't hear him coming until he was right on top of me.

I looked up at the sound of clattering gravel, expecting to see Myers coming down the trail, but instead found myself nose to nose with a black quarter horse.

The horse looked as surprised as me. Then I saw a rider lean over the horse's shoulder and a familiar unfriendly face appeared.

"You're in the middle of the trail, Dearcorn."

I took in a huge breath. "Willy."

"I should just run you over. I know it was your dad who snitched on me. Do you know how much trouble I got in?"

"I see you managed to keep yourself out of jail, for now." I was finally starting to get my breath back.

He leaned forward in the saddle. "I got out on bond. But there's a damn hearing I got to go to in the fall. You Dearcorns managed to mess me up pretty good. Maybe I ought to return the favor."

"I need your horse, Willy. Get off."

He looked at me like I had just asked him to donate a kidney without anesthesia. Then he laughed.

"Yeah. Like I'd even piss on you if you was on fire."

Not long ago this man had intimidated me into running from him like a frightened rabbit. I had always been afraid of Willy and his lack of conscience. But as I stared at his smirking face all I could think about was one thing. Hugo was in trouble.

This man stood between me and Hugo.

I stepped up to the left stirrup and wrapped my hand around the saddle horn. I knew Willy well enough to guess that he wouldn't dare go into the woods above our property with ill intentions on his mind without carrying a gun. And since I didn't see a rifle butt sticking out of his saddlebags, I knew what he was carrying.

It was a hot day for a jacket, but Willy wore one anyway.

I made sure I had a good grip on the saddle horn.

He leered down at me. "You sure are makin' this easy for me."

"There is one thing I have always liked about you, Willy."

He gave a suspicious laugh. "Yeah? What's that?"

"You favor short horses."

I slipped my hand under his jacket and pulled the pistol from his belt.

He tried to snatch my arm but I had already taken one step away and put myself out of reach.

I cocked the hammer back with my thumb and pointed the barrel at his nose. "Loy says you've been struck by lightning twice. Want to go for three?"

"What in the hell are you doin'?"

"Off. Now."

"Give me a second to—"

I grabbed his leg and shoved as hard as I could. Willy's arms flailed the air and he yelped, half-lunging, half-falling off the left side. The moment he hit the ground I was climbing into the saddle on the right. I scooped up the reins and urged the horse up the trail.

I kept the pistol gripped in my right hand and held the reins with my left. The horse's hooves clattered over exposed rocks and slipped on the powder-dry dirt as we thundered up the trail.

I rode hard, searching for anything helpful, but all I saw were trees and rocks, and not one sign of a small boy. I urged the horse harder.

We were almost to the top. Another hundred yards and we would be there, but the horse was frothy with sweaty foam and his head was starting to dip down with exhaustion. His footing was clumsy and his sides heaved with effort.

We needed to slow down. Loose stones and gravel littered the trail and the going was hazardous.

I tightened the slack on the reins to slow our pace. The horse dug in his front hooves, trying to stop, and without warning we went into a wild skid forward, the loose stones slipping and sliding wildly. I tried to lunge off but it was too late. A ton of horse and saddle tack came crashing to the ground hard with my right leg underneath.

I rolled sideways and the pistol fell from my hand as the horse's shoulder hit my right leg with a sickening thud. I felt my ankle snap on impact.

It hurt just as bad as getting shot.

It happened so fast I didn't even have time to scream from the pain before the air was knocked out of me.

The horse struggled for balance, heaved himself off of my leg and scrambled hard until he regained his footing enough to stand. He shook himself off and blew a sound of disgust in my general direction before dragging his reins to the side and trotting back down the trail.

For a moment all I could do was lie on the ground and try to stop the stars from swimming across my vision. I felt so nauseous I wasn't sure I could stand. Finally my breath came back and I could partially sit up.

The pistol was gone. Somewhere during the fall I'd dropped it and I couldn't see it anywhere. If Clifton had Hugo trapped at the end of the trail I had no clue how I could possibly help him now.

But I had to try.

As carefully as I could, I rolled to the left and eased myself up. The end of the trail couldn't be far now.

I reached out for tree limbs that draped down beside me and used them to haul myself up. My stomach lurched, but I managed to stay upright, and against all odds I kept my balance, standing precariously on my left leg.

My ankle was already swelling.

The high-top leather boot already felt tight, but it was probably the only thing keeping me upright.

I gingerly placed my right foot on the ground and was rewarded with a flash of pain. It was like standing on a row of knives, but on the third try I managed to grit my teeth long enough and hobble one step forward.

Half hopping, half lurching, I made progress moving ahead.

The thick trees hid the end of the trail from me, but as I struggled along the sounds of muffled voices drifted down. They were here. There wasn't any question.

I staggered around the last bend and froze when I saw them.

Hugo stood at the very end of the trail, backed up as far as he could go.

The ground flattened out across a broad expanse of rock maybe twenty feet across. The rock was smooth all around Hugo, and sloped down abruptly, becoming a sharp cliff only a few feet from where he stood. I knew what lay on the other side of the drop. We were standing on the top of a round shelf, and there was absolutely nothing to hold on to.

Clifton Myers had Hugo cornered and was just getting to the shouting.

"You see, young man? Running away achieved absolutely nothing. I want you to be reasonable and give me the damn backpack."

Hugo saw me stagger from the trees and because he already looked terrified beyond belief, his face hardly changed when I locked my eyes on him and lifted a finger to my lips.

He looked away from me quickly, both arms clutching the backpack with white knuckles, and took two stumbling steps backwards.

"It's a long way down, son," Clifton said.

My heart clenched when I saw Hugo skid to an uneasy halt. He was too scared to think straight. If I didn't do something fast he could easily fall right over the edge.

"Give me the backpack." Clifton moved forward a few steps, only stopping when Hugo's feet shifted uneasily.

His eyes were so wide I could plainly see that Hugo was close to shock.

"Do not make me come over there and take it," Clifton said.

There was nobody coming to help me this time.

All my helpless rage boiled to the surface and for one moment the pain in my shattered ankle vanished.

All I could think of was one thing: Clifton Myers had shot my grandfather in the back.

I didn't have a gun, or even a knife. But I had me. That was going to have to be enough.

I knew my ankle would only bear weight for a few strides before the pain would either knock me out or make me collapse. I had to move fast, and I had to make it count.

My left foot found purchase, I put my head down—and charged.

Clifton stopped advancing on Hugo and spun around when he heard my boots slapping down on the smooth stone. He opened his mouth to speak but nothing came out.

I hit him in the chest at full speed, squeezed with all my might and shoved off with the last of my strength.

The world dropped away.

They say when you are about to die your life flashes before your eyes. But the last thing I saw as I wrapped my arms around Clifton and pulled us both over the side of the cliff was Hugo's face falling away, his small mouth open, crying out as he watched us plummet over the side.

CHAPTER 22

I woke up dry-heaving, lying on a patch of wet pine needles, gasping for air.

My eyes snapped open and saw Clifton leaning over me, wiping his mouth, his face twisted with pain.

I tried to struggle away from him but he pushed me back to the ground. "Breathe, Marley. Just breathe. Alright? Take a few breaths and don't move."

There wasn't any choice. My entire body screamed with pain and all I could do was collapse on my back and shiver. I was soaking wet, through and through, and the ground beneath me was drenched.

Clifton trembled from exhaustion and dropped back on his haunches. He closed his eyes and used one shaking hand to wipe the mass of soaked blond hair out of his eyes. He turned back to me, still panting from effort, and scowled.

"Young woman, that was the single most insane act I have ever had the bad fortune to witness. Would you care to explain to me, exactly, what the devil it was you thought you were doing?"

It felt like someone had taken a blowtorch to my throat. I tried to speak, but it was more of a croak than actual words.

"You killed my grandfather."

Clifton stared at me. He couldn't even blink for a moment. "I most certainly did not."

"Badger Hand."

A flash of realization marred his expression. He dropped his head into his palms and sighed.

"Do you honestly mean to tell me you believe I am capable of murder? What possible reason could I have for shooting the only advocate I had in this wretched town?"

"He caught you planting the fakes."

Clifton laughed. "Your grandfather had no idea what I was planning to do. How could he expose me if he wasn't even aware of what I was about to do?"

"He was your friend," I said, trying to push myself up.

"And I was his."

He watched me struggling and pushed me back down with one hand. "Would you please stay still? You nearly died."

I fell back again, trying to make sense out of what had just happened.

The two of us were beside a deep-blue pool of water. Wet drag marks across the stones leading from the pool told me that Clifton had pulled me out, and the pain in my chest told me he had given me CPR. Lucky for me, Clifton had chased Hugo up the trail in June. Had this been October, the pool would have been mostly empty, and I doubted very much either one of us would be having this conversation.

I noticed that the pain in my ankle wasn't as bad. Probably because hypothermia was setting in.

"Considering what you just put me through, I would say it's quite remarkable that I didn't simply allow you to drown."

I shivered fiercely as I cast a dubious look in his direction.

"Yes," he said, looking at me with a lilting and condescending tone to his voice. "You are trying to sort it all out in your head, aren't you? If I am a mindless killer, why in the world would I salvage your miserable hide when I had the perfect opportunity to let you die?"

I coughed up another half cup of water. "I'm still working on that."

"When you come to the conclusion that you have just made a terrible error in judgment, please let me know."

"Hugo was terrified," I said.

"And in retrospect, I could have handled the situation better. I'm afraid that I am not very good with children."

"Or adults," I said, coughing the last bit of water out of my lungs. Finally, I started to breathe normally again.

Clifton peeled off his beautiful fringe leather jacket and let it fall in a sodden heap. "This was Italian."

I was shivering so violently I had bitten the inside of my cheek. "Is help coming?"

"The young man is calling from his aunt's residence. Until someone arrives to retrieve you, I'm afraid you are stuck with me."

I took in a few ragged breaths. "I thought you would hurt Hugo."

Clifton flashed a furious look my way, but then his face eased to an expression of irritation. "I suppose I can see how you may have thought that. But your actions here today . . ."

He waved a hand at the pool beside us and closed his mouth.

When he spoke, it was with reluctance. "Initially, the boy agreed to allow me to see the points in order to properly identify them. We rode together amicably enough in the car, and the boy insisted he would retrieve the points from the house and bring them straight out, but when he vanished out the back door I was concerned he intended to hide them. I thought it best that I take possession of them, for safekeeping."

All of the anger I'd felt had washed away the moment I'd hit the water. I still despised Clifton, but suddenly I had serious doubts about myself. Had I gotten everything wrong?

There was one way to find out.

"I have the Clovis points," I said.

He shot me a perturbed look. "They are not in the boy's backpack?"

"At the café."

"What is he guarding so valiantly, then?"

"Pelican Lake points."

Clifton snorted. "Worthless waste of time."

"An antiquities expert has seen the Clovis points. He told me you had them fabricated."

Clifton's mouth curved slightly, but that was the only indication he'd heard me at all.

Questions were swirling in my head, and I needed answers.

"Why didn't you come back to our ranch after that summer?" I asked.

"I seriously doubt you would believe me," he said.

I shivered so hard my teeth clattered together. "Try me."

Clifton settled his eyes on me and the look on his face was not what I expected to see.

"I was too naïve in 1977 to realize there is no such thing as a jade arrowhead. It wasn't until I

240

had studied archaeology, working for my doctoral degree, that I discovered what an amateurish mistake I'd made. I was willing to leave the Clovis points buried on your grandfather's ranch forever. Until that graduate student from U.W. came up here and forced my hand."

"So you came back to Killdeer to make sure your mistake wasn't ever discovered," I said.

"It was my attempt at damage control."

"Why didn't you come back sooner than this to try and clean up your mess?" I asked.

"Your grandfather meant a great deal to me. The old coot could grow on a person. Tough, respected. He loved a challenge. We were good friends, and I suppose the fact that he was dead was something I didn't necessarily want to face. It was easier to let it alone than to go back to the ranch and see where it had all happened. "

His tone was so defeated that, to my surprise, I believed him. Maybe he was conning me, maybe not, but in an instant I got the feeling I was finally seeing a genuine human moment from him.

Clifton looked disgusted. "I don't care if you believe me or not. That's the truth of it."

"Do you know who killed him?" I asked.

"How could I possibly know that?" he snapped. "I always assumed it was a fight over water rights or grazing leases."

"I thought he had caught you hiding the arrowheads and you'd argued about it," I confessed.

"Wherever did you get that idea? It's nonsense, in any case. No one knew about the Clovis points. Not even your grandfather."

He pulled a clump of moss out of the collar of his shirt, glanced behind me and his head fell back with relief. "Help has arrived at last."

Clifton stood up and waved both arms over his head. The backs of his knuckles were scratched and bleeding, but other than that he looked like he had survived the fall unscathed.

I tried to flex my ankle and realized it had gone numb.

A shadow fell across me and I smiled in spite of my injuries. "Hey, Loy."

"Hun? Hugo said you had an accident."

He dropped to the ground beside me and scooped up my hand.

"Something like that," I said.

"She and I wanted to take the express ride down from the trail," Clifton told him. "I'm afraid it's my fault, Sheriff. She warned me not to stand too close to the edge and I'm afraid I lost my balance and pulled us both down when I fell."

I tried to sit up. "Loy, that's not what—"

"She may babble nonsense at you, Sheriff. But it's entirely possible she hit her head when we landed."

"Let's get you out of here," Loy told me, getting to his feet and shifting his gun belt.

Hugo was walking towards us, towing the black horse I'd stolen from Willy. He looked frightened, but he also looked immensely relieved when he saw me sitting up.

Loy trotted a few paces away to retrieve the horse and I snagged Clifton's pant leg with one hand.

"What are you doing? That's not what happened and you know it."

"And I suppose you would enjoy spending the next twenty years or so in prison for attempted manslaughter?" he asked.

"Why are you doing this?"

"I told you. Your grandfather was my friend. Now keep your impulsive little mouth shut."

Loy lifted me into the saddle and I collapsed on the horse's neck. When we reached the caretaker's house I saw to my dismay that Finn's black Jeep was parked in the driveway.

Finn stood beside it, his face pale.

"Radio chatter," he said, explaining how it was he knew to be there.

Loy lifted me off of the horse and carried me like a sack to his sheriff's vehicle. I was starting to get feeling back in my ankle, which was a terrible, terrible thing.

Finn hovered behind Loy, managing to stay out of the way and yet maintaining a view of everything happening. "What can I do?"

Loy finished tucking me inside the Blazer and shut the door, but I could still hear what he told Finn.

"Go get her dad."

As Loy headed for the driver's side door, stopping to address Clifton for a moment, Hugo rapped on the window beside me. I managed to roll it down.

"He saved you," Hugo said, looking at Clifton with awe. "I saw him. He saved you from the water."

"I'm so sorry," I told him. "I made a really bad mistake."

"It's okay," he said. "You didn't know."

Loy started the engine of his truck and we left the house with sirens blaring. As if I wasn't already embarrassed enough.

We drove to Parkman to the hospital emergency room and when I felt the first blessed caress of morphine I came to my senses enough to ask Loy the obvious.

"What happened to Clifton? He should be here too."

"He said he had better things to do than hang around a hospital with a bunch of sick people," Loy said.

I was almost able to laugh.

The sheriff squeezed my hand. "You are going to be fine, Marley. But I don't think Wendy is going to let you babysit anymore."

CHAPTER 23

After X-rays and a plaster cast that made me feel like I was a fossil getting my very own field jacket, I was able to leave the hospital at last. Hobbling on a pair of crutches and feeling lower and more foolish than I ever had, I was told that I'd broken one of the bones in my ankle, and although I didn't necessarily feel all that lucky, the emergency room doctor had informed me it was a far better injury than having a separated tendon. At least this way I could avoid surgery.

My father drove me back to Leif's house, scolding me soundly about how dangerous it was to get carried away up on the hiking trails and how I needed to be more careful, and set a good example for Hugo, and about a dozen other things that popped into his mind concerning my personal safety.

I accepted his tirade wordlessly, all the while still grappling with how wrong I had actually been.

Clifton had stuck his neck out for me when he had absolutely no reason to do it. I couldn't help but believe he had not been the one who had killed my grandfather after all.

Luckily for me, the painkillers from the hospital helped me forget the fact that I was a complete twerp.

Three long drug-hazy days passed by before I was able to finally sleep through an entire night again.

The pain had subsided enough that if I held my right ankle just so, I could drop off into a blessedly sound sleep until I made the mistake of moving, and the sharp pang woke me again.

By Monday morning I managed to hobble downstairs on my own and tried to settle in on the couch for a day of mindless television to distract me from my troubles. I had bruises on top of my bruises above my cast. I hated to think what my ankle must have looked like.

As I got settled on the downstairs couch, Leif clucking over me like a barnyard hen, I had to face the fact that I would never know who had been the one who pulled the trigger thirty-four years ago. Pursuing it any longer wouldn't do a bit of good. And likely, at the rate I was going, it would kill me.

The couch was too warm, my tea was too cold and my bladder was too full. The day promised to be boring, long and tedious, and when the telephone rang I hoped that it was my doctor calling to inform me my driving privileges had once again been restored.

No such luck.

But the phone call did promise to put an end to my doldrums. Leif informed me that my father and Jimmy Burke would be stopping by to see me.

After they arrived I could see right away from the expressions on both their faces this wasn't simply a social call. I was a little surprised that Jimmy was still in Killdeer, and hadn't gone back to Wyoming, and as they both sat down I grew more and more suspicious.

Jimmy contented himself with the chair, and my father lounged on the love seat. The living room was an average temperature, but Leif had piled comforters and blankets on top of me all morning. The man was nothing if not thorough. I tossed my heavy blanket off and gingerly adjusted my leg. It was propped on a footstool and it ached like the dickens.

The cast was itchy, and over the last three days various visitors had stopped by to say hello, and a few of them had signed it.

Hugo had signed the cast with a black Sharpie marker. It said "Geronimo!" in block letters.

I didn't think it was very funny but Hugo thought it was hysterical.

"Word's got out, Kiddo," my father said. "I got contacted by an auction house and they want the dinosaur."

"That was fast. Who contacted you?" I asked.

"Bonhams & Butterfields is having the auction in Los Angeles on December 11. That only leaves me five months, maybe a little more, to study the specimen," Jimmy told me.

"Can you do it in five months?" I asked.

"It should have five years of research done on it after I get the thing properly identified."

"Yes, but you don't have five years," my father said.

"Dad, why are you so determined to sell it?" I asked.

My father propped his chin on his palm, one elbow resting on his knee, his tone cool. "Because that auction house says they can get big bucks for the thing."

My ankle suddenly didn't hurt as much. "Wow."

"Yeah, wow, but what about the science? What if I can't finish my research by then?" Jimmy asked.

"This auction is important," my father said, as if that answered the question.

"There will be other auctions," Jimmy insisted.

"Not as likely to attract the hordes of fossil collectors," my father replied.

"Hold it, hold it. Why not? I mean, what's so special about this auction?" I asked.

My father held out his hands. "It's got lots and lots of rocks."

Jimmy rolled his eyes.

It was all clear to me now. Jimmy and my father had come to visit me so I could mediate their dispute. In my painkiller-induced haze, I doubted very much that I would be able to do much good in the negotiation department.

"Dad, won't you have another chance to put it on the block?"

"Sure, but this auction is getting international attention. It will be specifically about fossils and such, so we stand a chance of getting the best bids."

"You sound like you spent a lot of time talking to the appraisers at Bonhams," Jimmy said.

My father sat back in the love seat. "Matter of fact, I did."

"Marley, can you talk your dad into seeing reason? I need more time."

"I've got another hospital bill that I won't be able to pay, and you are telling me that I need to talk sense into my dad when someone wants to hand him a big pile of cash?"

Leif had been leaning in the doorway to the kitchen, a cup of coffee in one hand, an interested expression on his face. When I looked his way he gave me a warm smile.

"Dad, can't you make the sale contingent on a window of delivery, or something?"

"I could, I suppose. But I know what Bonhams will tell me. They'll say if I do that it will discourage bidders."

I gave Leif a desperate look. "What do you think?"

Leif took a sip of coffee. He started with my father first, using his skills as a negotiator. "Nathan, how critical is it that you have access to those funds in six months?"

My father scratched the side of his face where a day's worth of stubble had accumulated. "I could sure use the money, Leif. I really could. Reimbursing Lewis Pritchett for his million-dollar bull has really set me back."

"Jimmy, what is the shortest amount of time it would take you to finish your thesis?" Leif asked.

Jimmy grumbled and rubbed his forehead with one hand. "Absolute minimum for study of this fossil? I'd like a year."

"I didn't ask that," Leif said, his voice level.

Jimmy shrugged. "If I had to, I could do it in ten months. But that is the worst-case scenario."

"Hey, what if a university or a museum bought the skull? Couldn't Jimmy study it in their facility?" I asked.

Leif shook his head. "Let's not speculate about the identity of the highest bidder. That's not a variable we can control. More than likely it will go to a private collector and that will be the last time it will see the light of day. I'm sorry, Jimmy. But if I were you I would do what I could to finish up your work inside that five-month time frame. Nathan, the best course of action you can take at this time is to sell the fossil and start investing that profit into something that will get you a regular, dependable income."

My father looked pleased, but Jimmy looked crushed.

Leif turned to me. "As for your medical expenses. Don't you think it's time you got yourself a health insurance policy? You do seem to be a bit accident-prone."

"Have you seen the premiums?" I asked.

"All the more reason that you and I should get married, sooner rather than later, Marley. I've got a very reasonable health-care plan."

My father's eyes shot towards Leif. "You want to marry my daughter?"

"If she'll have me," Leif replied.

"Why?" my father asked, incredulous.

"Hello? I'm sitting right here," I said.

"She's resilient," Leif said, a grin spreading across his face.

"But you've had her cooking," my father said.

"Dad. I can hear you," I said.

"I'll admit, she's a good housekeeper. But her temper? I could go on and on . . .," my father continued.

"You see me, right?" I asked Jimmy.

Jimmy just shook his head.

"I think it's a great idea," my father said. "You know, it's traditional here in Montana for the groom to give the father ten steers, after a date is set."

"What? No it's not," I said, trying to reach one of my pillows so I could smack him with it.

But Leif was loving the game and chuckled. "Only ten? She's a bargain."

"I wish I had another daughter, I'd charge you fifteen steers for two."

"I hate both of you," I said.

Jimmy rubbed his eyes with the heels of his palms and yawned. "I'm glad somebody is getting what they want."

The phone rang and Leif gave us an apologetic wave as he ducked down the stairs. I heard his door shut and knew he was probably on a business call.

"This is great news," my father said. "You and Leif. I think it's a good move."

I felt a bit sheepish that he had found out like this. "You really think so?"

"Leif is a good man. I couldn't have handpicked a better partner for you."

"Well, thanks, Dad. I think he is too."

"But you haven't said yes yet?"

"I just said we needed to talk about it a little more."

Jimmy made an exasperated sound. "What about the dinosaur, Nathan? What's your decision? I need to get moving on the research if you are only going to give me five months."

My father eased himself back in the love seat. He looked torn. "I need to make a call here don't I?"

"If the auction house is right, and this is going to be the best opportunity to sell the fossil for a good price, I think you should go for it, Dad."

Jimmy sighed and flopped back in his chair. "I should have stolen the thing when I had a chance."

I cleared my throat. "What he means—"

"It's fine, Nathan. It's fine," Jimmy said hastily. "I understand. I've got a huge student loan that I have to start chipping away at after I graduate.

Nobody needs to tell me how hard it is when money's tight."

"It's not personal, son. You understand? Being a rancher ain't easy. And I know I owe you a great deal because you found the thing, but I've got an opportunity here to set myself and my daughter up with a secure future. You got to see that takes priority, right?"

Jimmy gave my father a forgiving look. "I'd probably do the same thing."

After murmuring platitudes at each other for a while, my father and Jimmy left at the same time, shaking hands and both insisting that there were no hard feelings.

But I knew there were.

Leif came back to the living room after they were gone and settled beside me on the couch.

He wrapped one arm around me and planted a kiss on my forehead.

"You don't seem very happy," he said.

I leaned against him, grateful for the support. "I feel bad for Jimmy, that's all."

"Now, why would you be feeling that?"

"Look at all the vultures who came swooping down on my father's property," I said, trying to explain how I felt. "The BLM, the Forest Service, the Colorado people. Out of the lot of them, Jimmy is the only one who seems to have anything resembling integrity. And he's the one who is getting the short end of the stick in this deal."

"I can see how you might think that. But in fact Jimmy is fortunate to have made the discovery at all, from everything you have told me. It may not be an ideal situation, but he's got something very important to work on and it could have turned out quite differently."

"You think so?" I asked.

Leif gave my shoulders a hard squeeze. "He could have dug and not have found anything at all."

I allowed myself one wistful moment to imagine the peace and quiet we would still have had in Killdeer if the grad student had never reopened the quarry.

Still, maybe Leif was right. Perhaps the discovery was more important.

Even though the situation seemed to be turning out great for my father, a part of me wished that the dinosaur skull could stay in the family for a little while longer, if for no other reason than to give Jimmy time to finish working on his thesis. It was an enormous investment he had made, and just when he seemed to be getting close to the finish line it looked like his golden opportunity was being taken away through no fault of his own.

It was a sad reality, but it seemed that in the world of artifacts and fossils, nice guys did finish last.

CHAPTER 24

Tuesday morning I was starting to feel restless again. I'd spoken to my boss at the branch library and told her I would need to take the day off, but after that I would be able to work again, albeit at a slow pace.

By the middle of the week I figured I would be able to wean myself off the painkillers enough to work an entire day without falling asleep.

Leif had been amazing. He'd grilled pork ribs, fixed corn on the cob, fetched herbal tea and generally mothered me. By Tuesday afternoon I was shooing him away and telling him he needed to prepare for his trip to Panama the next day. He'd postponed it to accommodate my injury, but it was time for him to get back to work.

We didn't discuss it, but we both understood that after his return we would be sitting down to talk about our future. I wasn't certain how I felt about it. Of course I couldn't think of a better man than Leif Gable. He was kind, thoughtful, capable and, most important, he didn't micromanage my life. He gave me space to be myself but at the same time he was always available whenever I needed him. He was the perfect balance of attentive and respectful.

But he wanted to marry me. What did that say about his relationship judgment?

Scolding myself, I realized the most important question wasn't whether or not he had good relationship judgment, it was if I loved the man. Being trapped on the couch for four days had given me a lot of time to explore that issue, and the truth was that I did love him. My reservations about starting a new life with him were a product of my volatile experience with Finn, nothing more. Where Finn had been unpredictable and distant, Leif was reliable and present. It made no sense to me that I would shy away from making a commitment to Leif, because when I was with him I felt happy and secure.

If nothing else, my busted ankle had given me time to find clarity on that particular aspect of my life.

The doorbell rang and I jumped. I hadn't even heard a car drive up, and I fumbled for my crutches clumsily before managing to make it to the door.

"Hey, Hugo."

He stood on the porch, clutching a paper bag stuck with a bright red bow. His backpack was slung from one shoulder and he grinned when he saw me. "Hey, Aunt Marley."

Loy stood behind Hugo, thumbs hooked in his belt and a wide smile plastered across his face. Apparently things between the sheriff and Hugo's Aunt Wendy were going quite well if Loy was acting as chauffeur for the boy. "The two of us wanted to come by."

A quick and meaningful glance at Hugo told me Loy meant that the boy had wanted to come by, and the sheriff was simply a taxi service.

Loy sized me up. "How's the patient today?"

"I'm doing much better. Leif has taken very good care of me. I will probably heal twice as fast."

Hugo handed me the gift bag he clutched in his hands. "My Aunt Wendy says you need to learn how to knit since you will be stuck inside with nothing to do all day."

I took the bag and peered in. Two balls of creamy yarn were tucked inside, and a pair of pale wooden knitting needles rested on top of them.

"You tell your Aunt Wendy I said thank you." I set the bag on a small end table by the door and tamped down my guilt. There wasn't a chance I'd be teaching myself to knit, no matter how bored I got.

"Can you drive yet?" Loy asked me.

"Finally. I have to use my left foot for both the gas pedal and the brake, but I manage."

"I was hoping you could take Hugo back into town for me. I need to make a detour up to Fable and see about a missing motorcycle."

"Sure. I'd be happy to."

Leif had come up the stairs from his office and draped an arm over my shoulder. He was careful not to put any weight on me, and hugged me to his side. "Hello, Loy. Good to see you. Would you like to come in?"

Loy shook his head and took a step off the porch. "I better get. But thanks. See you later, Hugo?"

"Thank you for the ride," Hugo said mechanically. Obviously his mother had instilled in him the importance of saying "please" and "thank you" to adults.

Loy drove away and Hugo and I settled back on the couch just as the telephone rang.

Leif had disappeared into the kitchen, and since it was the house line and not his office telephone, I felt safe answering. More than likely it wasn't anything to do with business.

"Gable residence."

"Marley? This is John Taylor. How are you doing?"

"I've been better," I said.

"Oh. I'm sorry to hear that," he replied. "Is this a bad time to talk?"

"No, it's actually a really good time," I said, easing his concern.

"I was hoping you wouldn't mind me calling you at home, I got this number from your dad and he suggested I speak to you directly."

Hugo had settled on the big leather chair and had magically discovered the hidden TV remote. He was busy exploring the cable channels. I hadn't seen the remote for two days and somehow he'd managed to locate it in a matter of seconds.

John spoke into the phone with his signature quiet, deliberate tone. He sounded purposeful. Whatever he had to say, it was important.

"I drove out to the Cheyenne Indian reservation and I managed to get a few minutes with the man I was telling you about. He was . . . very helpful."

That was interesting. My curiosity was certainly piqued. "What did he have to say?"

"I asked him about Clifton Myers, and he told me that he remembered him. Clifton asked him to make a set of arrowheads the summer he was in Killdeer. Badger Hand seemed to recall that it was a set of fifteen."

"Fifteen?" I asked. "But there were only fourteen arrowheads in the hole. What happened to the other one?"

"Do you remember that box of Pelican Lake points that Hugo showed to me? Well, I recall there was one point with them that didn't match. It was beat up considerably and broken in half, but I would guess it is the missing Clovis point. Clifton somehow contrived it so that one of his fakes made it into that box, probably to lend his find authenticity."

"So that accounts for them all. Are you sure Badger Hand didn't make any more arrowheads for Clifton?"

"I'm sure. He said that he never saw Clifton Myers again."

Hugo was watching me now, suddenly interested in the conversation. He turned off the television.

"So, does this mean that the cache of arrowheads Clifton discovered in South Dakota was legitimate?" I asked.

"I did some research and apparently Clifton's site in South Dakota contained two dozen artifacts. Arrowheads, scrapers, you name it. It was a very comprehensive find. When I asked Badger Hand if he had fabricated anything other than arrowheads, he said that he hadn't. Now, I was talking to him through his granddaughter, and she was more interested in asking me about what kind of cell phone I preferred. Come to think of it, she could have been his great-granddaughter. In any case, the only thing I was able to find out is that if Myers planted fake arrowheads in South Dakota, he didn't use any that were made by Badger Hand."

"That's a surprise," I said.

"For me too. I suppose even a broken clock is right twice a day," John said.

"Thanks for finding out this information for me."

"You might not thank me after I tell you what else I managed to find out," he said.

"That doesn't sound good."

He made a glum noise. "It's not. I may have told you that I keep tabs on things pretty well in my area, and I've the benefit of a few friendships with some of the BLM staff at our local office here in Wyoming. Please don't let anyone know how you got this information, but I think that the Montana Bureau is planning to issue a notice of intent to impound the arrowheads discovered on your ranch."

"Can they do that?" I asked, incredulous.

"They can try."

"You realize how nuts that is," I said.

"Considering the fact that they are fakes? I do, but the Bureau doesn't know that."

"This is not good. If my father finds out about this, he will dig in his heels and fight them just for the privilege."

"Marley, the government has very deep pockets. I don't think that is a fight he can win," John said evenly.

I heard a sudden racket on John's end of the phone and his hasty voice came out in a rush. "Marley, I have to let you go. I just caught a bear in my pack-rat trap."

The phone went dead and I punched the button to hang up the receiver.

"I suppose the peanut butter did the trick," I muttered.

"What did he say?" Hugo asked.

I was sorting it all out in my head, but one thing was abundantly clear. I needed to forget about Clifton Myers and leave the man alone. I needed to let go of whatever personal vendetta I'd nurtured against him. And, honestly, I no longer had the will to ruin him. Nearly killing us both had erased my resentment.

"Hugo, do you still have those Pelican Lake points in your backpack?"

He scooped up his pack and unzipped it, letting the flap fall open. He pulled out the bubble-wrapped Pelican Lake points and set them on the coffee table. I eased myself down to the floor and the two of us unwrapped them until I found the one I was looking for.

"This is it," I said, holding it up to the light. It was the broken half-Clovis point that had been inside the wooden box for all those years.

"Does this one go with Jimmy's points?" Hugo asked.

"It sure does. John Taylor told me that all together there were fifteen. This is the last one."

It was a match for the other points that had been found at the dig site—at least, what was left of it was—and I carefully set it apart from the others. Irene still had possession of the wooden box, and when I was feeling up to it, the stray half-Clovis point would be reunited with the others.

So they were all accounted for, but now the question was, what in the world to do with them? The very thought of the BLM filing notice on my father made my eyes water. The legal wrangling could go on for months.

One solution would be to simply hand them over. But to who?

The notion of giving the arrowheads to Rob Powers at the BLM office turned my stomach, and even though she had apologized for her pushy behavior I wasn't crazy about giving them to Amelia Snow, either.

For a moment, I really considered taking them back up to the damn site and burying them again. But I shrugged that thought away when I realized an artifact thief wouldn't hesitate to trespass if he thought he could get away with it. Someone had shot Rufus and tried to steal the arrowheads once before, and if any arrowheads were discovered by a thief on our property, there wasn't a doubt in my mind that a greedy pot hunter would try it again given half the chance and we would never get any peace.

I didn't want those points anywhere near us. And as much as I personally disliked Clifton Myers, my heart wasn't in it anymore to ruin him. Revealing the arrowheads as fakes would only leave raw feelings, and who was to say the BLM would believe they weren't real?

There had to be a better way.

Then something occurred to me. What if the arrowheads were given to someone with the resources and an undisputed legal authority to take possession of them?

"Hugo, run up to my bedroom and look in the nightstand beside the bed. Grab me that address book in the drawer."

"Which one is your bedroom?" he asked, getting to his feet.

"The one with the big four-post bed."

He scampered up the stairs and was back in a flash. I scanned the address book for a number I'd never expected to need again, and punched it into the phone.

"Who are you calling?" Hugo asked.

"The Crow Indian reservation," I said, listening to the phone ring.

Hugo sat back down and watched me attentively.

A woman's voice answered on the fourth ring. "Kay-Hay."

"Wilma? This is Marley Dearcorn over in Killdeer. How are you?"

She didn't reply for a moment, and I supposed she was placing me in her mind.

"Dearcorn. Oh, yes."

"Is your son at home today? Could I speak to him?"

She fumbled with the phone and I could hear her talking to someone.

A man's voice came over the receiver and I recognized it at once.

"Yes?"

"Martin Flies Low? This is Marley. Marley Dearcorn."

"What do you want?" he asked.

Same Martin that I remembered. We were not exactly friends, but we had an understanding with each other. Martin's son had been killed on our land the previous winter. Somehow we had gotten through the ordeal, and though Martin had no love for me, at least he didn't hate my guts anymore.

"Listen, are you still friends with the secretary of the tribal council?" I asked.

He paused, probably trying to calculate exactly what it was I wanted from him.

"Yes."

"Good, good. I was wondering if you would be willing to do something for me."

He grumbled a few unintelligible words. Then he sighed. "What?"

I glanced over at Hugo and gave him a slight smile. "Martin. How would you like to stick it to the white man?"

CHAPTER 25

The ceremony was scheduled for 3 p.m. It was only 2:45 and the building was packed to capacity. Everybody loved a good show.

Killdeer had one true historical building still standing and the residents of our little town took every opportunity to use it when we could.

It had been a saloon, appropriately enough. Originally, prospectors had founded Killdeer, but the industry that had truly established the town had been logging. Loggers and gold miners had their priorities. The one historical building that had been built to last in Killdeer had been the one that served the most whiskey.

The historical building was large enough to hold 175 people, according to the fire inspector's sign by the door, but glancing around it was pretty obvious there were at least 200 people milling around and hurrying for the few chairs remaining.

Every window shade was pulled up, and sunlight poured in, dappling the old wooden floors with Appaloosa spots of brightness.

Casey Chastity stood at attention against the wall, her cameraman perched by her side untangling his gear.

She held her microphone like a hired gunslinger.

Rob Powers had taken up a position beside her on the off chance that she might spontaneously develop the urge to interview him. He had ditched his usual field hat and had opted for a British-style safari helmet. Once again he had managed to come off looking like a complete Twinkie.

Amelia Snow popped into view, partially hidden behind the doorway leading to the old restrooms. I hadn't noticed her at first—I had not seen the Forest Service truck parked on the street outside—and I hadn't realized Amelia was even in the crowd of onlookers until she had peeked out from behind the corner. She wore her standard moccasins, long braids, and today, for the occasion, she had pulled out her very best authentic deerskin shirt complete with elk-teeth accents. Two Crow men had come to the ceremony, most likely guests of Martin's, and they had given her strange looks, but were too polite to say anything. I wondered if any of Amelia's friends had ever screwed up the courage to tell her she looked ridiculous.

The ladies from the Historical Society were clustered around Hugo, fussing over him like grandmothers and reminding him of his important upcoming duty. Hugo looked determined. He seemed to be the only one who wasn't fawning for the cameras, and it occurred to me that the kid was a natural when it came to this sort of thing.

My father stood next to me, and I stood next to Martin Flies Low. We had managed to organize the ceremony in a mere three days and I was relieved it seemed like everything was going smoothly. The University of Colorado contingent must have had plenty of housing money left in their travel budget, because Clifton Myers and his anthropology students had arranged to linger in

Killdeer. They had taken up positions at the foot of the stage.

It was no surprise to me that Clifton had volunteered to officiate the presentation. Since my father had absolutely no interest in getting up in front of a large crowd of people in order to give a speech, it had all worked out for the best, and Dr. Myers would be representing our family.

The only person missing from the whole affair was Jimmy Burke. I wished he could have returned from Wyoming to see the ceremony. I was proud of my crazy idea for how to deal with the arrowheads, and I wished that the grad student could have seen how it all turned out in the end.

I sensed a presence beside me and I turned to see Deputy Wilcox standing on my left and surveying the crowd with an air of annoyance.

"Nick. I didn't know you were a student of history."

The deputy spared me a scowl. "Loy told me to come and do crowd control. For what? A bunch of little old ladies from the Historical Society and a gang of geeks from a university? I've got better things to do."

"You know what I like the most about you, Nick?" I asked.

He pretended to examine his badge and ignored me.

"It's your positive attitude. It's really inspirational," I said.

A stage had been set up at the end of the great hall with stairs on either side. It was wide enough to support a row of chairs, mostly filled with local Historical Society members, and of course, the mayor of Killdeer. David Jordan beamed at his constituents from his post on the stage. For the most part the Historical Society ladies ignored him but he seemed oblivious to their snubs and grinned at the crowd happily.

Hugo kept glancing in my direction, looking slightly stiff in his department store blue suit, as the moment of the ceremony crept closer and closer. I caught his eye and gave him a thumbs up.

Clifton Myers stood behind the women from the Historical Society with a solemn demeanor, looking like he had done this very ritual a thousand times before.

Martin Flies Low waited beside me, fidgeting with nervous energy. I could hardly blame him.

I had told Martin the truth about the arrowheads. He knew that without question they were not genuine artifacts. But after I had explained to him that a local pot hunter had tried to steal them, and that the local BLM office wanted to confiscate the cache, Martin had agreed to this elaborate ruse. It gave him an opportunity to prevent the government from getting what they wanted. We had agreed to pretend they were the genuine article, and Martin had assured me that after the ceremony the arrowheads would all be destroyed. Neither one of us wanted to take the chance that they might make it back into circulation again.

The president of the local Historical Society stepped up to the podium and watched the crowd expectantly. She reminded me of Queen Elizabeth in her pale blue dress and pillbox hat.

She smiled at the assembled group and spoke into the microphone.

Her voice carried to the back of the room and everyone settled down to listen. "Thank you for coming. Today is a great day for those of us who possess a desire to preserve the past, and for those who wish to honor the ancestors of the ancient people who have called this land home for generations. Today, we wish to repatriate the items that were once held in the hands of the forbearers of the local Crow Nation, and now I would like to introduce Dr. Clifton Myers, the man who discovered these wonderful treasures."

"He didn't discover them," I said with a groan.

"Who cares who discovered them?" Martin asked. His back was ramrod straight as he prepared to play his part in the ceremony. He was dressed in a snappy western suit and tasteful silver bolo tie, and he wore a sharp Stetson cowboy hat that probably cost more than half of my wardrobe. Martin was not the most personable man I had ever met, but he sure knew how to dress.

He kept his eyes on the podium as he spoke. "This isn't about recognizing the people who discovered the arrowheads, remember?"

I grumbled but I didn't press the issue.

My father put a hand on my shoulder and glanced down at my crutches. "How are you doing? Need to go sit down yet?"

"I'm alright. I should have taken a pain pill before we came down here but I don't think this will take very long."

"Thank God for that," Nick said, tilting his head back and shuffling both feet impatiently.

Casey Chastity and her cameraman were busy worming their way to the podium in order to get a better view of the presentation.

As she squeezed between the Colorado anthropology students, I noticed Max staring at her shamelessly. She eased past him and his face broke into a lecherous half-grin.

Apparently Max was not any worse for wear after I had assaulted him in Lil's. I would be apologizing to Irene for months after that fiasco. I had flat refused to apologize to Max, though, no matter how out of line I had been. When he caught sight of me looking at him he glanced away and pretended he hadn't seen me.

"Thank you, Miss Tipton," Clifton said as he stepped forward. He settled at the podium, doing his best to affect an expression of reverence.

Martin started to move to the front of the crowd towards the stage, and Amelia Snow quietly stepped into the spot he had vacated. It was a tight squeeze. I noticed with satisfaction the building was buzzing with excitement.

Word of the arrowheads from the Dearcorn Ranch being returned to the Crow Nation would spread through the valley like wildfire. Everyone would know now that our ranch was no longer a good place to hunt for artifacts.

"How in the hell is he managing to keep a straight face?" My father was staring at Clifton with a frown.

"Dad, shh. This is a great day for history, remember?"

Amelia glanced at us over the rims of her thick glasses. "This is what should have happened a long time ago."

I was about to ask her what she meant by that statement, but Clifton erupted into his speech.

"I became a scientist due to my insatiable curiosity about the world around us. In the past, the desire to collect and display artifacts sometimes outweighed the greater and nobler need to respect the religious and cultural treasures of the ancient people who populate this area. But we have before us an opportunity to right what was once wrong, and to that end, I would like to present to Martin Flies Low of the Crow Indian Nation an invaluable discovery that was made here in Killdeer Valley. Hugo?"

Hugo came forward. It was his job to hand the arrowheads to Clifton. It had been Clifton's idea, because he had wanted Hugo to feel included. I supposed it was his way of saying sorry to Hugo for their misunderstanding.

The large picture frame case was almost too much for Hugo to lift by himself and Clifton deftly darted a hand underneath to steady it.

Clifton took the case and I was duly impressed with how the display had turned out. The arrowheads had been mounted on a piece of black velvet cloth inside a beautiful oak frame.

"What is that?" asked Amelia. "Is that a display case?"

She was staring at the framed arrowheads, wearing an incredulous expression.

Martin moved to stand at the edge of the platform and reached out to accept the frame from Clifton. Wordlessly, Martin took the arrowheads and lifted them over his head so that the crowd of people could see them. Several people stepped forward to snap photographs.

Clifton leaned into the microphone, making sure to turn his best side to the cameras. "Martin has informed me that he will donate the arrowheads to the Custer Battlefield Museum. They will be proudly displayed as an example of the mastery possessed by the ancient peoples who once lived here."

Amelia gasped beside me and covered her mouth with her hand. "They can't do that."

What was she so upset about? Hadn't she wanted the artifacts to be well cared for?

Of course, I wasn't about to tell her that this entire presentation was just a show. So her reaction didn't make a bit of difference in the grand scheme of things. But still . . .

"They should have been left alone," Amelia muttered. She shoved her glasses back up on her nose and spun around. I watched her march out of the building with her head shaking back and forth with disgust.

"She have something against black velvet?" my father asked.

Martin had stepped up onto the platform and was busy posing for photographs with Clifton.

Hugo stood watching Martin Flies Low with an expression of awe. To Hugo, Martin was the Indian's Indian, with his piercing eyes and proud profile.

The boy was never going to forget this experience.

Finally Hugo came down from the stage so he could avoid the jostling adults.

He gave me a quick hug. "That was great. Can we do this again next year?"

"Your mother is going to let you come back?" I asked.

"Sure. We can do it all again next summer."

I hugged Hugo back and ruffled his hair. "Hopefully next time you come to Killdeer it will be a bit less exciting."

He darted off to join his Aunt Wendy. She tucked him under one arm and gave me a wave.

I felt my ankle throbbing and knew it was time to sit down. "Dad, I'm going back to the car. Take your time in here, and when Hugo is ready to escape let me know and we can go get an early supper."

My father snagged the deputy's shirtsleeve. "Do me a favor and walk my daughter to her car, would you?"

Nick's lip curled up. "Why?"

"Protect and serve," my father said cheerfully. "And besides, she will give you an excuse to get out of here."

"I'll take that," Nick said.

I never thought I would live to see the day, but as I clumsily made my way outside, Nick Wilcox held out his arm and helped steady me.

"Please don't make it a habit to be nice," I said as we shuffled to my SUV. "You wouldn't want to spoil your image."

"It'll never happen again."

The two of us slowly made our way across the green lawn, struggled down the high curb and began to cross the street. Luckily for me, no one else was leaving the presentation just yet and the street was quiet. We started towards my vehicle, which was parked along the opposite curb, and I was grateful I didn't have to hurry.

I heard a car door slam. Amelia Snow had climbed inside a huge battered blue diesel pickup truck parked against the curb five or six spaces behind my SUV. No wonder I hadn't seen her Forest Service truck. She was driving her own vehicle today. Amelia sat in the seat, staring straight ahead, her face livid. She furiously wiped a tear off her cheek and pounded the steering wheel with a fist.

Her reaction seemed overblown. Hadn't her goal all along been to see the arrowheads returned to the local tribe?

I stopped in the middle of the street to reposition my grip on the crutches, and Amelia started the engine of her truck.

She pumped the gas once, and I heard something that made me freeze.

I heard a whistle.

A loud—distinctly mechanical—whistle.

"Did you just break your other ankle, Dearcorn? Can we get out of the middle of the street or what?" Nick asked, looking at me petulantly.

I stood where I was, staring straight at Amelia's big diesel truck. "What is that? That whistling sound."

"It's a turbo," Nick said. "Turbo diesel. My cousin had one that sounded like that. I think it's annoying but he loved it."

"The truck is whistling?" I looked at Amelia's angry face and felt my heartbeat speeding up.

"It's the intake system," he told me. "They push a lot of compression and they suck a lot of air."

I spun away from Nick and hobbled my way right down the middle of the street straight towards Amelia. She didn't seem to register I was there and threw the truck in gear.

I heard Nick scramble after me. "Whoa! What are you doing?"

Amelia hit the accelerator. The big diesel belched smoke and nosed out of the parking space into the street with a lurch. Her eyes were unfocused and it was obvious she didn't even see me. She spun the wheel, pointed the truck down the street and punched the accelerator.

And came straight at me.

I stopped dead in her path. I was so angry I didn't even care if she ran me over, there was no way I was letting her drive away.

Nick leapt up beside me just as the bumper of the truck came within striking distance and slammed a hand on the hood of the truck.

"Stop!"

Amelia hit her brakes and blinked with shock. I saw the color drain from her face.

The deputy grabbed my elbow and gave it a shake. "You want to explain to me exactly what in hell you are doing?"

I glared straight at Amelia. "She shot Rufus."

"Lewis Pritchett's bull? Are you communing with the dead or something?"

"Nick," I said, my voice fierce. "You have got to trust me."

Amelia was still staring at us with amazement. The deputy's eyes darted from her to me, and he scrutinized my determined expression.

To his credit, Deputy Wilcox hesitated for only a moment. He automatically checked his sidearm and walked around the front of Amelia's truck.

"I'd like you to turn off the engine and step out of the vehicle."

Amelia set her jaw and for one horrible moment I thought she was going to ignore Nick and run us both down. Then she saw the look on the deputy's face, his hand resting on his pistol, and thought better of it. She carefully put her truck in park and the engine died, much to my immense relief.

"What are you stopping me for?" She opened the door and swung her short legs out.

"I need you to stand next to your vehicle and keep both hands where I can see them at all times," he said, poised to react.

She eased herself to the ground with both hands raised, walked around the open door, turned to face her truck and held her hands apart at her waist. She glared at me viciously over her shoulder.

"Do you have any weapons inside your vehicle?" Nick asked.

The color came back to her face in a rush of anger and she didn't respond.

"Are there any weapons inside your vehicle?" Nick repeated. His tone was harsh.

"You know I carry a rifle in my truck. In the back." Her eyes had narrowed to mere slits.

Nick's forehead creased with concern. "I'm going to need to take a look at it."

My anger broke the dam and rushed over the spillway. Before I could stop myself the words came out in a torrent. "How could you do it? He didn't deserve that. How could you shoot him?"

She waved her arms, defiant. "He wouldn't listen to me. I never could get him to see reason. No one else on your ranch would defend them. I had to do something!"

I shook my head, dumbfounded. "He wouldn't listen to you?"

How could a bull listen to someone?

Nick was looking back and forth between me and Amelia, confused.

"I didn't have any choice," she said. "Clifton wrapped your grandfather around his little finger just like he did everyone else around him. I was the only one who saw what was really going on."

One of the crutches fell out of my grasp and clattered to the pavement.

Horrible realization hit me like a blow.

Amelia wasn't a pot hunter.

She was a murderer.

The words came out of my mouth seemingly of their own accord. "You couldn't get my grandfather to see reason. He was going to continue to let Clifton dig up graves on our land."

Her lower lip started to tremble. "I tried to talk to him. There wasn't anything else I could do. Neither he nor Nathan ever took me seriously. He didn't give me any choice!"

Nick was trying to decide if he should draw his weapon or his handcuffs.

"Why did you shoot him in the back?" I felt sick inside.

She let out a sob, her body shook once from a spasm of regret. Her voice came out like a tiny wail. "He . . . he laughed at me."

"You killed my grandfather because he laughed at you?"

"I killed him because he had no respect for the dead!"

"Amelia Snow, you have the right to remain silent . . ." Nick handcuffed her stoically, his voice calm and professional.

As the second cuff went around her wrist, I looked to the far curb and saw my father standing there watching the whole thing.

He looked stricken.

It was clear he had heard every word she'd said.

Nick noticed my father and held up a hand. "Nathan, I need you to step back."

Amelia spat her words at him like a viper. "You make me sick. They couldn't defend themselves and you stood by and did absolutely nothing to stop him."

My father took two giant steps and lunged for Amelia. Nick was ready for it and grabbed him by the arms. It was all the slim deputy could do to hold on.

"Nathan, stop." The deputy grappled my father but he was losing ground fast.

Clifton Myers appeared from nowhere and grabbed my father in a firm shoulder lock, pulled him off of the deputy and dragged him back.

"Come with me right now," Nick told Amelia. He hustled her out of my father's sight and dragged her by the elbows to his sheriff's truck.

When Amelia was gone Clifton finally relaxed his hold on my father and released him.

"Nathan, my boy. Rise above this."

"Why?" my father asked. He was in shock, but at least he was under control once more.

"She thought the site was a grave," I told him. "She thought Grandpa didn't do enough to protect it."

"My God," Clifton's shoulders slumped down. "How could that possibly be worth the life of another human being?"

I managed to retrieve my fallen crutch and leaned on it gratefully, feeling light-headed. "She's the one who shot Rufus. Jimmy said he heard a whistling sound the night someone tried to vandalize the site. Her truck made that sound when she started it. That's why I confronted her. She didn't know I was talking about the bull. She thought I was talking about Granddad and she just blurted it all out."

Both of them stared at me wordlessly. Finally, it was Clifton who spoke.

"I suppose we have to admit that for once a lack of concise communication produced positive results."

"Dad, I'm sorry. If I hadn't gone poking into this—"

"Marley, I don't ever want you to apologize again for asking questions. You hear me? Never again."

Hearing those words, I should have immediately felt vindicated. But as I watched my father slump down on the curb and curl his face into his hands to hide his sobs, I only felt a horrible weight of sadness.

Grief this deep drained the life out of everything it touched. My father was so shaken by what had happened he looked like another person to me, and I was so stunned I didn't even know how to comfort him. But Clifton Myers eased to the ground beside him with quiet fortitude and managed somehow to do what I couldn't. He gave my father silent support while honoring his pain.

I hobbled to the curb beside them and sat next to my father. The three of us stayed there well after all the other cars had filled up with chattering people and driven away. Nobody approached us. We were left to ourselves.

It was a long time before we managed to rise again.

CHAPTER 26

"It's a paddle." I put a hand over my father's arm "Not a fan. If you keep waving that thing you will be the proud owner of a fourteen-thousand-dollar meteorite from Arizona."

Our little group from the sticks sat together like tourists in a strange land, surveying the wealthy Los Angeles auction attendees.

Jimmy Burke sat on the other side of my father, staring at his paddle. "Number four? How did I get number four?"

"What's wrong with that?" I asked.

"Why couldn't I have gotten number six-eight-seven or something?"

"I have four ninety-two," my father said proudly.

I grabbed his arm again. "We know. Everyone in the building knows. You've been flapping that thing around like you are trying to help land a jet on an aircraft carrier."

"I think you may have driven the price up on that trilobite," Jimmy said.

"Where did Leif get that?" my father asked.

Leif sat beside me, sipping a rich-looking red wine.

His paddle was on the floor, sensibly stowed beneath his seat.

"Where'd you get the hooch, Gable?" my father asked.

I covered my eyes. "Dad. It's not hooch."

"It's a merlot," Leif said, leaning forward to chat with my father. "A Bogle reserve, I believe."

"Where did you get it? Is it free?"

"Dad—"

"It's medicinal," my father said. "Calms my nerves."

"Are you nervous?" I asked.

My father gestured to indicate the general crush of bodies in the large room. The space was filled to capacity. People stood at the back lined up along the wall like shy freshman at a homecoming dance. Bid callers stood at strategic locations around the packed room scanning the crowd, and it was sweltering hot even though it was December.

"Why would I be nervous?" my father asked. "In five minutes we could see Jimmy's dinosaur flop, and go home penniless."

"If it doesn't make the reserve you can keep it, Nathan," Jimmy pointed out. "I'd be fine with that outcome."

"Do you think that will happen?" I asked.

"Look at this crowd," Jimmy said miserably. "They'd bid on a pitcher of margarita mix if you held it up."

My father grunted. "Even if it sells, we can look forward to leaving the building and being killed instantly when we try to drive in this L.A. traffic."

Leif draped an arm over my shoulder and gave me a squeeze. "I've got to go make a phone call. I'll be right back."

He gave me a quick smooch on the forehead and set his wine glass under his chair. I had to slap my father's hand down again when he started to point at something with his paddle, and I didn't see which way Leif went, but I hoped he would be finished with his phone call in time to see the skull auctioned.

"Where's your husband going?" my father asked.

"We're not married yet."

"You and Leif are getting married?" Jimmy asked, leaning in to hear me better. "When?"

"We are still talking about it, but yes. It looks that way."

"You seem to be really laid-back about the whole thing," Jimmy said. "Didn't he pay your dad the ten steers yet?"

I was about to say something about turning Jimmy into a steer if he kept it up, but the auctioneer was suddenly announcing the final call on the meteorite.

"Fourteen-five? Do I hear fifteen? Going twice," he said.

He rapped the podium with his gavel. "Sold for fourteen-five to number . . . ? To number one eighty-five."

I was impressed with the entire operation. First of all, the auctioneer wore a suit. And his gavel had no handle. It was simple and elegant, like a carved wooden paperweight. When he concluded a sale he rapped it once on the podium politely. Very classy. In fact, two auctioneers stood at the podium, lending an air of professionalism to everything. They didn't appear to hurry. They enunciated carefully into a microphone instead of shouting out the bids like a pig caller the way all of the auctioneers from back home had a habit of doing. I had never seen an auction where the items up for bid were worth more than my father's house. Usually I was standing at the back of a small crowd of onlookers in someone's backyard while two dairy farmers rolled around on the ground fighting over who would get to bid on the heavy-duty Wilton shop bench-vise and matching pipe wrench.

This was the same planet, but a different world.

The woman on the other side of Jimmy was wearing a fur coat.

I wore a pair of black slacks and a blaze-red jacket, with a pair of simple black pumps. Glancing around at the other women in the audience of bidders, I should have been wearing about twenty pounds of platinum just to meet the minimum dress code requirement.

I self-consciously fingered the tiny pearl earrings I'd worn to spruce myself up a bit, and allowed myself a moment of self-pity. Likely, I would never be a guest at a champagne party on a yacht in the South Pacific.

But when I looked over at my father, sitting in his seat holding his paddle like it was a giant lollipop, I couldn't help but scold myself for feeling glum. I would never get another chance to see something like this again and shouldn't squander the moment by comparing my mother's hand-me-down pearls with the blinding glare from the sea of diamonds glittering in the crowd.

Since we had an item in the auction of some note, we had been invited to sit in the second row from the stage. At least, that was what Leif had told us as we had taken our seats. I had no doubt that someone in the auction firm was an old college buddy of his, or perhaps Leif had once been the CFO of the company who used this auction house from time to time and he had pulled in a favor to get us up front.

When it came to Leif Gable, it was always safe to assume the most outrageous scenario possible in any situation, and then double it. He truly was a worldly person.

I wondered what my mother would have thought of the two of us, Leif and me. I tried to imagine what she would say. Since I remembered my mother from the perspective of a nine-year-old girl, which is how old I had been the day she was hit and killed by a drunk driver, I had to temper my imagination with my current wisdom.

I had just turned thirty-five, but sometimes I felt as if I was still nine years old emotionally. Leif had draped his black wool coat over the back of his chair to claim his seat. It was still there, the tails brushing the floor. Although it was forty-seven degrees outside, cold for L.A., the room was stifling hot and I felt overdressed. The woman in the fur coat must have had a pair of underpants packed with ice. She wasn't even sweating.

I put my hand on the collar of Leif's jacket and stroked the smooth fabric with my fingers. I decided that if she had gotten a chance to meet him, my mother would have liked Leif very much.

The auctioneer was checking on the progress of the next item. The wall behind the auctioneer had a sliding panel that allowed workers behind the scene to carefully set up large items backstage. When he saw the go-ahead signal from a woman wearing a silk pencil skirt and emerald green blouse, he addressed the crowd.

"The next item up for bid has taken a 150,000 years to arrive, but we didn't mind the delay," the auctioneer said with a wry smile.

The panel smoothly slid aside to reveal a gleaming, toothy grin.

When I saw the skull I stood up with wonder. "I wish Hugo could have been here to see this."

"Lordy have mercy, living snakes alive," my father said, dropping his paddle to his lap.

I tugged the grad student's shirtsleeve. "Jimmy, it looks fantastic."

The dinosaur skull looked nothing like it had the day I had seen Jimmy slapping plaster over it back home up on the dusty ridge. It had been cleaned, reconstructed and mounted on a block of striking red stone. The skull itself was nearly black and gleamed under the lights from the stage. Each tooth glimmered. An audible and appreciative gasp rippled across the crowd.

"Yeah, even I have to admit it turned out pretty darn good. I mounted it on a piece of stone called Red Dragon marble. I thought it would really make the bones stand out. Nice, huh?"

"If a monster can be beautiful," I said, "this one is."

The auctioneer spoke into his microphone to quiet the crowd. "This skull represents one of the best examples of a rare carnivorous dinosaur that once prowled the Jurassic. It was discovered in the wilds of Montana on the remote Dearcorn cattle ranch, and was excavated with full rights of ownership held by the landowner, and it is offered here today."

"Wilds of Montana?" I asked.

Jimmy sat forward in his seat. "They just say that to get people to bid higher. It sounds exotic."

"This complete fossil skull of Allosaurus fragilis represents one of the largest members of that species ever found," the auctioneer said grandly.

"Jimmy, it's not a megalosaur?" I asked.

"Megalosaurus. No, it's not the species I was pinning my thesis on," he admitted.

"What about your degree?" I asked.

"Oh, I'll get my master's," he said. "Someone with the title Doctor from the University of Colorado agreed to let me have access to all of his old field notes from the seventies."

My mouth must have dropped open because Jimmy tapped the side of his nose with one finger conspiratorially and nodded. "I guess he wasn't such a creep after all."

"May we start the bidding at one hundred? One hundred. Then may I have fifty?"

One of the bid callers lifted a hand. "Fifty!"

"Seventy-five? Do I hear seventy-five?"

I caught from the corner of my eye a fluttering motion beside my father.

"Seventy-five!"

"Jimmy what the hell are you doing, son?" my father asked.

Jimmy lowered his paddle. "Pushing up the price for you, Nathan."

"Are you out of your mind?" I asked.

"Do I have one hundred?"

"One hundred!" said a bid caller.

"Who's bidding?" I asked.

The three of us scanned the crowd but there was so much activity we couldn't see anything.

"You, sir, will you give me one-fifty?"

"Who's he talking to?" Jimmy asked.

"That fella over there," my father said, pointing with his paddle to a man in the third row wearing a flannel shirt.

The auctioneer pointed at my father. "Sir, I believe you are bidding against yourself."

"Dammit," my father said. "Take this thing away from me."

I snatched my father's paddle and tossed it underneath Leif's seat. Where was he? He was missing it all.

"Do I have two? Will you bid two, sir?" the auctioneer asked.

"Two!" cried one of the callers.

"And two-fifty, then. Do we have two-fifty?"

"I thought it would go for more than two hundred fifty bucks," my father remarked.

"He means two hundred fifty thousand, Nathan," Jimmy said patiently.

"Holy schmoly!"

"Three then? Do I have three?" the auctioneer asked the man in the flannel.

The man hesitated for a moment, then nodded and raised his number.

"And we have three. Will you go three-fifty, then, sir?"

"Is he talking to someone on a phone bid?" Jimmy asked, craning his head around to scan the room. "I can't see who he's talking to."

"Three-fifty. The bid is three-fifty to you, sir. Do I have four?"

Flannel man hesitated again. Even though he looked as out of place as I felt, he radiated confidence. His arms were folded across his chest tightly and his fingers tapped out a measured cadence on his arm while he considered. He wanted the skull badly.

The auctioneer coaxed him along. "The bid is three-fifty to you. And to you, sir. Do I have four?"

The man relented and lifted his paddle with a flourish. If he was going to blow the bank he was going to do it with gusto.

"And the bid is four hundred thousand dollars. Four hundred thousand. Do I have four-fifty?"

"Four-fifty!" cried the bid caller.

The man in flannel slumped in his seat. Could he go that high?

"Someone is going to write me a check for four hundred thousand dollars." My father reeled in his seat.

"Dad, put your head between your knees."

"Four-fifty, sir. The bid is four-fifty," the auctioneer said.

The man in flannel laughed. "Yeah, I know what it is."

"Will you bid four-seventy-five? Do I have four-seventy-five?"

"I will bid four hundred sixty thousand," the man said. It was plainly his total budget.

The auctioneer held his response for a moment. He nodded to the man. "Four hundred sixty thousand. That is the last bid."

"I think they've topped out," Jimmy said.

"Four-sixty-five!" shouted one of the bid callers. "Four hundred sixty-five thousand!"

The auctioneer turned back to the man in the flannel shirt. "Sir, you've come this far, you may as well complete the journey."

The man shook him off with a wave and a grimace.

The auctioneer beseeched him again. "We all want you to have it. You've been such a good sport."

The crowd laughed and the man looked at his paddle with desperation.

It was breaking his heart, but he had to let the skull go.

He shook his head no, and lowered his gaze, indicating that he was done.

"The bid is four hundred sixty-five thousand. Going once. Going twice . . . sold!"

"Who is it?" Jimmy asked, finally rising up in his seat to search the crowd.

"I never did see who it was," I said.

The crowd applauded politely.

A few people took that moment to dash out of their seats and make a run for the bathrooms before the next items came up for bid.

I patted my father on the back. "Deep, slow breaths. Deep, slow."

"Your grandfather always said we'd never make a dime off of the critters he had on the place." My father eased himself up so that he could lean back against his chair. "I guess he was wrong after all."

I felt an arm circle around my waist and Leif was suddenly hugging me from behind.

"Where did you go? You missed it all," I said.

"I had to call Massachusetts. What was the final bid?"

My father held his hand apart in a grand gesture. "More than four hundred thousand dollars."

Leif smiled appreciatively. "Good for you, Nathan."

"Does everyone want to stay until the end?" Jimmy asked. "We could go get some Thai food. Does anyone want Thai food?"

"It's going to be nothing but leftovers from that movie star's estate," I said. "I don't know about anyone else, but I can't think of a place I would ever wear a sapphire tiara."

"Dinner's on me," my father announced.

We ambled through the milling crowd and I realized when we were halfway to the door we had to check in our paddles.

"I'll catch up," I said, squeezing Leif on the shoulder to get his attention.

"What's wrong?" he asked.

"I forgot Dad's paddle. I'll be right back."

I trotted to the second row and sat down on the seat so I could feel beneath it without presenting my butt to the rest of the crowd.

My fingers touched my father's paddle almost at once, and then I remembered that Leif had left his under his chair too.

I scooted over one seat and felt along the floor, but I couldn't seem to come up with Leif's paddle anywhere.

Since there was no one else in the row I could drop to my knees and look under the seat. When I did, I saw the wine glass that he had left under his chair but nothing else.

I stood up and searched the area carefully.

Maybe it had been kicked from under the seat in all the commotion?

"Sweetheart, we should go," Leif said, easing into the row and giving me a gentle tug.

"I can't find your bidding number."

He leaned in against me and brushed my ear with his lips. "You won't. It's back on the auctioneer's table."

"What?" My eyes must have grown as wide as saucers. "You?"

"We don't need to tell Nathan about it," he said, hugging me to him and steering us towards the door. "I made a deal with Jimmy in the hallway just now that he could have as much time to study the fossil as he needed. But then it will be donated."

"Donated? To who?"

"A friend of mine works for a little museum in Washington, D.C., and I told him they could have it."

"What's the little museum?" I asked.

Leif chuckled and kissed my cheek. "The Smithsonian. Now, where should we go for dinner? Sky's the limit."

"I won't tell Dad on one condition," I said, giving him a quick kiss.

Leif was suddenly serious. "Name it."

"He gets to be the best man at our wedding."

His smile was so big it crinkled around his blue eyes. "That's a deal."

I tucked myself under his arm and we walked out together so we could get started on the rest of our lives.

FOR GLENN—
REDEFINING WHAT IT MEANS TO BE A
WORLD CLASS MAN.

A fourth generation Wyoming native,
Jessica McClelland is a librarian, avid archer and
spent a decade hunting dinosaurs in the
Jurassic formation in the foothills of the
Bighorn Mountains, a stone's throw away from
where the Johnson County Cattle Wars occurred.
She is the author of the Marley Dearcorn novels, a
series of murder mysteries set in
South Central Montana.